One November Night

By

Madeleine Grainger

Acknowledgements

This book – my first published novel – has taken almost a lifetime to come to fruition. It wouldn't have happened without the valued support of dear friends and family. I owe an enormous debt of gratitude to my friend, Nicola, for her unflagging encouragement over many years. Grateful thanks, also, to my friend, Sarah, for her editing and helpful suggestions. To my partner, Keith, thanks for believing in me and helping me to believe in myself; and to Denise, Vicsy, Mary and all those who have assisted in my incredibly long journey, in one way or another, heartfelt thanks for enabling me to realise a dream. Finally, thanks to Publish Nation for making this happen.

CHAPTER ONE

November 2014, Yorkshire

The November night was sinking over the village of Flintby like spilled black ink from an overturned bottle. Rain from a recent heavy shower shimmered in puddles illuminated by the few streetlamps which stood guard along the high street. Many of the working population of Flintby were gradually making their way home, some from the neighbouring town of Granton, just over four miles to the north-east, others from farther afield. A winter stillness was settling over the whole village.

Three hundred yards before Flintby gave way to surrounding fields and farmland, stood St Mark's Church of England Primary School. A solitary lit window, on one side of the building, punctured the solid blackness of the night in a neat square. Behind it sat Melissa Fairley, head teacher, who was finishing up for the day.

Cocooned in her office, in the calming silence that followed the departure of all the children and staff, Mrs Mel, as she was fondly known, relished a couple of hours, alone, to review the day's activities and to plan for what lay ahead. Christmas was approaching fast, and she was about to enter her busiest time of year. With a Nativity play to stage, end-of-term reports and parents' meetings to organise, she joked to her staff that she needed an extra couple of hours in her day.

She checked the time. It was just after five-thirty, so Morgan should be home from school by now. Her husband, Gareth, was working late tonight, she seemed to remember him telling her. She still had heaps to do, but some of it she could take home with her, to work on after supper. The rest would have to wait until tomorrow. She needed to switch off for a few hours and head home.

At least, she congratulated herself, she would be in before seven, on one night this week. Her daughter, Morgan, had her A

1

levels coming up soon and it was going to be a difficult time for her. However crazy her own schedule was, she was determined to be there for Morgan, even if it was just to talk about anything and nothing. Her daughter was developing into a confident, level-headed young woman, thank goodness, but you could never be sure these days. There were so many more pressures and distractions than when she was Morgan's age. After a quick tour of the building to check all was well, she pulled on her quilted, winter coat and headed out to the car park.

On the opposite side of the road to St Mark's, and closer to Flintby, stood a terrace of three properties. Seaforth Cottage sat comfortably in the middle of the three, home to former dairy man, Ted Dunlop and his late wife, Betty. As Melissa Fairley was tidying her desk, Ted stood in his small kitchen, at the back of the cottage, washing up a dinner plate, cutlery, and mug from his solitary evening meal. At his feet, his eighteen-month-old border collie, Maisie, was staring up at him, her head cocked to one side, her soft brown eyes fixed on him, laser-like.

"Alright, young 'un," Ted said, shaking off his wet hands and drying them on a towel, "give me a minute. I know what time it is." Making his way into the narrow hall, he lifted his outdoor clothes and Maisie's lead from their pegs by the front door and pulled on his waxed jacket and woollen cap. Maisie threaded herself between Ted's legs in a figure of eight, panting and barking with excitement at the prospect of her evening walk.

"Steady on, Mais. You'll have me over, dancing about like that." Ted fumbled with the zip fastening on his well-worn waxed jacket. "It's bloody cold out there tonight, lass. Give me a chance to get me coat on."

As Ted's arthritic fingers struggled to fasten his coat, Maisie raced up and down the small hallway, alternately barking and whining at Ted as he carefully slipped his feet into Wellington boots.

"Calm down, lass. We'll be out there soon. Those rabbits and squirrels'll be waiting for you, don't you worry."

Ted drew back the bolts on the front door and turned the key. As he did so, his gaze settled on the face of a plump-cheeked, smiling woman, framed in a photograph, hanging on the wall beside the coats. He leaned forward to plant a kiss on the cold oblong of glass covering the photo.

Momentarily he closed his eyes and pretended Betty was with him again, calling out a cheery goodbye or a caution to take care on this chill, winter night. Then he opened them again and shook his head, looking away. Silly old buggar, he said to himself. She's not here and you won't be seeing her again in this life.

As soon as the door was open wide enough, Maisie wriggled through the gap and bounded out into the cold night. Ted bent to grab her collar, so that he could attach her lead, but she was too quick for him. His fingers snatched at the air as Maisie charged down the path and onto the road, barking with excitement at the myriad scents to be explored with her highly sensitive nostrils. Intuitively, she knew her route and headed off down the road towards the fields beyond the school, where she and her master regularly walked.

"Maisie," Ted yelled, hobbling after her. His old knees were stiff and painful tonight, and he cursed his feeble effort to try and run after his dog. He grabbed the whistle from his pocket and blew her recall signal repeatedly, in between shouting louder and louder.

"Maisie. Wait!"

Ahead of him, he could just make out the white blaze on his dog's forehead as she briefly looked back at him. Drawn on by the attractions of the hedgerows and woods, she resumed her quest, trotting briskly towards the old farm gate which marked the entrance to their usual walk.

Suddenly, Ted felt a sharp, stabbing pain in his left knee. His leg buckled beneath him as he sank to the ground like a deflated balloon. He lay as still as possible, for a few seconds, gingerly checking whether he had broken anything. Sickening pain shot through his left hip, where he had hit the unyielding tarmac, but he believed himself to be intact.

Cursing his feebleness, Ted forced himself to crawl over the damp road to the grass verge. Damn it, he muttered, as he heard the distant sound of a car engine approaching from the village. Later, he would wonder whether it was at that moment that Maisie's animal instincts sensed danger from the advancing vehicle or perhaps she was drawn by her owner's plaintive cry.

3

Whatever the reason, she suddenly stood still, gazing back towards Ted as he struggled to rise to his feet.

Barking furiously, the young dog turned and headed back in the direction of her master, up the middle of the road, wagging her tail as she drew nearer to him. With every muscle and sinew in his body, Ted slowly hauled himself to his feet, his left hip and knee shouting with pain. The car was so close, now, that its headlamps illuminated a patch of road in front of him, like theatre lights trained on a stage, where a drama was about to unfold.

Suddenly, Ted became aware of movement to his left. He turned to briefly glimpse a dark-clad figure darting out from the school car park, about 100 yards farther down the road from where he stood, swaying uncertainly on his feet.

Whoever it was ran straight out towards Maisie, who was still in the centre of the road. The night's silence was suddenly shattered by the ear-splitting scream of tyres, as the driver of the vehicle slammed on the brakes. The noxious smell of scorching rubber filled the air.

Unable to move, as if frozen to the spot, Ted looked on in horror, as the car skidded past him, out of control, to an eventual halt. Before it stopped, there was the terrifying sound of several tonnes of metal smashing into fragile flesh and bones, closely followed by the sight of a body propelled into the air, before it landed with a sickening thud, on the hard tarmac. A high-pitched pitiful cry could be heard above the screech of the car's tyres.

Shaking himself into action, Ted hobbled up the road, ignoring the pain coursing through his left side. Maisie, now at his heels, after bounding swiftly out of the path of the vehicle, barked frantically to alert anyone who might hear her. Ignoring the pulsating throb in his knee and hip, the old man commanded himself to reach the injured person and the driver as quickly as possible, to see if he could help.

The car's engine was idling steadily, cooling metal ticking a beat in the frosty air. As he approached the driver's side of the vehicle, Ted saw a figure slumped over the steering wheel, unmoving. It was impossible to tell if the person was dead or alive. He reached out a shaky hand to open the car door, but before he could connect with the handle, there was a deafening roar of the engine and a startling spin of wheels as the vehicle pulled away from him, almost knocking him off his feet again.

For a few seconds Ted remained standing in the road, struggling to comprehend what had just happened. Shaking his head in disbelief, he turned to look at the body lying motionless on the ground. Without illumination from the departed car's headlights, it was pitch dark. Even so, he could see that the person's head was twisted at an unnatural angle to the rest of the body, as was one of the feet. He bent down to take a closer look.

Despite the thick, padded coat, with an oversized hood pulled over the head, Ted was in no doubt whose lifeless body lay in front of him. It was Melissa Fairley, headmistress of Flintby Primary School. She must have spotted Maisie trotting up the middle of the road in his direction, whilst at the same time noticing the approaching car. Like him, she must have thought the car was going to strike the unsuspecting animal. With only seconds to spare, she had made a brave but doomed attempt to run out and grab Maisie and to pull her out of the way of harm. In doing so, she had been struck by the car, which had been unable to stop in time to avoid her.

His fingers trembling, Ted bent down to feel for a pulse on the woman's neck, though he knew it was hopeless. Death had come to her the minute that car tossed her into the air, like a bundle of unwanted clothing. She'd had no chance against the weight of metal that hit her with such tremendous force.

"Dear God!" Ted called out over the lifeless body. In trying to save Maisie, Mrs Fairley had lost her life. The thought was running through his mind in a continuous loop. He knew it would haunt him for the rest of his days.

Wincing as he straightened up from leaning over Mrs Fairley's body, Ted stared down the road after the car, as if he might still be able to see it. It had been going at a fair old lick, he told himself, but whoever was behind the wheel hadn't had a chance to avoid the figure that sprang out into the centre of the road.

It wasn't the first time an accident had occurred in this spot, Ted recalled, with anger. The bend in the road before the school was so poorly lit, it was near impossible to see anyone crossing there, or walking up the road from the direction of Granton.

Villagers, and Mrs Fairley herself, had been complaining about it for years. The driver probably didn't see a person running out in front of him, dressed head to toe in dark clothes, until it was too late. But why did he or she just drive off like that? Ted couldn't comprehend such a cowardly act. To leave the scene without even checking on the person who'd been hit, or trying to get help, was unforgivable, in his opinion.

Ted was shivering now, and his hands were shaking uncontrollably as he pulled his mobile phone from the pocket of his coat and clumsily punched out the number for emergency services. Struggling to find the words, he eventually managed to report what had happened. He agreed to remain at the scene until the police and paramedics arrived.

It seemed like no time had passed, after he rang off, before Ted spied the blue, flashing lights of emergency vehicles flickering in the distance, becoming brighter with every second. They were tearing down the hill towards him from the direction of Granton. They'd be here any minute, he told himself, as the winter cold penetrated deep into his old bones, making him shiver and shake, all over.

Until the police and ambulance reached him, Ted stood guard over Melissa Fairley's body, Maisie now quiet and watchful, by his side. He wasn't a religious person, but he was compelled to say a short prayer for the soul of this poor woman and her family. They'd be needing everybody's prayers, he figured, after what had happened here tonight.

CHAPTER TWO

"So, you didn't get the registration of the vehicle, Mr Dunlop?"

Ted shook his head. Back in his cottage, he was clutching a mug of tea with extra sugar, between his shaking hands. One of the police officers, who had brought him home from the accident scene, had stoked the dying fire and made him a hot drink, but he just couldn't get warm. His hands and feet were numb, and the rest of his body felt as if it was slowly freezing over.

Questions came at him, thick and fast. Did he notice the make or model of the car which struck Mrs Fairley? How about the colour? What about the driver? Male or female? Young or old? What was he or she wearing? Were they well-built or slight?

He hadn't even gathered the most basic of information about the car and driver, so couldn't help at all. It all happened so quickly, Ted tried to explain. There was the dog, the car, then the body. He didn't notice anything else before the vehicle drove off into the night.

Ted could see that the young fellow asking all the questions was becoming frustrated with him, though he tried to hide it. All Ted knew was that Mrs Fairley would still be alive if he had only put Maisie on the lead before he left the house. That knowledge sat with him like indigestible food in his gullet.

"Ok, Mr Dunlop," said the young man, "thank you for your help. If you do remember anything else, be sure to give us a call, won't you?"

Ted nodded.

"Is there anyone who can pop in on you later, Ted?" The female police officer, who had remained silent for most of the interview, was speaking to him now. "A relative or a friend, maybe?" she asked, looking hopefully at him. He shook his head again.

"I have a son, but he lives down south, miles away. I'll give him a call later. Tell him what's gone on. Betty, my wife, she passed a couple of year ago. It's just me and Maisie, now."

"Well, I'll give you a call tomorrow, if that's alright Ted? Just to make sure you're ok? You've been through a lot today. It's

7

bound to be a shock. We can arrange more help and support, if you need it."

Ted looked at the young woman's earnest face, as she and her colleague made to leave. She looked kind and genuinely concerned about him. Most likely it was pity she felt for a decrepit old man who was losing his wits. No use to man or beast. Worse than that, he felt responsible for the death of a young woman so much more deserving of life than him. The unearthly sight of that poor woman played over and over in his mind's eye. He saw her body hurtling through the air and smashing onto the hard road, her life extinguished in an instant. He may not have knocked her down like the driver of the car that hit her, but it was his fault she died.

"We'll see ourselves out, Ted," the female officer said. "You stay there and keep warm by the fire." He nodded and waved a hand in acknowledgement, his brain still churning the events of the evening.

Hearing the front door open and close, Ted rested his head on the back of the chair and closed his eyes. He was weary to his bones. The second his eyes shut he was back there again, on the road, hearing the car approaching from the village and experiencing the grip of fear as Maisie trotted on ahead of him, seemingly unaware of potential danger.

Was there anything else he could recall that might help, he asked himself? Wracking his brain for a nugget of useful information he might have overlooked, he pictured himself hobbling over to the car, reaching out to open the door and catching a glimpse of the driver. The car engine was still running, the lights illuminating the road ahead.

The person at the wheel was wearing a top with a hood over his or her head, he recalled. It had been impossible to tell if it was a man or a woman from the little Ted could see of them. But wait a minute – the right hand on the wheel. Ted remembered seeing it there, resting beside the slumped form of the driver. There was a ring, a gold signet ring, on the person's little finger, he was sure of it. But then, was he sure, or did he just want to offer up more to the police, having been of no help so far? His head was in a muddle, and he was feeling dizzy, but he should ring that nice

8

policewoman anyway to tell her about it. She could decide what she wanted to do with the information.

From the small coffee table beside his chair, Ted picked up the piece of paper on which a contact number for the police had been written. He made to stand up but fell straight back down into his chair. His energy had completely drained away. What was wrong with him?

Suddenly, he felt an excruciating pain in his chest, as if a concrete block was pressing down on him, squeezing the breath out of his body. He gasped as pain gripped him, moving down his left arm. Maisie looked up suddenly, her soft, brown eyes trying to read her master's face and movements. Anxiously, she placed a paw on one of his feet, her ears flattened against her head, as she sensed trouble. Tense and rigid, she watched as Ted cried out in agony, his body writhing in pain. She jumped up, barking frantically to attract attention, even after her master's body became unnaturally still. Drawing no response, she gave out a small whine as she scratched at Ted's worn, old slippers and licked the hands that hung lifelessly over the arms of his chair. The clock on the mantelpiece ticked on relentlessly. In her last vigil at Seaforth Cottage, Maisie laid her head proprietorially on her master's feet.

CHAPTER THREE

Morgan Fairley stepped down from the school bus and jogged the few yards round the corner to her house. As she approached, she saw it was in total darkness, meaning her mum and dad must both be out at work.

The pack on her back was heavy with homework which she really should crack on with until one or other of her parents arrived home. Morgan sighed and looked longingly across the road to her friend Brady Forrester's house. Lights blazed in every window, and she could see Mrs Forrester moving around the kitchen, preparing food for Brady and her younger brother, Dylan. She and Brady had been friends since primary school, and although they were at different secondary schools, now, they were still each other's bestie. Morgan often hung out at Brady's house until one or other of her own parents returned from work. She quickly texted Brady to see if it was alright for her to come over.

Get your sweet ass over here. B

Morgan smiled and waved at Brady who was already opening the front door of her house.

"Hi Brades. Hi Mrs Forrester," said Morgan as she stepped over the threshold.

"Hello, Morgan," Emma Forrester called from the kitchen. "You timed that well. I've just put pizza in the oven for Brady and Dylan. There's more than enough for them both. Would you like to help them eat it?"

Morgan inhaled the delicious smell of pizza dough and melting cheese wafting in her direction from the kitchen. Her stomach grumbled with hunger. "That would be great," she said. "Thanks Mrs Forrester."

"Up you go then, I'll give you a shout when it's ready."

Granton Police Headquarters stood at the top of the town, fortress-like in location and appearance.

At seven o'clock on a winter's evening, most of the windows were still illuminated in the building that never slept. Police officers, members of the public and those apprehended, swarmed in and out like bees to a hive.

Detective Chief Inspector Gareth Fairley clicked on the latest email from his superior. His heart sank as he noticed the length of the attachment. Another policy document for him to read and disseminate to his team. His enthusiasm to spread the word might be all the greater if he didn't know that it would likely be followed up in a month's time by another such document, carrying completely different instructions.

Out of the corner of his eye, Gareth saw a figure framed in the doorway of his office. It was Jenna Waite, his detective sergeant, newly promoted to the role. He beckoned her in, grateful to have an excuse for deferring his longread, at least for a few moments.

Jenna was one of his most promising young officers, much deserving of her recent promotion. Gareth always enjoyed discussing a case with her. She was one of the few, on his team, who were able to think out of the box. Her efforts had contributed greatly to some significant convictions over the past year. He wondered what she would bring to him today.

"Come in, Jen," Gareth said, seeing Jenna was hesitant to enter. "You look like you've seen a ghost, or was it Mad Mick Thompson, our most persistent offender?" He laughed at his own joke, though he didn't raise the flicker of a smile from Jenna. Was she sickening for something, Gareth wondered? She certainly looked pale. There was a nasty bug sweeping round the department at the moment. He could ill afford to spare one of his best officers when they were all so busy.

"Have a seat," Gareth said, pulling out a chair. He was concerned Jenna was about to faint on him.

"I'm fine," Jenna said, remaining by the door. "I've just taken a call from Traffic, boss. It's Mrs Fairley. She's been in an accident."

For a moment, Gareth wondered who she was talking about. He didn't connect himself to her words.

"Who?" he asked, aware that he sounded rather stupid.

"It's your wife, sir. Melissa. She's….she's dead, sir."

Her words hurtled towards him like a cannon ball from a gun, shattering his life, in the space of a few seconds.

11

"What?…I mean…where? What happened? Are you sure it's her? It's probably a mistake. She'll still be at school," Gareth said, glancing at his watch whilst running his fingers through his hair, as he tried to absorb the enormity of what Jenna had just told him.

"It was a hit and run, sir," Jenna said, biting her lip and looking anxiously towards her boss. "Traffic took a statement from an old guy, who was out walking his dog. He saw the accident, but can't provide any useful details. Forensics are at the scene, looking for evidence."

"Right, right," Gareth said, as if Jenna had just passed on routine information, rather than the details of his wife's untimely death.

"She's next door, sir," said Jenna, hesitantly. "In the mortuary. They're asking for you to go and identify her."

"Yes, yes of course," Gareth said, fighting to gather his thoughts. Was this a terrible, bad dream from which he would awaken any minute? It had to be. What Jenna said couldn't be right. He'd go to the mortuary, straight away, so he could confirm it was a case of mistaken identification. Some other poor family had been robbed of their Mrs Fairley.

"Is there anything I can do, sir?" Jenna asked.

"No, thank you Jenna. I'll take care of everything," Gareth said, making a futile attempt to tidy his desk. "Just keep this to yourself, for the moment, will you?"

Jenna nodded, remaining silent. She sensed that her boss hadn't properly absorbed what she had just said. Who could blame him? He'd just had the worst news imaginable. How could anybody be expected to take that in?

Jenna moved aside as Gareth brushed past her, pulling on his coat. Heads looked up from computers as he passed, but no-one spoke. Many of the team had already heard, even without Jenna saying anything to them. News spread like a forest fire inside Police HQ.

He'd have to break it to his daughter, Jenna reflected, as she watched her boss walking out. Morgan was only a teenager. God! What a terrible thing to happen. Jenna didn't know how she was going to be able to concentrate on her work after this. Slowly and thoughtfully, she returned to her desk, picturing the DCI having to identify his dead wife. It made her blood run cold. How the hell was he going to cope with this, she wondered? Sitting back down, she pretended to look at some paperwork, silent tears slipping down her cheeks.

CHAPTER FOUR

It was the cold, inhuman silence of the mortuary that struck him most and stayed with him for weeks afterwards. Gareth wouldn't be able to warm himself, no matter how many layers of clothing he put on.

How many times had he stood here, in this deathly room, looking on, as the forensic pathologist carried out the macabre exploration needed for a criminal investigation? Was it hundreds of occasions? Maybe even thousands, over the course of his career.

In the dispassionate search for evidence as to how a life had come to be extinguished, DCI Fairley had ceased to reflect on the person of the deceased. His interest was limited to the usual concerns. How and when did the person die? What evidence was there as to the cause of death? Who were the next-of-kin to be informed? It wasn't that he didn't care. He had a job to do, and he couldn't afford to allow sentiment into it, otherwise he'd never be able to solve crimes and apprehend criminals.

Countless times Gareth had watched relatives or close friends arrive at the mortuary, white-faced and fearful. Now it was he who stood in the shoes of the recently bereaved, like them, unable to take in what he was being told. Sooner or later, he would wake up from this nightmare and there would be his wife and daughter, the two constants in his life. The job was important, but his family defined him. He was the husband of Melissa and father of Morgan. That was it.

"Are you ready Gareth?"

Charles Taylor, the pathologist, was a friend of many years. Gareth had been relieved to see his face as he entered the mortuary. He nodded in reply.

Slowly and respectfully, Charles lifted the blue sheet which lay over the body on the autopsy table. Gareth stood behind him, as the figure on the table was revealed.

"Oh God!" Gareth doubled over, as if he had been kicked in the solar plexus. "Oh my god, no!" he shouted. "Melissa! No!"

"I'm so sorry, Gareth," said Charles, his gloved hand resting on his friend's arm.

Gareth Fairley gazed at the pale, delicate beauty of his wife's face. He noticed the perfect arch of her brows, the high cheekbones over which her flawless skin was smoothly stretched and the full, generous lips, so often parted by a smile or a shout of impromptu laughter.

He reached out, to brush aside the dark brown curls she had always tried so hard to tame. As his fingers slowly released the silky strands, they bobbed back into lively ringlets. How bizarre that hair appeared to have life when the body's pulse had ceased beating.

Charles drew him away. "It looks as if she died when her head hit the ground, after she was struck and knocked over. There are internal injuries and broken bones, but they're not sufficiently serious to have killed her."

Gareth felt the bile suddenly rise from his stomach as it contracted involuntarily. He rushed to the sink where he vomited, noisily, several times. When he'd finished, he wiped his mouth with the paper towel his colleague handed to him.

"Have some water," Charles said, handing Gareth a plastic cup. He took a sip, shocked by its icy chill.

"Are you ok to drive home?" Charles asked, a look of deep concern etched on his face. "I can take you. I'm nearly finished here. I'll only be a few moments."

Gareth shook his head. "No, thanks Charles. I'll be alright. I have to get back to Morgan."

Charles nodded. "Of course. But please ring me if you need help – anything at all. You and Morgan are more than welcome to stay with Amanda and me tonight, if that would help."

"No. Thanks again, Charles, but I need to be on my own with Morgan. I'll call you if I need anything."

"Ok, mate. I'll ring you in a couple of days, but I mean it – if there's anything, anything at all we can do, please let me know."

Gareth shook his friend's hand, awkwardly, as if they were concluding a business meeting rather than signing off on his wife's death. He looked at Melissa again, just as beautiful in death as she had been in life. There were bruises and scratches on her forehead, but they didn't dim her beauty. He bent and kissed her gently, murmuring his final farewell. A sob caught in his throat, and he rushed from the room. He didn't want his friend to witness him breaking into pieces.

Walking away from the tomb-like mortuary, Gareth Fairley asked himself, repeatedly, how he would live in a world without Mel in it?

His wife had been the counterbalance to all the evil and depravity he faced, every day, in his job. Being with her had cleansed his soul and made it possible for him to continue trying to bring some order to the awful chaos of humanity that sometimes threatened to overwhelm him. Hers was the voice of calm reason when he raged about another teenage knife crime incident, a terrifying rape ordeal or the desecration of a home after thieves stole precious, irreplaceable keepsakes and possessions. She had always encouraged him to debrief with her, never flinching or retreating from the brutal facts he regularly offered up to her. She was the kindest, most generous, selfless person he had ever known.

In a few months, she would have been fifty, with a big party in the planning. She was far too young to die, with so much yet to offer. The world, and he, could not afford to lose her.

Gareth climbed into his car and locked himself in. For several minutes he sat completely still, the image of his dead wife burned onto his eyelids. The feeling he'd had of being inside a horrible dream was beginning to fade; in its place, reality was creeping over him like a cold, damp fog.

As he sat, cocooned in his car, Gareth recognised that his greatest challenge lay before him. He must tell his seventeen-year-old daughter that her mother was dead. Morgan and Melissa had been more like friends than mother and daughter. How could he possibly try and fill the gaping hole that Melissa's death would leave in Morgan's life? How could he even begin to try and compensate for her loss? The prospect of what lay ahead absolutely terrified him.

He started the car and pulled slowly away from the kerb, a million colliding thoughts whirring around his head. How did the accident happen? Who was responsible? How was he going to take care of Morgan on his own? Melissa had organised her life – both of their lives. He didn't know where to begin.

Gareth still felt sick to his stomach, his gut clenched in a tight knot. He thought of Eileen, Melissa's mother, who had lost her husband, Derek, only a few years ago. That had been bad enough for her, but this would hit her terribly hard, as it would Mel's older sister, Jessica, and her family. So many lives blighted by Mel's sudden and untimely death.

It was all too much for him. He felt like winding down the car window and screaming and shouting until his voice gave out. Up ahead, he noticed the lights of The Windmill pub. It was a bit of dive and not somewhere he usually frequented, but at least he might not be recognised there. He needed a quiet corner in which to sit and contemplate what he was going to say to his daughter. It was wrong, he knew, but at least Morgan would have a few more minutes of blissful ignorance before he had to tell her that her life had just been changed forever.

CHAPTER FIVE

Morgan peered out of Brady's bedroom window, across the road to her house. Still, no-one home. She glanced at her phone. It was after seven o'clock in the evening. She checked all her messages, but there was nothing from either of her parents. This had never happened before. Anxiety crept over her like insects under her skin.

For the umpteenth time Morgan tried her mum, but the call went straight to voicemail. She'd already left several messages but received no response. It was always difficult to reach her dad when he was at work, but she messaged him anyway, hoping he would check his private phone.

Dad – I can't reach Mum. Do you know where she is? I've left messages but she hasn't called me back. I'm scared. Can you ring me?

"Is everything alright Morgan?" Emma Forrester asked, entering the room. "I'm not throwing you out or anything – you can stay as long as you like, you know that. It's just, there doesn't seem to be anyone in yet, over the road. Is everything ok, love?"

"I don't know, Mrs Forrester. I've been trying to contact mum and dad, but neither of them have come back to me. I'm really worried."

"I'm sure everything will be fine, Morgan. They've probably both run into traffic, or they can't get a signal to message you."

Morgan nodded, biting her lip. Brady was trying to interest her in a funny YouTube video, but she couldn't concentrate. She was glued to the bedroom window, peering down the road in the hope of spotting one or other of her parents. With her nose flattened against the windowpane, she could crane her neck round to the junction where cars turned into her road. With each car that entered, Morgan prayed, with every ounce of her being, that it would be her mum or dad. Crushing disappointment and heightened fear washed over her with each successive vehicle that passed her by.

Gareth drove slowly home from the pub, eking out every second remaining until he had to face Morgan. He was over the limit, he recognised, after a couple of whiskies, but he had needed the fiery burst of alcohol in his system to motivate himself to go home.

As he turned into Wentworth Avenue, Gareth could see that his house was still in darkness. He hated himself for the relief he felt that he might still have a few moments alone, at home, before Morgan returned from her friend's house, across the road. He knew she was there, because he'd received about a dozen messages and missed calls from her, which he hadn't had the guts to answer. God help him, but he was hoping he might have time to grab another stiff drink to calm his nervousness and bolster the courage he needed to speak to his daughter.

In the pub, and all the way home, Gareth had wracked his brain to find the words to explain to Morgan that the happy, mostly trouble-free life she had lived until now, was over. Although he had been trained to deal with situations like this and had attended at more homes than he cared to remember to break bad news, he had no idea how to do the same for his daughter. Even as he pulled onto the drive, he still did not know what he was going to say to her.

Gareth looked up at his unlit house, its darkened windows like sightless eyes. Only this morning, it was his place of refuge and happiness. Now it appeared grim and uninviting. Without Mel inside those walls, the place could never be the same. She breathed life into it, made it a home. How was he going to replicate that, now the beating heart of the place had been torn out? He didn't know where to start.

Gareth glanced across the road. He could see Emma Forrester in the kitchen, looking over in his direction. What must she think of him, leaving his daughter to worry and wonder?

In minutes, Morgan would come flying through the Forresters' front door and across the road, full of questions to which he had no good answers. Hastily, Gareth scrambled out of the car and dashed into the house. Without turning on the lights, he headed straight down the hall to the kitchen and the central island where the wine rack was housed. Grabbing a glass and bottle opener, in seconds he was knocking back a large glass of red wine and then another. As Gareth felt the alcohol trickle into his veins, there was the sound of a key turning in the front door lock.

CHAPTER SIX

Morgan dropped her rucksack on the hall mat, threw on the light and headed towards the kitchen, anger blazing from every pore.

"Dad! What the fuck?" she demanded, language she had never used to his face before. Coming from his daughter, it sounded shocking to Gareth, even though he was used to hearing it all day and every day, at work.

"I've been trying to call you.... and Mum. Loads of times. What's happened? Why did neither of you pick up or answer my texts? Where's Mum?"

Gareth took a deep breath, feeling his heart pounding in his chest, as he steeled himself for what must come next.

"I think we need to go and sit down," he said, putting his arm around his daughter and steering her towards the living room. She batted him away.

"I don't want to sit down. Tell me what's wrong? Something's happened to mum, hasn't it?" Morgan balled her fists and tensed her whole body, as she used to, occasionally, when, as a child, she couldn't have her own way. Invariably, then, her tantrum was about something inconsequential – being denied a television programme she wanted to watch, or having bedtime strictly enforced when she wanted to continue playing with her toys. Either he, or more often, Mel, prevailed over her childish objections and the upset was soon forgotten. If only he could turn back the clock to those simple, happy days.

At length Gareth spoke. "Your mum's been in an accident," he said, the blood pounding at his temples. "She's....she's gone."

"What do you mean, she's gone?" Morgan asked, her eyes darting across his face, as she tried to read there what she couldn't understand from his words.

"She's dead, love. She was knocked down by a car. She died at the scene."

Gareth cursed himself for putting it so baldly, as he watched his daughter's mouth drop open in horror. The colour in her rosy cheeks faded to a ghostly white and her knees buckled. He rushed forward, to prevent her falling, and wrapped her arm around his neck to steady her.

"Breathe deeply, love. Keep breathing." He guided her into the living room and lowered her gently into a chair.

"Head between your knees. Keep breathing." He ran back into the kitchen and filled a glass with water.

"Drink this."

Morgan took the glass from him but didn't drink. Gareth clasped her free hand, gently rubbing it as he watched anxiously for any further signs of faintness.

"What happened?" she asked, her voice barely audible.

"It was a car accident, just outside the school. She seems to have run out to save a dog from being hit by an approaching car and got knocked down herself."

"What? Why would she do that? Who did it? Who knocked her down?" Morgan's mind was whirring. It felt as if her brain was about to explode, unable to assimilate the information being thrown out like bricks hurled in anger.

"We don't know love. He, or she, drove off after the impact. Ted Dunlop, who lives nearby, saw what happened but didn't get any details of the driver or the vehicle. We're checking CCTV from the school, but I don't think it's going to be much help."

Whilst her father was speaking, Morgan suddenly let out a blood-curdling cry. Drawing her knees tightly into her chest, she rocked backwards and forwards on the chair, as if she were working herself into a trance. It was a terrifying keening sound - primeval, to his ears. Gareth felt helpless and completely out of his depth.

"Hush, love, hush." He rubbed her back, as he had when she was a baby, crying from colic. It made no difference. Morgan was inconsolable.

"I want to go and see her," said Morgan, her face screwed up in grief, snot and tears pouring down her face.

Gareth was appalled. He couldn't allow Morgan to go to that inhospitable place to see her mother lying on a hard table, pale and lifeless. Better by far that she remember her mother as the vibrant, life force that she had been to all who met and knew her.

"You can't love," he said. "Not now."

"Why not?"

"There had to be a post-mortem, love. She's not as she was." He told himself it wasn't an outright lie. He had to embellish the truth to protect his daughter from being haunted by the last image she had of her mother, just as he would be. She was much too young to process such a sight immediately after receiving news of her mother's sudden and shocking death.

"Better to remember her how she was in your happiest memories."

Morgan's face crumpled. She was pulling and twisting her hair as if she was preparing to yank it out. It was killing him to watch her distress, whilst feeling powerless to offer any comfort. All his training in victim support and he couldn't provide a crumb of comfort to his own daughter.

"You should have told me, as soon as you knew," she said, thrusting her face at him. "I could have come with you. To say goodbye. Why did you leave me waiting and worrying for ages?"

Morgan jumped up, grabbed her bag and thumped up the stairs to her room. "I hate you," she yelled. "I wish it was you that was dead instead of mum." With that, she slammed her bedroom door with such force, it shook the whole house. Briefly, she opened it again.

"And I can smell you've been drinking," she shouted, before banging her door shut once again.

Standing in the hall, Gareth was paralysed – unable to say or do anything. Grief was tearing at his heart with razor-sharp claws, but as painful as that was, he had one thought, in that moment. He had failed his daughter in the worst way possible. Instead of putting her welfare above everything else, when he heard about Mel's accident, he had been a coward, wallowing in self-pity for what he had lost. He could hardly believe that he'd taken himself off to the pub, leaving Morgan to worry and wonder about why she couldn't reach her parents.

23

Gareth felt sick, he had a banging headache, and his thoughts were in turmoil. He couldn't see any light in front of him, towards which he could steer them both; only a long, dark tunnel of misery and pain. Hating himself for it but unable to resist, he returned to the kitchen, where he poured himself another glass of wine and kept pouring until the bottle was empty.

CHAPTER SEVEN

One year later

Morgan lay staring up at the ceiling, trying to decipher the shapes made by the damp patches in each corner of Todd Hopkins' bedroom. One of them stretched across the full width of the room, like a cloud of smoke drifting from an unchecked fire.

Switching her gaze to the side walls, she took in the fingers of black mould creeping down from the corners where the roof was leaking. Three months – maybe more – had passed since a man from the local council came to inspect, declaring the problem to be water ingress. No shit, she thought, as she listened to his musings whilst she lounged on Todd's bed. Assurances had been given that the problem would receive urgent attention, but no action had been taken. In the meantime, the air in the room had become increasingly rank. Since the only window was jammed shut - the frame rotten and spongy and the window latch missing - the situation seemed unlikely to improve. Morgan couldn't care less. It wasn't her house.

She glanced at her phone. Eleven thirty-two am on 12 November 2015. A whole long year since her mother died.

People said the pain of loss lessens over time. Not for her. If she closed her eyes, Morgan could smell her mum's perfume, feel her warm, reassuring embrace, and hear her calm, steadying voice. Wide-eyed, all she could see was the bleak emotional landscape she now inhabited, in which she would never be able to laugh or cry with her mother again.

The body beside her stirred and groaned. In a moment, Morgan knew, there would be the stench of foul breath on her neck, a hand clamped roughly on her breast, then animal-like thrusting inside her until he came. She had learned that Todd Hopkins couldn't start his day without swift and selfish sexual release. Since they met and became some sort of dysfunctional couple, she had allowed him to use her whenever he wanted. She never refused or resisted him. Whilst, occasionally, his insatiable appetite had inexplicably sparked in her a fierce, reciprocal desire, mostly she just felt empty and hollow.

Predictably, Todd began to claim those parts of her body which he needed for his own gratification. He didn't even bother to turn her over to look at her as he entered her from behind. Morgan clung to the edge of the sagging single bed until, as Todd thrust faster and more powerfully, he roared out his climax. Within a few minutes, after he caught his breath, he made to move on her again, but she rolled away from his grasp and climbed out of bed.

From a backpack propped up in the corner of the bedroom, Morgan took out a pack of baby wipes and a small towel she kept in there.

The Hopkins' family only bathroom was rarely vacant because the house was always overflowing with itinerant adults and children, most of whom she didn't know or recognise. Even when it was free, she went in there as infrequently as possible. Just like every other room in the house, it was liberally decorated with mould around the window and on the walls. Several shared toothpaste tubes spewed their colourful contents onto the washbasin. Every surface, including the floor, was covered with plastic bottles and pots of gel, their tops encrusted with dribbles of hardened soap or cream. Most were either empty or dried out. No-one seemed to bother throwing anything away.

As for the loo, bath and sink, they looked as if they hadn't been cleaned in months. Evil stains, lurking around the toilet rim and taps, made her retch whenever she had to use them.

Dressing hurriedly in her uniform black T-shirt, ripped jeans and Doc Martens, Morgan thought about how it had been before her mum died. She had lived a charmed life amongst people who loved and encouraged her, making her believe she could do anything she chose. Roll on one year and look at her - living in a human jungle, directionless and debased. What on earth would her mother make of her now?

Morgan looked down at Todd as he lay snoring in bed, sexually sated, his long, lanky body sprawled across the space she had just vacated. He'd probably stay there until lunchtime, she considered, until he eventually hauled himself out for some dishonest labour.

He was in commodities, he had told her, when she first awoke to find herself in his bed. She had no recollection of how she got there. When he produced a small wrap of crack cocaine, waving it tantalisingly beneath her nose, she had realised what he meant.

Of course, he had recognised the craving that oozed out of her every pore, as he swung the small plastic pack in front of her like a metronome.

She had moved in with him, at 27 Balmoral Gardens, only because he fed her addiction and for no other reason. She had known he was trouble. On the rare occasions when she was not in a drugged state, she was constantly on edge, tapping into a subliminal sense of danger in being around him.

In the house, he kept a knife stuffed down the side of his bed. He took it out with him to his 'business meetings', as he described them. Morgan didn't like to dwell on how that worked. She found the best way of coping with it, and with life in general, was to blot it all out with something from the smorgasbord of chemicals Todd always had to hand. For a precious few hours, she could be in a much better place, until the drugs wore off and she had to face the relentless cycle of misery and despair all over again.

Today was different, though. No powders, no pills, just a swig from her water bottle. Peering in her small makeup mirror, Morgan added more mascara and black eyeliner to what remained from the day before and dragged a comb through her short blonde-black hair. It was the most effort she had made in ages. Without looking back, she slipped out of the room, down the stairs and out of the battered front door. Even from the street, she could hear several voices raised in argument inside the house, shouting over the background noise of pumping music. She broke into a run as she caught sight of her bus approaching the stop at the end of the road.

Just in time, she leapt onto the forward platform, then made her way to a seat at the rear. Pulling her sleeve over her fist, Morgan wiped clear a circle on the steamed-up window. She gazed out at rows of cowering houses, clinging together in the grey, dreary cold of a November day. With her headphones firmly fixed in her ears, she set herself to ignore everyone around her as she tried to forget who and where she was.

27

"Do you want this one, love?" the bus driver called out.

Morgan hadn't noticed there was no-one else left on the bus. The miserable streets of Denley, where Todd lived, had given way to the neater gardens and larger houses near Granton cemetery, where the bus was coming to a halt. She jumped up from her seat, waving acknowledgement to the driver as she alighted from the bus.

A bright winter sun suddenly pierced the thick cloud cover, casting shafts of light across the pavement where she walked. It seemed inappropriate on this day of sorry pilgrimage. The earlier greyness suited her mood better.

Morgan tried to remember the weather a year ago to the day, but that detail had escaped her. When her memory travelled back there, she saw only darkness.

Walking through the cemetery gates, she relished the peace of the place. So many people, yet never a word spoken. No raised voices, no anger, just a quiet calm. The clamour of daily life ceased at the gates and only birdsong broke the silence. She took her time to stroll through the avenue running through the middle of the site. Her mum's plot, planted with a rose bush, was down a path to the right. She could find it with her eyes closed, so often had she visited. Bad days, birthdays, Christmas, anniversaries - all brought her here, in search of solace.

Morgan was about to turn down the path to her mum's plot when she noticed there was someone sitting on the bench her nan had dedicated as a memorial to Grandad Derek, who had died several years earlier. Immediately, she stopped in her tracks and stepped behind a neighbouring tree.

"Shit!" she muttered, under her breath. Though he had changed since the last time she saw him, when she slammed out of her family home more than six months ago, there was no mistaking that she was looking at her father.

Morgan was shocked that her instinct was to immediately run into his arms, as she used to when she was little. Pressed tightly against his burly frame, she had always felt safe from all harm. It surprised her that the sight of him stirred such a powerful emotion of longing after all that had happened. But it didn't last.

28

With the next beat of her heart, the familiar anger and bitterness came rushing in, sweeping aside all gentler emotions.

Morgan turned and began to walk away, as unobtrusively as possible, hoping he wouldn't notice her. As she headed off in the opposite direction, she heard her name echoing across the silence.

"Morgan!"

She walked more quickly, trying to put distance between them, but she heard him running up behind her.

"Morgan!" Footsteps following her. A hand on her arm. She shook him off and broke into a run, anxious to get away.

"Morgan, please!"

"What?"

She spun round, her face fixed in an angry glare. The sight that confronted her made her gasp. In place of the dapper, well-groomed man she remembered, the person she was looking at could have been a homeless beggar, down on his luck. His hair, which had grown long to his collar, was greasy and unkempt. It looked as if he hadn't been near a hairdresser in months. He was wearing a pair of dirty, faded jeans and a lightweight quilted jacket, on which both pockets were grubby and torn. His face was puffy and the eyes that looked directly into hers were bleary and blood-shot. Obviously still drinking, then.

"I was hoping – well, I'm not sure hope is the right word – I thought you might come today. I've been here since the gates opened. I just wanted to see you, to see how you are."

Morgan gave a bitter laugh. Should she tell him how she really was – treat him to the details of how degraded and sordid her life had become? Would he like to know that she could barely make it through a day without some mind-altering drug that helped her to forget her shitty life?

She could go on to tell him about her new boyfriend Todd, whom he probably already knew as a small-time drug dealer. Theirs was a relationship of mutual convenience, she could explain. It was based on his insatiable desire for sex and hers, for a continuous supply of the pills and powder on which she now depended.

She guessed that none of that was what he would want to hear.

"I'm great, dad. Really great. How about you? Still drinking?"

The blood-shot eyes looked away into the distance behind her. Morgan knew she had hit home. In no time at all, she had taken them back to where they were, her and her dad, in the months following her mother's death. Words had flown between them like arrows, each one finding its mark and leaving a painful wound.

"Please Morgan. Not today. Can't we just be kind to each other, at least for one day?"

And there it was. Just when she thought she was achieving a state of numbness, in which nothing could hurt her, she discovered the molten anger that bubbled away at her very core, threatening to explode without warning and scorch everyone in its path.

"Kind? What, like you were to me when you left me distraught, thinking both my parents were dead? Kind, like when you didn't tell me about mum until you were good and ready, by which time it was too late for me to say goodbye? Does being kind mean leaving your daughter to tidy away your empty whisky and wine bottles whilst you drink yourself into oblivion? Does being kind mean leaving me to fend for myself whilst you slump into a self-pitying stupor? Is that what kindness is all about, dad? 'Cos if it is, I'm not interested, thanks all the same."

Morgan was shaking and boiling over with rage. She couldn't stop the angry words from flying out of her mouth like heat-seeking missiles directed to eliminate their target. She watched as her father started sobbing like a baby, crumpling over as if protecting his body from her verbal hammer blows.

What a fucking disaster! All she had wanted, on this dreadful anniversary, was to spend a few moments alone with her mum. Imagining Mel could hear her, she would reveal her innermost fears and anxiety about the hopeless downward spiral of her life. She would speak of her despair about the future, as she struggled to find a way forward for herself. Estranged from her dad and now in a seemingly endless drift from day to meaningless day, she would beg for her mum's advice on what she should do.

"Please Morgan," Gareth continued, pleading with her. "I'm sorry for being such a rubbish father. I've let you down. I know I have. Please love, let me make it up to you. Let me help you."

Morgan laughed out loud. "Help me? Are you joking? Have you looked at yourself lately? You're a fucking mess. You can't help yourself, never mind anyone else. I'm fine without you, dad. Just leave me alone. That's all I ask."

She turned and ran, as fast as she could. No chance her dad would catch up with her, in the state he was in. Dashing out of the cemetery gates, she spotted the number 16 bus that would take her to her nan's house. She stuck out her arm and jumped on, only pausing for breath when she found a seat.

Briefly, Morgan glimpsed her dad, standing stock still, at the cemetery gates, watching as the bus disappeared from his view. He looked distraught, his face a picture of misery and pain. A pang of guilt plucked at her heart. As much as she blamed him for the way she was feeling, she knew it wasn't all his fault. If her mum had been sitting next to her now, Morgan knew what she would have said.

"Cut him some slack love. You know what he's like. He's no good with the emotional stuff. He can't handle his own feelings, never mind anyone else's. It's partly the job. He shuts off to protect himself, so he can carry on doing what he does. If he didn't, he wouldn't be able to cope with all the evil and horror he faces every day."

God! It was all such a mess. She could see no way out of it now. Even if she tried to forgive him, her dad would soon be on her case again about dropping out of school, hooking up with Todd and wasting her life. That was rich, coming from him. Most days he'd gone to work pissed, when she still lived with him. That was if he bothered to go in at all. From what she had seen this morning he didn't look as if he'd sobered up, so she wouldn't be taking any lectures from him about "applying herself", as he liked to call it.

Morgan sighed and peered out of the bus window. The promise of a sunny morning had faded, obliterated by thick, grey cloud that stole the light. It was fitting, really, on this most miserable of days. She would stay at her nan's tonight, her only safe place. She couldn't face going back to Todd's. He was bound to be pissed or drugged up, or both, so he wouldn't miss her. She'd have a long soak in the bath to wash off the accumulated grime of Todd's house, then an early night in the deliciously comfortable bed her nan always kept made up for her. Thinking of the crisp fresh smelling bed linen and her nan's home-cooking perked up her spirits slightly. Right now, it was as good as it got for her.

CHAPTER EIGHT

Gareth Fairley opened his eyes and looked about him, trying to orientate himself. His senses registered the familiar dry mouth, dull headache and scratchy eyes that usually plagued him on waking. Looking down, he noted he was fully dressed, with his shoes on, lying on the sofa where he had fallen asleep. The light was fading in the room, so it must be late afternoon. A swish of traffic outside told him that it was raining.

Slowly, he heaved himself upright from his prone position and swung his legs to the floor. Beside him, on a small coffee table, stood a half-drunk glass of whisky next to an empty bottle. Without a further thought, he drained the contents in one gulp. Instantly, he felt more alert.

Then he remembered. Today was the first anniversary of Mel's death. His favourite photograph of her lay on the floor beside him, where he had dropped it a few hours earlier, after drinking himself into a stupor. Many more photographs were displayed around the living room. She was everywhere he looked, each photograph reflecting a moment in their wonderful life together.

One of his favourites was of Mel, sitting on the beach in the south of France where they took their first holiday, only a couple of months after they met. She was leaning back on her elbows, looking straight at the camera, her light brown hair hanging away from her in a thick, luxuriant curtain. Her mouth was parted seductively, as if inviting a kiss. The memory made him ache for her now, as intensely as he had then.

Gareth had met Mel when he was thirty-two and she, five years younger. After a disastrous first marriage at nineteen – which quickly ended - he had tumbled from relationship to relationship, shying away from commitment. All that changed the night he met Mel at a mate's party. She had taken his breath and his speech away, so that he could barely string a sentence together in their first conversation. It had taken a supreme effort to gather the courage to ask her out and he had messed that up.

Fortunately, she had given him the benefit of the doubt and they were married a year later, when Mel was a few months pregnant with Morgan. They had been deliriously happy and excited on their wedding day. Now, as he gazed at the photographic representations of so many precious moments, the room seemed to pulsate with Mel's absence.

Gareth gave an involuntary sob, his face crumpling into folds of misery.

"I'm so sorry, my darling," he said, aloud, as if Mel were sitting in her favourite chair by the window.

Just as he did every day, Gareth berated himself for his perceived failure to find the driver who hit his wife and drove off, leaving her for dead. A whole year had passed without a single lead to the despicable coward who ruined his life and that of his daughter, not to mention his mother-in-law, Eileen.

Although Ted Dunlop, the only witness, stated that Mel had run out in front of the driver, who had no chance to avoid a collision, he didn't believe it. His wife was a highly intelligent woman and a devoted mother. There was no way she would do exactly what she told her pupils and daughter not to do – step out into the path of an oncoming vehicle. It wouldn't happen. Old Ted Dunlop's recollections must have been incorrect. He was an elderly chap, who'd had a fall immediately before the accident. Before any of his officers could patiently try to tease out his subconscious registering of important facts, that might assist the investigation, the poor old fellow died, probably from the shock of his ordeal.

To Gareth's great frustration, there was no CCTV footage covering the road along which the car must have travelled through Flintby, and the school's cameras did not reach as far as the accident spot.

Appeals were put out for information for months after the incident. Someone must be aware of a car which had recently sustained damage at its front, he said to camera, at a news conference for the regional television news. Requests for assistance were sent to neighbouring forces, asking them to pass on anything at all which might be relevant. There had been a deafening silence on all counts, which made the rage inside him grow. It lodged, like a festering tumour, in his gut. Eventually,

34

he could not bear to confront what he saw as his own impotence and ineptitude. Increasingly, he stayed away from the office and drank himself into oblivion at home.

Today had been a terrible day. Not only was it the first, awful anniversary of his wife's death, but his attempt to meet and speak with his daughter, at the cemetery, had gone spectacularly wrong. The look on her face when she saw him, told him all he needed to know about how low he had sunk in her estimation, and how badly he had failed her. The image of his earlier encounter with his daughter was burned onto his eyeballs, and he had been unable to think about anything else all day. He had coped, or rather failed to cope, in the usual way – by drowning himself in alcohol until he passed out. What a way to honour his wife's memory and to support his only child.

Hauling himself to his feet, Gareth staggered upstairs to the en-suite bathroom. Catching a glimpse of himself in the mirrored cabinet above the sink, he was shocked by his appearance. He couldn't remember the last time he had looked at his reflection. There he stood, a bleary-eyed, unshaven wreck of a man with mottled, puffy skin and sagging jowls. He could easily be mistaken for one of the street-sleeping drunks he used to pick up from time to time, slumped in the urine-stinking alleyways of Granton. Christ, was this really him now?

Suddenly his stomach lurched and flipped watery bile into his mouth. He heaved and spat into the toilet bowl, quickly flushing away the foul-smelling vomit. What a bloody mess he was – no good to his daughter, his colleagues or anyone else. What was the point of him even being here?

He watched his shaky hand reach out to the cabinet, as if guided by a remote force. Opening the door, Gareth was confronted by an array of half-empty blister packs of tablets. Most were either sleeping pills or anti-depressants, prescribed for him by his doctor. He'd taken a few from time to time, then abandoned the course, preferring to lose himself in a bottle of wine or whisky.

It would be so easy to end it all and be done with this shit, he reflected. All he had to do was empty the innocuous-looking sugar-coated pills into his mouth, strip after strip, until they had all gone. He could wash them all down with that half bottle of whisky beckoning to him from downstairs, then lie back on the sofa and drift slowly out of this world. Sweet oblivion and an end to all his pain. Forever.

His fingers reached towards a packet of anti-depressants, drawn like iron filings to a magnet.

Morgan. Her voice, her face, in front of him, as vivid as if she were standing right there in the room.

Morgan.

"Christ!" he shouted out loud to the wretch of a man in the mirror. "What sort of heartless, selfish bastard are you?"

Here he was, contemplating his suicide, with no thought of the impact on his daughter. How could he leave Morgan to cope with the death of another parent? None of this sorry mess was her fault, yet he'd left her to struggle on, alone, whilst he wallowed in self-pity, unable to move through his grief. Even if she never spoke to him again, the least he could do for her was to stay alive.

One by one, Gareth emptied the tablets into the toilet, flushing repeatedly until they had all gone. He raced back down the stairs, into the living room, grabbed the bottle of whisky from the coffee table and poured its contents, and those of every other bottle of booze in the house, down the sink. His heart was thumping and his tongue felt as if it was shrinking inside his mouth, as the pungent smell of alcohol filled the kitchen. He didn't know how he was going to cope without it, but he knew he sure as hell needed to try.

He crossed the hall, into his home office, where books and papers lay scattered about the floor and desk. Somewhere he had a pamphlet listing the names of therapists and counsellors whose services were available to serving police officers. It had been pressed on him by HR at one of the many meetings to which he had been summoned, during the past year, to discuss his performance. Frantically, he turned out documents onto the floor as he hunted through every drawer of his desk, searching for the information sheet. Finally, crumpled in a corner, he found what he was looking for.

Anxiously straightening out the creases in the pamphlet, he was relieved to find that he could still read its contents. Thank God he'd had the foresight to keep it, subconsciously anticipating, perhaps, that he might one day need to refer to it. If he'd given in to his first instinct to throw it away, he would have been too embarrassed and ashamed to have asked for another.

Inside the pamphlet was a list of names, two of which had been ringed for him by Jan, his HR manager. Clearly, she, too, believed he might need to seek help. It wasn't surprising. He'd been a mess for months, now.

It went against the grain for him to seek help from anyone. Reflection and introspection were not part of his makeup. During their marriage, Mel had been the only one to whom he had ever confessed his private worries and concerns and even she had to work hard to persuade him to open up to her.

He used to think that it was the job that had been the making of him, but really it was Mel. She had softened the wild streak in him and restored his faith in human nature, which he so often needed after dealing with some of the worst examples of it. He owed his success to her steadfast encouragement and unwavering belief in him. How quickly it had all fallen apart after her death.

Bringing his mind back to the moment, Gareth scanned the pamphlet he was holding. He read the biography of Patricia Fellowes - one of the names signposted for him - and researched her profile on the internet. Before he had chance to change his mind, he tapped her telephone number into his phone and listened to the ringtone. It was after six, now. Probably she would have finished work for the day. Would he have the courage to try again tomorrow? He honestly didn't know. Just as he was about to give up, a slightly breathless voice answered.

"Patricia Fellowes."

"Patricia, this is DCI Gareth Fairley of Granton CID."

"Hello Gareth," said the calm, reassuring voice at the end of the line. She sounded as if she had been expecting his call for some time. "What can I do for you?"

Biting his lip, he willed himself to respond.

"I need your help," he said. As soon as the words left his mouth, it was as if he had been unclamped from the dead weight of guilt and grief he had been dragging around for the past year. He'd taken a first step towards a better place. He knew it wasn't going to be easy to overcome his demons, but at last, he felt ready to try. More than ready; in fact, he was desperate.

"I'm so glad you called me, Gareth. When can we meet?"

"As soon as possible," he replied.

CHAPTER NINE

Eileen Garrett lived in a neat, three-bedroomed terraced house, close to the centre of Granton. She and her husband Derek had bought it shortly after they married, sixty years ago. It was the only house they had ever owned.

Five years had passed since the love of her life had died, succumbing to lung cancer after being a smoker for many years. Ironically, he gave up when he retired, at sixty-five, but it didn't save him. He was a few days short of his seventy-fifth birthday when he passed away, after several years of suffering. It was no age, these days, Eileen sadly reflected when she sat alone, poring over her photograph albums. Look how many people go on into their nineties and beyond, she commented to her friends over cups of tea and sympathy. Why couldn't she have had Derek a few more years? It didn't seem fair.

Though she missed him every day, Eileen was glad Derek had died before suffering the loss of his beloved Mel. Always a family man, he was devoted to his daughters, Melissa, and her older sister, Jessica. He would never have coped with the loss of his youngest child. It would have broken him, as it nearly had her. If it wasn't for Morgan, she would have willed herself to sleep, and not to wake up.

There was no favouritism in how she felt about her only granddaughter. She loved Jess, her husband Charlie and their two boys, more than she could ever say. But they were a strong, cohesive unit – always had been. They would cope and thrive. She didn't need to worry about them.

With Morgan and Gareth, it was a different story. It broke Eileen's heart to see two of the people she loved most in the world pulling in opposite directions, but her strong-willed granddaughter was adamant she didn't want any more to do with her father, and Gareth seemed unable to get through to her. Seeing the state he was in, it wasn't surprising.

Gareth visited regularly, helping her with shopping and odd jobs - for which she was grateful - but the smell of alcohol on him was almost overpowering, at times. It was a wonder he hadn't lost his driving licence. She didn't know what was happening with his job, but he never seemed to be at work these days. He was always on sick leave, which wasn't like him at all. He loved his job, always had.

Most of all, though, Eileen worried about Morgan. It wasn't just her granddaughter's changed appearance that concerned her. Most youngsters went through a rebellious streak; it was part of growing up. Goodness knows, even Melissa had challenged her and Derek at times. No, what kept her awake at night was that lad Morgan had hooked up with – Todd Hopkins. He lived in Denley, a rough area, on the outskirts of Granton, and home to more than its fair share of criminals. Eileen could well imagine what Morgan was getting up to with him, and none of it was good.

"Worrying about it won't change anything," Eileen said aloud. She often talked to herself these days. "Gareth and Morgan'll have to sort it out between them. It's the only way."

With a sigh, Eileen slowly climbed the stairs. It took longer these days and seemed to require much more effort than it used to do, though she would never admit it to Jessica. Her eldest daughter would only go on at her again about buying a bungalow in the Midlands, near her.

She felt tired and low today and had barely slept the night before. Memories of that terrible night, a year ago, had played over and over in her mind. She remembered Gareth's phone call, giving her the devastating news, that Melissa had been killed in a car accident. It would be etched on her memory for as long as she had the ability to remember.

Sometimes Eileen felt as if her life had frozen at that point in time. It was impossible to believe a year had already passed since her daughter died. At any minute, she expected Melissa to ring the doorbell before letting herself in.

"Only me!" Mel used to shout, in a sing-song voice, before heading straight for the kitchen to make them both a cup of tea. "I'll put the kettle on." What Eileen wouldn't give to hear those words again. The pain of her loss came flooding back each time she had to confront the fact that it was never going to happen.

She should have gone with Morgan to the cemetery, today, Eileen told herself. She should have laid flowers for Derek and now for Melissa too, but she couldn't face it. Morgan seemed to find it helpful to spend time there, but she drew no comfort from it. All it did was to remind her of what she had lost.

Instead, she preferred to go through the ritual of changing the sheets on her daughter's bed and dusting her room. Surrounded by Mel's favourite photographs and posters still clinging to the faded wallpaper, it transported her to happier days when Melissa was growing up in this house and she and her sister used to run between each other's rooms, shrieking and laughing and frequently arguing, their favourite music filling the house. Occasionally, Derek would half-heartedly tell them to turn it down, but he didn't really mean it. He had loved the energy and vibrancy his girls brought into his home.

Eileen picked up a photograph of Melissa, taken just before she went off to university. She traced a finger over her daughter's beautiful, broad smile. How could someone drive off, after knocking her down, leaving her poor, broken body lying on a cold, hard road, not even afforded the basic respect of the driver's time and attention to check on her, report the accident and stay with her until help arrived. What sort of human being behaved like that, she asked herself?

Cursing her arthritic hands, Eileen bundled up the bed linen for washing and placed it at the top of the stairs. Only Morgan slept in Mel's room now, and she never knew when that was going to be. It didn't matter to Eileen. If Morgan felt comfortable to stay with her, she was only too glad to be able to offer a hot bath, a decent meal and clean sheets, no questions asked. From the state of her, whenever she turned up on the doorstep, Eileen didn't think she was getting any of that at Todd Hopkins' house.

Slowly, Eileen picked her way down the stairs, carrying the large bundle of bed linen. Thoughts of Morgan, Gareth and her daughter swirled around her head on this dreadful first anniversary.

Whether it was because she wasn't concentrating properly, or not looking where she was going over the top of the washing, she couldn't say, when she was later questioned. All Eileen could remember was her foot slipping suddenly off the edge of the middle stair, then herself bumping painfully down to the bottom. She couldn't grab hold of anything to soften her fall because of the tangle of sheets, pillowcases and duvet cover she was carrying. Landing with a thud at the bottom of the stairs, she felt a shooting pain through her right hip, as if someone had thrust a spear into her side. Instantly, she knew what had happened. She had broken her hip and now she was unable to move or call for help. The telephone was out of reach, and her mobile, which she rarely used, was sitting on the small table beside her chair, on the opposite side of the living room.

There was a part of her that welcomed the sickening pain in her side. She might die here if no-one found her. The thought didn't trouble her at all. Death held no fear for her. It was life and all its complications that made her head spin and kept her awake at night. She could so easily leave it all behind. It would be a blessed relief, she acknowledged.

A surge of tiredness swept over her like a sedative, coursing through her veins. The familiar furniture and mementoes around her were starting to blur and become unrecognisable. It was only the throb of pain around her hip that prevented her from drifting into an unconscious state.

Faintly Eileen heard a bell ringing. Was that real or was it inside her head, she wondered? She was too tired to think about it. Just so very, very tired.

CHAPTER TEN

Morgan strode up Victoria Terrace to her nan's house. She was still fuming over the encounter with her father. How dare he trespass on the quiet time she so desperately needed with her mother? On this day of all days, as well. How typical of him to think only of himself and what he wanted.

Arriving at the shiny, red-painted front door of number 34 Victoria Terrace, Morgan rang the doorbell. She didn't like to let herself in, for fear of giving her nan a shock.

Still muttering to herself, she waited at the door, listening for the sound of her grandmother shuffling towards the door in the cat slippers Morgan had bought her last Christmas. She rang again, unable to identify any sign of life from within the house.

She glanced at her phone and saw it was lunchtime. Eileen rarely ventured out these days unless it was with her or her father. Morgan knew he visited regularly and took Eileen shopping once a week. Peering through the frosted glass panels in the top half of the door, she knocked and called out.

"Nan! Are you in? Can you hear me?"

Still no sound from inside the house. She couldn't peer through the letterbox to check, because her bloody father insisted Eileen get rid of it. There'd been a gang of teenagers going round the area, shoving fireworks through letter boxes, he said. You need one of those boxes you fit on the wall, he said. So, he bought her one, fixing it himself to the left of the door, where it was no bloody use to her now.

Morgan knocked louder, just in case Eileen couldn't hear the bell for some reason.

"Nan!" she shouted again. Straining to look through the heavily obscured glass, she picked out a dark blur, on the floor, near the bottom of the stairs. Her heart was in her mouth as she realised it must be her nan, lying there.

Frantically, Morgan searched in her pack for the front door key she usually carried with her. She swore out loud when she realised she had left it at Todd's house, safely tucked away in her spare pair of boots. How could she have been so stupid as to

43

forget it? Wracking her brain, she remembered Nan hid a key in the back garden, in case of emergencies. She raced round to the back of the house, hurled herself against the sticky old garden gate and after throwing over and kicking aside a few plant pots, finally found the key. Thank God! she cried out loud.

In seconds, Morgan was inside the house, where she found her nan in a crumpled heap, at the bottom of the stairs, resting on a soft mound of sheets. Her lips were moving, though barely a sound emerged. It was obvious to Morgan that her grandmother was beginning to lose consciousness. I'm sure that's bad, she thought, crouching down beside her, to try and make out what Eileen was saying.

"Nan, it's me. Morgan. Don't worry. Everything's going to be alright. I'm going to call an ambulance. Just try and tell me what happened."

Eileen's bloodless lips moved slowly, but still Morgan couldn't make out what she was saying. She was afraid to move her, for fear of causing greater injury, so she gently stroked her head and kept talking to her, whilst attempting to explain the situation to the emergency services operator as best she could.

It looked as if her Nan had fallen down the stairs and possibly broken something, Morgan told the questioning voice on the other end of the line, but she couldn't be sure.

After what seemed like hours, but was probably only minutes, an ambulance arrived. Morgan continued to talk to her nan, but without getting much sense back from her. Two paramedics gently examined Eileen, provoking plaintive cries as they gently checked her over.

"Looks like it might be a fracture, I'm afraid," said one. "We can give her some pain relief, but we're going to need to take her in. Does anyone live with her here? If it's a fracture, she's going to need some help when she comes out."

Morgan was struggling to hold back her tears. Her poor Nan. She couldn't believe her family's bad luck.

"She lives alone," Morgan said. "My grandad died a few years ago. But I visit often and so does my dad and my aunt Jess."

Suddenly, it struck her how frail and vulnerable her nan looked. It was easy to forget she was nearly eighty years old. She always seemed to be the strong one. Without her, Morgan would never have made it through the last year. She had come to rely on Eileen's quiet wisdom and unquestioning love. Now, Morgan suspected, it would be her nan who needed the support. They were all going to have to rally round to look after her. Quite how she was going to work that out with her father, she had no idea. Right now, she didn't want to think about it.

"Ok thanks," said one of the paramedics, as he and the other guy gently lifted Eileen onto a stretcher. They'll look into all that at the hospital. We need to get her in as soon as possible."

"Can I go with her?"

"Yep. Hop in. You can help us with details on the way. Now, let's get this young lady to some help."

CHAPTER ELEVEN

December 2015

In the compact kitchen of Eileen's house, Morgan and her aunt Jess were squaring up to each other.

"I can look after her," Morgan protested. "I live here now, and I can be with her the whole time. I can keep her safe."

"Morgan," said her aunt, softening her expression, "I appreciate you want to be there for nan, and I think it's wonderful that you do, but we have to be realistic. Since the fall, she's really gone downhill, and the doctors say she's not likely to improve. She needs more care than you can give her, however hard you try. Besides, I don't mean to be harsh, but it really is time you were finding your own way and making a future for yourself. It's what your mum would want. I can almost hear her saying it to me."

Seeing Eileen lying at the bottom of her stairs after her fall, lying fragile and broken, like an injured bird, had shaken Morgan from her catatonic state and given her focus. It was as if a lump of ice around her heart had suddenly shattered and melted, allowing emotion to flow freely again. She had ended the toxic relationship with Todd, sweated and screamed her way to being clean, and moved permanently into her grandmother's house, visiting her every day whilst she was in hospital.

With a new sense of purpose, Morgan had blagged her way onto a crash course to re-sit her A levels the following summer and had taken a part-time job in a coffee shop in Granton, to pay the bills on her nan's place. Although her father paid her a monthly allowance, she was determined not to touch it. She would stand on her own two feet from now on, she vowed to herself; she didn't need any help from him.

"I think she'll get better if she comes back home," Morgan pleaded with her aunt. "Being in hospital for nearly a month has made her depressed."

Jessica sighed in the face of Morgan's obstinacy. Her sister had been the same when she believed strongly in something.

"Look, I understand how you feel about it, but nan's going into respite care for a couple of weeks and that's all arranged. Harley Grange Care Home is highly rated and, better still, it's only a few streets away. Nan will still feel at home, in an area where she's lived most of her life.

Morgan gave a dismissive snort. She was deeply unhappy with her aunt's decision, but it was pointless arguing with her any longer. Her aunt Jess held Power of Attorney for Eileen, so had the last word on what happened to her.

"Well, I'm going to be round there every spare moment I have," Morgan responded. "If she's unhappy, in Harley Grange, I want her to come straight back home and I'll look after her."

Jessica nodded. There was no point in sharing with Morgan the fact that Eileen was booked into respite care until such time as a permanent room became available at Harley Grange. Jessica had talked it over, at length, with her husband, and with Gareth, and they had all agreed it was the best way forward for Eileen. Despite that, and particularly after hearing Morgan's impassioned views, Jessica could not help agonising as to whether she was doing the right thing for her mother.

In silence, heavy with unspoken words, Morgan and her aunt packed a few of Eileen's prized possessions to take to the care home, ahead of Eileen's arrival.

"Why bother if she's coming back home in a couple of weeks?" Morgan asked defiantly.

"Just to make her feel more at home and less disorientated when she arrives at Harley Grange from the hospital," Jess said, with an air of certainty she didn't feel. She suspected that Morgan was already guessing that her nan was going into the care home permanently and was building up to an accusatory showdown, at any moment.

After arranging Eileen's possessions in her room at Harley Grange, Morgan and her aunt drove to the hospital to collect Eileen and take her to the home.

On Eileen's arrival, the staff fluttered around her attentively and Jess and Morgan did their best to inject some cheer and jollity into the day, but Morgan could see that Eileen was stricken with anxiety and confusion. It broke Morgan's heart to see the puzzled look on her nan's face as she ran her skeletal hands over familiar objects now arranged in a strange space.

Morgan felt sick to her stomach to see her nan look questioningly at them both. Did she feel betrayed, Morgan wondered, her head pounding with the tension of the day? Whatever it was that was going on in her nan's muddled mind, Morgan was even more determined to spend every spare waking moment she had with her grandmother, to try and restore her lovely smile and wicked sense of humour. Kissing her nan on the head as she and her aunt left, to allow Eileen to be settled by the carers, Morgan prayed that her efforts might be successful, and she would catch a glimpse of her nan again one day soon.

Josie Simmonds proved to be the answer to everyone's concerns. With her pink hair and multiple piercings, she was an arresting sight. Her infectious laugh reverberated around Harley Grange, dragging a smile from even the most taciturn resident.

Eileen took to Josie instantly and it was obvious that Josie had won her trust. Within a week of leaving hospital, Eileen was taking faltering steps again, supported by Josie and her walking frame. More importantly, Josie lifted Eileen's spirits - something Morgan had been struggling to do. Keeping the promise she had made, Morgan spent every spare moment at Harley Grange, helping with her grandmother's care as much as she was allowed. Not only did it give her peace of mind, but she found she enjoyed it.

"You could do this for a living you know," said Josie, one day, after Morgan had helped her to give Eileen a bath. "You're a natural."

Morgan laughed, though secretly she was quite pleased. She admired Josie and her no-nonsense but infinitely caring attitude towards Eileen. The pair were rapidly becoming friends and Morgan valued Josie's forthright opinions and advice. Whenever she tried to think about her future, Morgan became mired in hopelessness. Beyond re-sitting her A levels, she didn't know what she was going to do. Josie's throwaway remark made her think.

For the first time since her mother's death, Morgan settled into a rhythm around study, and visiting and caring for Eileen; she even went on a night out with Josie and a couple of the other carers whom she had come to know well from her frequent visits to Harley Grange.

In the week before Christmas, Morgan and Josie managed to bundle Eileen into Josie's car - her slight frame swaddled in warm clothing - and take her out to a nearby garden centre for tea and a mince pie. It was all Morgan could do to hold back her tears, as she watched her beloved grandmother nibbling daintily on a mince pie and drinking a cup of tea. Eileen looked almost happy, Morgan reflected, as she observed her chattering away inconsequentially to Josie. Seeing her nan like that filled Morgan's heart with unaccustomed joy. Perhaps, she reflected hopefully, life might be starting to improve at last.

Two days later, it seemed that Morgan's hopes for a brighter future might be realised in some small part.

"I hope you don't mind," said Josie, who was hovering in the reception area of Harley Grange when Morgan arrived to visit her nan. "Bev, the manager is doing her pieces over the staffing rota for Christmas. We're short-staffed anyway and people want time off with their families, so she's looking for all the help she can get. I mentioned you might be interested in a care assistant role. What do you think?"

"Me?" said Morgan in surprise.

"Yeah. We were talking about it only the other day. You're a natural for this work. I've been doing this job a few years now, so I do know what I'm talking about."

"But I have no experience – no qualifications," Morgan protested.

"Don't need any," Josie responded. "You'd be doing what you do now – helping out at mealtimes, taking the drinks trolley round, talking to people. The only difference would be that you'd be getting paid for it."

Morgan experienced a flutter of happiness at hearing Josie talk about her in this way. Although only five years older than her, to Morgan, Josie seemed much more mature and capable. She had a steady relationship, a young child and she worked full-time at the home. She was the sort of person, Morgan considered, who overflowed with kindness and compassion for others. If she thought Morgan could fit in at Harley Grange, then it would be cowardly and churlish not to at least try for a position.

"Ok," said Morgan. "How do I go about this?"

By the end of the day, Morgan was the latest recruit at Harley Grange.

"You're saving my life," said Bev, the manager of the care home. "I've been tearing my hair out over the staffing for Christmas. It will really make a difference, and all the residents know and love you already. I need to recruit more full-time, qualified staff, but it's so difficult these days. I know you're studying and hoping to go to university, but we can work around that. The job's yours for as long as you want it."

Though Morgan harboured a lingering ambition to follow in Mel's footsteps and become a teacher, she recognised that possibility was some way off. She was learning to live more in the moment and, for the time being, a position at Harley Grange would be perfect for her. She would give up her part-time job at the coffee shop in town and fit in her studies around her new role. Best of all, though, she would be able to see Eileen every day, if she wanted; and that was, by far, the greatest incentive for accepting Bev's offer.

"Ok," said Morgan. "When do I start?"

"Tomorrow?" Bev responded, looking hopefully at Morgan.

"I'll phone my boss at the coffee shop and if I can square it with him, I'll be here then, all present and correct."

"And I will be very pleased to see you," said Bev, giving Morgan a beaming smile.

CHAPTER TWELVE

Todd Hopkins zipped his hoodie tightly up to his neck and thrust his hands deep into the pockets. The bus shelter opposite Harley Grange Care Home had one of its glass panels missing and a chill north wind was slicing through him. At least it made a change from the pelting rain and hailstones that had showered him a few moments ago. He hopped from foot to foot, trying to encourage some warmth back into his ice-cold toes.

Just when Todd thought he was going to freeze to death, a familiar figure appeared in his sights. As Morgan descended the drive from the building directly opposite, Todd checked the time on the illuminated screen of his phone. It was nearly six o'clock.

He let Morgan draw some way ahead of him before emerging from his hiding place and falling in behind her. Darkness was his friend in this, the depth of winter. He was pretty sure Morgan would be going down the next road on the right, then on to Victoria Terrace. Having tailed her along that route numerous times, Todd knew there were huge, old trees and generous front gardens offering places to conceal himself, if necessary.

It had taken him several weeks to track Morgan down after she slipped out of his bed never to return. Sad fuck that he was, he had already bought her a Christmas present of a bracelet she liked. All she left him was a shitty little note, stuffed under his bedroom door.

"Dear Todd," it read.*" I need to get my head together or I'll go mad. Thanks for letting me crash at yours. Have a good life. Morgan xx*

He had stared at it for ages, thinking the words might rearrange themselves into a different meaning that made sense to him, but the message remained the same.

He had tried her mobile, but she never answered. Sobbing and pleading, he had left loads of messages for her, begging her to come home. Thinking about how pathetic he must have sounded made him cringe.

He had told himself she would be back; that she wouldn't be able to cope without him and the medication he freely supplied to her. It hadn't happened and she didn't reappear. When he realised she wasn't coming back, he went on a bender for several days, indulging his misery in a mind-blowing mix of drugs and alcohol. Even his mum, Shelagh, was worried.

"You're gonna kill yourself, Todd," she said, when she found him vomiting copiously into the toilet. "You need to stop."

"Leave me alone," he said, waving her away, before taking refuge in another helping of pills and booze.

When he had emerged from near obliteration, all Todd wanted was to talk to Morgan. He was pissed that she'd dumped him after all he'd done for her. When they first met, she had said she had nowhere to live, so he'd taken her back to his mum's house. Shelagh hadn't been bothered; she never knew who was living under her roof from one day to the next. Morgan was just another troubled soul he had added to the bubbling cauldron of dysfunctional and itinerant humanity, which regularly resided at 27 Balmoral Gardens. Anyway, Morgan had fitted right in, and they'd been good together. She'd have to make it up to him, but he would forgive her, if she agreed to come back.

Feeling listless and edgy, Todd had begun searching for Morgan all over town. Throughout the grey days and long nights of winter, he had haunted the streets of Granton, visiting all the pubs and clubs they used to go to and asking around after her, but no-one seemed to remember her. He had trawled through social media but could find no trace of her. It was as if she had disappeared off the face of the earth.

Then one day, in early December, he had spotted Morgan, walking up the hill out of Granton town centre. Todd recognised her instantly, even though she had changed her appearance. She looked different from the waif-like creature he first saw in The Feathers, where he regularly hung out. The dirty-blonde hair and heavy black make-up were gone, and now her hair was brown and shiny and her skin sort of glowed. She was wearing ordinary faded jeans and an oversized hoodie, but the DMs gave her away. The sight of her had almost winded him. She was even more beautiful, and he had realised that he wanted her as much as ever.

The urge to run up to her and stop her in her tracks was overpowering. Todd had so many questions for her. Why did she run out on him like that? Why didn't she want to be with him anymore? Of course, he knew there was no point confronting her in the middle of the street. She'd tell him where to go, then scarper. He had to figure out a way to hold her attention and he was working on that.

Todd had followed her home from Granton, on that occasion, to the little house on Victoria Terrace, where he had stood watch at a safe distance. He had observed the lights come on, before curtains were drawn and Morgan disappeared from his sights. He had lingered, watching, until the winter cold ate into his bones and drove him away.

Undeterred, Todd had returned, day after day, until he had discovered not only where she lived, but also that she was regularly visiting a care home, a few streets away from Victoria Terrace. There had been no pattern to her visits, so she must be going in to see someone there, he decided. She had gone on about her nan a lot, when they were together, so he guessed it might be her she was going to see.

Then, in the last few days, there had been a change to Morgan's comings and goings. He knew because he had hung around from early morning until long after darkness had fallen. She arrived and left the care home at the same time each day, once going off with a scary bird with pink hair. Was she working there now, he wondered?

At the end of each vigil, Todd had returned home or taken himself off to the pub, where he mulled over his observations for that day. After each reflection, he had returned to one big, unanswered question. Was Morgan seeing someone else? As far as he could tell, from all the time he had spent watching her, she was living alone and had no social life. That wasn't the Morgan he knew; she had always been ready to party. A theory was forming in his head, but he needed to test it.

After following Morgan home from Harley Grange this evening, Todd had taken up his usual vantage point behind the wall of a house, a few doors up from Morgan's and on the opposite side of the road. He watched as she let herself in to number 34, disappearing through the front door. The rain was hammering down on him now, almost dousing the burning desire in him to confront Morgan so that they could have a talk. All he had to do was cross the road and ring the doorbell, he told himself.

Maybe it was the worsening weather, or perhaps it was something else that deterred him, but he didn't cross the road, turning for home instead. He was beginning to formulate a plan, but he needed more time to think about it. Soon, Todd promised himself, soon he and Morgan would be having that chat, and it would be on his terms.

Pulling his damp hoodie tighter about him, Todd broke into a run, jogging all the way back to Balmoral Gardens.

CHAPTER THIRTEEN

In Harley Grange Care Home, the bustle of the morning routine was subsiding as those residents who had made it to breakfast were transferred to one of the spacious sitting rooms, or back to their own room, if they preferred.

With an air of resignation, Eileen Garrett allowed herself to be helped from the breakfast table and wheeled in her chair to the largest of the two lounges, which overlooked the well-tended gardens at the rear of the property.

Eileen didn't seem to care where she sat, Morgan noticed. Her face was blank and expressionless most of the time. Morgan liked to settle her nan into a wing-backed chair, positioned in one of the bay windows which overlooked the gardens. From there, Eileen could observe the variety of birds and wildlife that ventured into the garden to help themselves to the seeds and fatballs put out for them by residents and staff. Occasionally she would point to and correctly name one of the birds or comment on the small dramas that were played out between the larger birds and their more diminutive relatives. Those were Morgan's most prized moments, when she was given a glimpse of her nan as she used to be.

"Ooh look, nan. Your favourite chair's free. Let's get you sat down before Bernard nips in."

Eileen smiled at her granddaughter but made no comment, as Morgan wheeled her into position and helped her to transfer to a chair. Having settled her nan comfortably, Morgan looked up to see a female resident, newly arrived at the home, like Eileen, steering purposefully towards them in her motorised wheelchair. With admirable skill and precision, the newcomer manoeuvred the chair around tables and seating areas, finishing with a three-point turn before coming to a halt opposite Eileen.

"That was pretty nifty, Phyllis," said Morgan, looking on.

"Years of practice on two wheels m'dear," Phyllis responded.

55

"Whenever I see you in that chair, I picture you tearing around London on your motorbike on some top-secret mission," said Morgan.

Phyllis let out a shout of laughter. "Well, they did call me fearless Phyllis."

Phyllis Edwards, who had moved into the home a couple of weeks before Eileen, was rapidly becoming the life and soul of Harley Grange. She had been a despatch rider during the Second World War which provided her with a fount of gripping stories about her escapades during those difficult years. Morgan had noticed that Eileen paid rapt attention whenever Phyllis was around. In turn, Phyllis appeared very comfortable in Eileen's company. Morgan was grateful for anything or anyone who could form a connection with her nan and put a smile on her face.

"You're up and about early this morning, Phyllis," said Morgan.

"I'm a lady of leisure now," Phyllis retorted, in her broad Yorkshire accent. "What can I say?"

Morgan laughed.

"Actually, my great-niece, Eliza, and her son, Dominic are visiting this morning, so I've made a special effort. What do you think of my outfit?"

"Very colourful, Phyllis. You bring light into our lives," she said, smiling as she observed the ensemble of colours that Phyllis had put together. She was wearing green trousers, an acid yellow, loose top and a deep purple scarf tied jauntily around her neck.

Phyllis hooted with laughter again. Even Eileen smiled.

"I don't think we've met Eliza yet, have we?" Morgan remarked.

"No. She's always working, poor lamb, so it's difficult for her to get here. Dominic, her son, and my great-great nephew, comes home regularly from university, which bucks her up. She's a nervous little thing, Eliza. She wasn't like that when she was a little girl. It was her wretch of a husband who ruined her, running off with another woman, young enough to be his daughter. He was an absolute bastard, that one. I told her so before she married him, but she didn't take any notice. He'd turned her head."

Morgan smiled to herself. Phyllis had an opinion on everything, including matters of which she had no experience.

Although never having married herself, she nevertheless freely dispensed marital and relationship advice to the staff at Harley Grange. It didn't surprise Morgan to hear that Phyllis had done the same with her great-niece.

"Now Dominic is a different kettle of fish altogether," Phyllis continued. "A delightful boy and nothing like his mother. He's training to be a doctor, you know. A very clever lad. I don't know why he bothers to come in and see a silly old woman like me, but I'm very glad he does. He's about your age, Morgan, I should think, and very handsome. I'm sure he's going to be very rich as well. I must introduce you."

"Thanks Phyllis, but I'm not in the market for new friendships of any description. Too busy working and studying. No time for anything else."

"You know what they say, Morgan – all work and no play….."

Morgan smiled but did not respond. Her life had been anything but dull and she was certain that Phyllis would not be able to cope with the details.

"No time to chat, sorry Phyllis," Morgan said, keen to shut down Phyllis' attempts at matchmaking. "People to see and places to go."

Phyllis waved airily at her. "Off you go then, my dear. But remember what I said."

Hurrying down the corridor to assist with another resident, Morgan passed two visitors, whom she didn't recognise. One of them - a petite, bird-like woman with a furrowed brow and anxious expression - was talking to a young guy who towered above her. He was leaning in towards her, listening attentively, as she chattered away, seemingly without pause for breath.

This must be Eliza and her son, whom Phyllis had just been talking about, Morgan thought to herself, as she passed them. The young man looked up, as they drew level, and gave a shy smile. He was certainly good-looking, just as Phyllis had said. To her surprise Morgan found herself smiling broadly in return.

Instantly, her gaze was drawn away by the sight of Bill - another of the residents - tottering across the corridor, without his walker. Still clinging to false notions of his capabilities, he liked to nip out of his room, when he thought no-one was looking, to take a stroll around the home. He refused to accept he was unsteady on his feet and prone to falling. Never having broken a bone, despite numerous falls, he mistakenly believed he was invincible. It meant the staff had to be doubly vigilant that he didn't manage to set off on one of his solitary strolls.

Today, Morgan noticed, Bill looked alarmingly wobbly - staggering along, as if drunk. She hastened towards him, just in time to prevent him falling heavily to the floor. Battling to overcome his protestations, she gently persuaded him back to the safety of his room and coaxed him into his chair. Though Bev had given her a busy schedule for the morning, Morgan sat with Bill, for a few moments, making conversation. She hated to see residents sitting alone in their rooms, staring blankly out of the window. However busy she was, she always tried to make time for conversation.

Glancing at her watch, she saw she was already running late. She had a million jobs to do that day, starting with a residents' review meeting with Bev. I'll have to put a spurt on, she said to herself. Josie had a day off, to take her mum to hospital, which meant they were short staffed. It's going to be a late one, Morgan thought to herself, as she mentally ran through her duties for the rest of the day. Hurriedly, she made her way to the manager's office, all thoughts of Phyllis and her visitors as far as possible from her mind.

After her first, brief encounter with Dominic Cooper, Morgan seemed to continually bump into him around the home.

Sometimes she found him seated between Phyllis and Eileen, entertaining them with jokes and amusing stories; at other times, she came across him in the reception area or passed him in one of the corridors. It happened so often that she found herself wondering if it was entirely coincidental or engineered by Dominic to find a pretext to talk to her. That's what Josie and several of her colleagues repeatedly suggested, relentlessly teasing her about it during her rest breaks.

Increasingly, Morgan would exchange a few words with him, even though she was always pressed for time. Despite herself, she couldn't help noticing that same engaging smile that first drew her attention. It spread slowly up to his eyes then across his whole face, seeming to demand a smile in return.

"He definitely fancies you," said Josie one day, as they were eating their sandwiches together during their lunch break. She and Morgan had just finished helping residents to their tables and assisting those who needed it, to eat their meal. Dominic had wheeled Phyllis to her place at the table she shared with Eileen. He waved and smiled at Morgan before leaving the two friends to their lunch.

"I've told you, Jose, I'm not interested," Morgan replied, through a mouthful of sandwich. "Just drop it will you. I have enough trouble with Phyllis going on about it."

"I'm just saying," said Josie, munching thoughtfully. Morgan had revealed the details of her past during a drunken girls' night out in town. Josie had found herself in floods of tears at the thought that her friend had endured so much trauma in her young life. It just didn't seem fair that one person should have had so much bad luck. This Dominic fella – or Dom, as he asked them to call him - seemed really nice, and he was obviously interested in Morgan. Josie couldn't help wishing for some happiness for her new friend, after all she had been through.

Ah well, she sighed, recognising Morgan's determination to steer well clear of a personal relationship. You can lead a horse to water, but you can't make it drink. Only Morgan could decide when she was ready to open her heart again. It was no-one else's business, and she would say no more about it. Finishing up her sandwiches, she arranged to meet Morgan again at their tea break, before heading off to do the Meds round.

CHAPTER FOURTEEN

Morgan lay in her bath, attempting to soak away her stress. She had lit candles, poured scented oil into the water, and set her phone to play some of her favourite music.

It had been a dark day at Harley Grange.

After sharing her lunch break with Josie, as usual, she had gone to check on Fred, a lovely old chap of whom she had quickly become very fond. He had complained of a headache, at lunch, and didn't eat any of his food. Gratefully, he allowed Morgan to assist him back to his room, where he lay down on the bed for a rest. She drew the curtains and promised to check up on him after half an hour. Fred had waved a hand, weakly, to acknowledge her concern, then closed his eyes, drifting instantly into sleep. Morgan had slipped out of the room quietly, leaving the door ajar and setting her watch alarm for thirty minutes. Fred had appeared unwell for several days, and she was worried about him. She had mentioned her concerns to Josie, who had arranged for the doctor to visit the following day to check on Fred.

When her alarm went off, Morgan had dropped what she was doing and hurried back to Fred's room. She knocked lightly on the door before entering. When there was no response, she had pushed open the door a few inches. Her hand flew to her mouth.

"No! Please no," she cried out.

Fred lay motionless and pale on top of his bed. His mouth had fallen open, and his eyes stared, unblinkingly, at the ceiling. Instantly Morgan knew he was dead, though she didn't want to believe it. Moving over to Fred's bedside, she had checked the pulse at his neck. There wasn't even the faintest movement. Tears sprang to her eyes as she pressed the emergency buzzer, above the bed, to summon assistance. In seconds, she heard hurried footsteps hastening towards her along the corridor. Lynette, another of her colleagues, had rushed into the room, swiftly followed by Bev, who carefully checked Fred for vital signs before pronouncing time of death.

Wordlessly, Morgan's colleagues had swung into the well-rehearsed procedures they had for dealing with the death of a resident in the home. Morgan hovered at the edge of the room until Bev had asked her to leave them and take a break in the staff room, where she would join her later.

Stifling a sob, Morgan had hurriedly left the others to their grim task and rushed outside into the garden. It was bitterly cold, but she had been desperate for air, fearing that she might faint.

The shock of Fred's sudden death had badly shaken her. In an instant, Morgan was back in the hallway of her old family home, looking at her dad, ashen-faced and dishevelled, as he broke it to her that she would never see her mum again. More than a year had passed since that day, yet the emotions of loss came flooding back to her as vividly as if it were yesterday.

An arm about her shoulders had suddenly brought Morgan back to the present. Bev was leaning in towards her, speaking quietly and guiding her back inside the building. Morgan's mind and senses were numbed, but she had allowed herself to be led along the corridor to the manager's office, where she slumped into a chair, as Bev had busied herself making tea for them both in the small staff kitchen next to her office. Sipping on the strong, sweet drink, Morgan had begun to feel better.

"I'm sorry you had to see that, Morgan, so soon into the job. It must have been awful for you, after all you have been through."

They had talked for a while, then Bev scribbled a number on a piece of paper and handed it to Morgan. "I want you to go home now and give this number a ring," she had said. "It's a counselling helpline you can contact at any time. Will you do that?"

Morgan had taken the scrap of paper and stuffed it into the pocket of her uniform. The last thing she wanted was to be home alone, revisiting her sorrow. She had insisted she wanted to finish her shift, and then she would go home and have a bath and an early night, to which Bev had reluctantly agreed, making her promise to call her on her mobile if she was struggling.

Welcoming the warm water lapping gently to her chin, Morgan sank back into her bath, after adding another capful of the scented aromatherapy oil which Josie had given to her when she was offered the job at Harley Grange. One of her favourite playlists, like balm poured on her soul, streamed softly around the house.

Fred's sudden death had stirred the grief that was never far from the surface. Although Bev had offered to talk it through with her and she knew she would have Josie's ear should she ask for it, the sad events of the day reminded her of just how alone she was. With her mum gone, her dad out of her life and her nan increasingly in a world of her own, she had no family and no partner, with whom to share the troubled emotions that once again pressed on her like a heavy burden she could not throw off.

Morgan sighed, topping up the water for a longer soak and laying her head back on the rim of the bath. Despite all her efforts to relax, her mind was racing at a hundred miles an hour over the events of the day and the other worry that constantly gnawed away at the back of her mind.

For weeks now, Morgan had experienced the disturbing sensation of being followed wherever she went, which was at its most acute when she walked the short distance between Victoria Terrace and Harley Grange.

Only last night, as she walked home from work, Morgan had been convinced she heard footsteps behind her. On hearing what she thought was the crack of a twig underfoot, she had spun round suddenly, like a child's spinning top. As she had done on each occasion when she sensed that there was someone following her, she had paused, scanning for any further noise or movement. She had hesitated, barely breathing, as she strained to listen out for any tell-tale sound that would confirm or negate her fear, but there was nothing.

It was merely the rustle of the tall hedges that bounded the substantial properties neighbouring Harley Grange, she had told herself; or maybe a cat, darting from garden to garden, on its evening hunt. Unpersuaded by her own arguments, she had half-run, half-walked back to Victoria Terrace, not pausing to gain her breath until she had shut the front door of number 34 behind her.

Once safely indoors, with curtains drawn and lights illuminated, Morgan tried to reassure herself that she was imagining things, and it was just her mind and senses playing cruel tricks on her; but she hadn't been able to shake off a growing feeling of unease.

Deciding that her train of thought had ruined her mood, Morgan pulled out the plug and watched the water whirl noisily down the drain until she was sitting in an empty bath, hugging her knees.

If she and her dad still had any kind of relationship, Morgan would have turned to him to offload her worries about being followed. Once upon a time, he would have been full of advice and reassurance; but that route was barred to her, as there was no way she was going to look to him for any help. He'd shown that he was so wrapped up in his own misery that he had no time for her. She had learned, the hard way, how to look after herself.

CHAPTER FIFTEEN

Todd was tingling with excitement as he packed a few essentials into his backpack. After his last visit to Morgan's house, he'd begun to form a plan for his future, but he had some work to do to make it happen.

Slipping past the lounge door, he was halted by his mother's smoky voice calling out to him.

"Where you going, Todd?"

"Out", he replied, briefly, his hand on the front door lock.

"Fetch us some ciggies on your way back will you, love?"

He grunted indistinctly as he opened the door. His mum was always touching him up for money in one way or another. If it wasn't fags, it was booze, a takeaway or a loan until benefits day, which she never repaid. He was sick of it, sick of being put upon by his mum and everyone else in this dump. Everything was going to get better for him soon, he told himself. All he had to do was hold his nerve and stick to his plan.

Today, he was heading for Victoria Terrace when he knew Morgan would be out at work. Checking the time on his phone, Todd saw it was 3.30pm. The light was already fading from a grey day, which meant it would be dark by the time he got to Morgan's house in about forty-five minutes. Perfect timing for what he needed to do.

Todd took a circuitous route, doubling back occasionally, diving behind trees and hedges and making to walk up driveways, just as he did when following Morgan. There was CCTV everywhere these days – on houses, garages, shops and offices. It was second nature to him now to dodge and dive, wherever he went, whether on business or not.

Arriving at the rear of Morgan's house, Todd discovered there was an alleyway running behind the terrace of houses in which number 34 stood. It was perfect for his purposes, being little used, and a place where he could hide out to spy on Morgan, when she was at home. Not wide enough for vehicles and blocked off at one end, it wasn't much more than a bin store and rubbish dump.

There was no lighting at all, and neither the streetlamps nor house lights cast any illumination on the dark, uninviting strip of cracked concrete.

Todd took up position, leaning against a garden wall from which he could see the back of number 34.

The house was in total darkness, the black eyes of the upper floor windows staring balefully at him. He checked the time again; still another hour before Morgan would be home from Harley Grange. Plenty of time to carry out a more detailed inspection.

A wooden gate was set into the back wall of each property in the terrace. Todd tried the latch on Morgan's gate and pushed hard, but it wouldn't open. Cursing his lack of bulk, he leaned against the gate, barging his shoulder against the immutable wooden panels, all the while listening for any sign of life which might indicate he had been overheard. He heard only the swish of traffic on the damp surface of the road running alongside the terrace of houses.

"Mitzi," a wavering voice called out. "Mitzi, where are you?" There was the sound of food being rattled in a bowl. Some old bird, trying to get her cat in for the night, he guessed.

He had to make a move. People were coming home from work, turning on lights, letting out pets.

Beside the gate was a refuse bin, with the number thirty-four painted on the side. Todd eyed it up. He reckoned he could easily hoist himself up on that, climb over the wall and access the garden that way. He didn't like the idea. There were too many people appearing at upper windows, peering out into the late afternoon, before closing blinds or drawing curtains. He didn't want to risk being seen scaling the wall.

One more try, then it would have to be the bin. Todd heaved his bony shoulder against the gate one more time, summoning what little strength he possessed. To his surprise, it gave way, yawning open with an almighty creak. Again, he stopped and listened, his senses alert to any change around him.

"Yes!" he whispered, pumping his fists. Now for the next phase of his plan.

Flattening himself against the back gate of number 34, Todd scrutinised the property. It was critical that he avoid being observed or identified from any of the neighbouring houses. He had dressed in his work uniform of black jeans, hoodie and balaclava. Only his eyes and nose were visible to anyone who might be looking out over the gardens.

The layout of Morgan's house was quite simple – two up and two down, with a single storey extension at a right angle to the back wall, jutting out into the neglected rear garden. A half-glazed wooden door and adjacent window were set into the extension. He edged along the fence that separated number 34 from the house next door and darted across to the kitchen extension. Todd tried the handle, several times, but the door was firmly closed and unyielding.

On the back wall of the house were two casement windows, at ground floor level, both of a decent size, with side opening. One of them was cracked open an inch. Looking at it, Todd reckoned he could easily jemmy it open and squeeze into the interior. Being skinny had its advantages.

He peered through the nearest kitchen window and found himself looking at a small kitchen-diner, leading into a living room at the front of the house from which a flight of stairs led to the upper floor. The kitchen was neat and tidy – that was different. Morgan had been a messy bitch when she lived with him at Balmoral Gardens. Was someone else tidying up after her, he wondered? He moved back over to the extension.

Through the glass pane of the door, Todd could tell that he was looking into a utility room. On the wall opposite the door hung a row of coats, with boots and shoes stacked on a rack beneath. It was impossible to tell if the clothing was male or female. He was desperate to know if Morgan was shacked up here with some other fella. For that, he needed to have a proper look round, upstairs and down, but not now.

There was the sound of activity in neighbouring houses. Time for him to make a swift exit. He would have to come back another day to satisfy himself that Morgan was living alone and not seeing anyone else.

From his surveillance, when tracking and watching Morgan, Todd had convinced himself that she was single. Increasingly, when he thought about it, he was coming to believe that she wasn't interested in being with anyone else, because she wasn't over him. The thought caused a strange ripple of joy in his chest. He had never really known true happiness until he met her, and he desperately wanted that feeling back again. He loved her, and he should have told her that when they were together. He was convinced that if he had done so, she might never have left him like she did. He couldn't wait for the opportunity to make everything alright again.

Deciding that he'd hung around long enough, Todd slipped away down the garden, as quietly as a stalking cat. He emerged into the back alley, closing the gate behind him, and jogged towards the street. There he came to a sudden halt and looked backwards towards the rear of number 34. A thought occurred to him.

Retracing his steps, Todd stopped in front of the bin, situated beside the back gate, lifting the lid to peer inside its murky depth.

He muttered to himself as he sifted through the contents of the bin. There were several knotted plastic bags of general rubbish forming mounds inside its dark depth, topped with discarded teabags and other kitchen detritus. Lower down were a couple of magazines and a bunch of envelopes, some of them unopened. On an impulse, he leaned over the rim of the bin and reached down to grab a handful of envelopes.

It was too dodgy to hang about and read the mail now, Todd decided, stuffing the envelopes inside his hoodie. He heard several people talking, as they approached the entrance to the alley. He froze, flattening himself into the recess of the gate and praying that none of the people were planning to enter the alley. They passed by, walking on up the street. Time to make a run for it before he was disturbed. Zipping up his hoodie, to secure the stolen envelopes, he bolted from the alleyway as fast as if he was running from a deadly fire.

CHAPTER SIXTEEN

Rain was hammering down on the pavements by the time Todd ran from Victoria Terrace in the direction of home, this time taking the shortest route. He was sick of being soaked to the skin and just wanted to escape another dousing.

The exterior lights of The Feathers flickered in front of him, like baleful beacons at sea. Todd hurtled through the front door, desperate to escape the rain.

Inside, the atmosphere was hardly more inviting. Sparse decorations heralded the approach of Christmas and aged fairy lights were already flickering to extinction.

"Usual Todd?" the landlord called out to him. Todd nodded, paid for his drink, then went to sit down. He had a wide choice of tables, as the only other patrons were an old bloke sitting at the bar nursing a pint, and a youngish couple having a row in the opposite corner to him. So much for coming in for a bit of peace and quiet.

Todd took a gulp of his cider, then pulled out the bundle of envelopes from inside his hoodie. He was excited to learn of the information they might contain about Morgan. He wanted to know what she was up to, and these envelopes might contain some clues.

The first one he picked out carried advertisements for mobility aids and was addressed to an Eileen Garrett. He remembered Morgan used to speak about her nan, but never mentioned a name. It was probably her that was Morgan was visiting in the care home where Morgan was working now. He tossed the envelope to one side and moved on to the next one, addressed to Morgan Garrett. He opened it and scanned the contents. It was all about teacher training courses. Did Morgan want to be a teacher? She had never mentioned it to him. She said she'd failed her A levels and dropped out of school. Bit weird, he thought.

The next envelope really did surprise him. The address on the front read:

Morgan Fairley, 34 Victoria Terrace, Granton, Yorkshire.

Who the fuck was Morgan Fairley, Todd asked himself? The printing had been smudged by the rain, but he could read it, clear enough.

He continued sifting through the remainder of the post. There were a couple more addressed to Morgan Fairley and one more addressed to Morgan Garrett. In place of the earlier flutter of happiness he had experienced, he now felt as if he'd swallowed a brick.

Opening one of the more official looking envelopes, Todd found himself holding three pages of bank statements. He skimmed the document, reading down to the total funds figure at the foot of the third page.

Christ! Whoever Morgan Fairley was, she had just over three grand in her bank account. That was mad. His Morgan was always complaining she was skint. What the fuck was going on here?

He ordered another couple of drinks, his head whirring with possibilities. No longer obsessing over whether there might be a chance for him and Morgan to get back together, he was now trying to figure out if his girlfriend had been lying to him the whole time she had been with him. He'd always thought she had an air of mystery about her, but he'd kind of liked that. It kept him interested in her when other girls bored the tits off him.

Tipping the remainder of his cider and the vodka chaser he had ordered down his throat, Todd wiped his mouth with the back of his hand. Had he been well and truly fucked over, he asked himself? Was the person he'd known as Morgan Garrett, and Jesus help him had fallen in love with, was she actually someone called Morgan Fairley, with a very different back story to the one spun to him? Now he really did have to confront her, and not by knocking politely on the front door.

Suspicious that he might have been duped or taken for a ride, Todd vented a wave of rage that rolled through his entire body. He jumped up, kicking the pub door open and lurching out into the street. With no-one on whom to visit his anger, he let out an almighty roar that hurt his throat.

If there was one thing Todd hated, it was being made to feel any less than he was. Ever since he was a kid, he'd fought to be

69

ascribed his place in the world. With a hopeless mother and a father who didn't even want to know him, he had grown up with a massive inferiority complex which he lugged around with him like a deadweight. It had made him super sensitive to any slight or disrespect which he perceived to be directed his way.

"Fuck!" he yelled, in a long exhalation. Passers-by turned to look at him, their faces registering a mixture of curiosity and fear.

He shrugged up the hood of his thin jersey top. It was still raining hard, so he was going to get soaked after all. He darted out into the heavy evening traffic, jaywalking between approaching vehicles. A volley of horns and shouted abuse greeted him. Todd laughed out loud and showed the finger to the occupants of all the cars that beeped him. Seeing how easily he could annoy people made him feel instantly powerful.

Whilst jogging home as fast as his unfit body would allow him, he churned what he knew about Morgan.

Her dad was a copper, she had told him, and she hated his guts. Nothing strange about that and he had never asked her about it. But what if she was working for her old man under cover, or something? His thoughts were racing out of control.

Todd sped up as the rain pelted his face and body, adding to his fury. Random thoughts, like loose coins, rattled and rolled around his head, not coming to rest. There was something he knew about the name Fairley, but it wouldn't come to him. He needed a toke and another drink to make him think straight. He was going to figure out what that bitch Morgan had done him for, and he was going to make her pay for it.

CHAPTER SEVENTEEN

Arriving back at Balmoral Gardens, Todd leapt the stairs to his room, two at a time. Throwing back the bedroom door, he ripped off his damp clothing, dropping it in a soggy pile in the corner of the room. From his wardrobe, he grabbed a twist of weed and rolled himself a spliff, slipping naked under his duvet. He took a deep inhale in an effort to calm himself; his head was all over the place, and he needed to think straight.

Suddenly, as if the cannabis had rewired misfiring signals in his brain, the recollection came to him.

"DCI fucking Fairley," he shouted to the space around him, sitting bolt upright.

In an instant, five years rolled away, and Todd was back in a small, windowless interview room at Granton Police Station, sitting on an iron-hard chair, in front of a drink-stained table. Opposite him were two police officers, one skinny with a pathetic beard creeping around his chin and the other, almost filling the room with his broad shoulders and solid frame.

"Todd, this is Detective Chris Barlow and I'm Detective Chief Inspector Gareth Fairley," the big guy said. "We're here to question you about a large quantity of cannabis found on your person when you were apprehended by Detective Barlow on Silver Street in the city centre."

Todd had only just started buying and selling drugs in and around Granton, and it had taken ages to set up a deal with a supplier. He'd been so keen to acquire the product, he hadn't noticed Detective Bastard Barlow and his copper mates lurking about, until they grabbed him as he left a meet. His suppliers had been nimbler on their feet and had split up in all directions, throwing the officers off their trail. Hence why he had ended up alone, sweating in fear, in front of DCI Fairley and his sidekick.

For what had seemed like an eternity, but was only a few hours, Todd had been questioned, relentlessly, about his activities and those of his suppliers up the chain into which he had manoeuvred himself. He had known diddly squat about the chief executives of his business back then, but that hadn't stopped Fairley and his henchmen from pushing and prodding, bombarding him with questions and accusations until his head spun. They had taken him for a weak link, he quickly realised.

Fairley had an air of suppressed anger about him, Todd recalled. He thumped the table a lot, when he didn't like Todd's responses, and thrust his face forward, threatening Todd with all kinds of retribution if he didn't give up what he knew.

"I don't know anything," Todd had pleaded repeatedly. "I was told to ask for X Man – no name given. A guy I met in The Woodman, once, got me into the business. He told me when and where to meet X the first time. After that, X fixed the meet each time. That's all I can tell you."

He had been tempted to spin a story, just to get out of that dismal, sweat-smelling interview room, but he had the sense to realise that would land him in even more trouble. He had given up the little he knew, then continued to protest his ignorance. Eventually, Fairley had let him go, warning him that his detectives would be watching out for him and if they got a sniff of criminal behaviour, he'd be on the waiting list for a prison sentence before he could sneeze. He hadn't doubted them for one moment and laid low for several weeks, using his enforced holiday to figure out how to improve his business model. He must have got something right, because there had been no more traumatic encounters with Gareth Fairley since that memorable occasion.

Back in the present, Todd grabbed his phone and searched against the name of DCI Fairley. There were pages of entries, with photographs.

"Bastard!" he muttered, as he continued to scroll through. Clearly, DCI Fairley was good at catching criminals, according to the numerous reports of his successful investigations. No surprise there – the bloke was a mean fucker. Todd continued swiping his screen until one particular headline caught his attention.

"Senior police officer's wife killed in hit and run." He read on.

icle from a local newspaper described the known facts ⸌ut the incident, which didn't amount to very much. Little had been learned about the driver of the vehicle involved, but there was lots of stuff about the lack of lighting on a dangerous stretch of road. Todd skim read the whole piece until he came to the points of interest. Fairley's wife was a headteacher, and the couple had a teenage daughter, unnamed, who attended Granton Grammar School.

"Fuck it!" Todd threw his phone across the room, where it landed on his damp clothing. Reading that piece confirmed his suspicions. His Morgan must be Fairley's daughter. What were the chances of there being two Morgan Fairleys in a place like Granton? That meant Morgan had been lying to him the whole time he'd known her.

For a fleeting moment, Todd thought he was going to cry. He had given Morgan a home, money and a plentiful supply of drugs. In return, the only person he had ever loved or cared about had pissed all over him.

Soon, though, his self-pity and sadness were swept away by molten anger bubbling up from his guts. No-one took him for a mug and got away with it.

Having watched Morgan and scoped out number 34 Victoria Terrace, Todd knew what was possible, but his plan must change. It was no longer a matter of slipping into the house to take a little look around. Morgan - whoever the fuck she was - must pay for treating him like shit and pay big. Not only was he going to help himself to that three grand she had sitting in her bank account, but he was going to give her a scare she would never forget.

Rolling himself another spliff, Todd lay back on his pillow. Tendrils of sickly-sweet smoke weaved a wreath around his head, as he set himself to formulating a scheme of retribution. He knew it had to be faultless, and it had to go without a hitch. For sure, if he messed it up, Morgan's old man would have his guts this time.

CHAPTER EIGHTEEN

On a bright, cold morning in early December, Gareth Fairley walked out of Granton Police Headquarters for the last time. He was flanked by his solicitor on one side and a union rep on the other, each one dragging behind them a suitcase, bulging with files and papers.

"Well, I think that went as well as it could have done," said Gareth's solicitor. "It's a generous settlement."

Gareth nodded, tight-lipped. His thirty years of service in the force had just come to an ignominious end and it was all his fault. Flattering words had been spoken by his solemn-faced superiors about his huge contribution to policing in Granton, and his success in tackling serious and organised crime. It was all a farce, since everyone at the table knew what was really going on. He was being discreetly retired for his incompetence, poor judgement and lack of self-discipline.

Gareth couldn't complain. His bosses had been more than fair, offering him first counselling, a leave of absence, then a generous early retirement package. He had chosen the latter, recognising, when the proposal was put, that his career was over. He had lost the confidence and respect of his team and his superiors. There was no way back from that, he knew.

"There are some formalities to conclude," said the solicitor. "I need to review the final agreement and check the changes we made today, but I don't anticipate any issues. I'll give you a shout when the agreement is ready for your signature and that'll be the end of it."

Gareth shook hands with the other two men. What would they say, he wondered, if he were to ask for their advice on what the hell he should do with himself from now on? He had no job, no wife and a daughter who didn't want to know him. He suspected that they, like him, would be at a total loss.

"Thanks, James, and you, too, Bob. Thanks for all you've done," Gareth said, trying to keep his voice as firm and steady as he could. "I'll wait to hear from you."

Driving away from the building that had been his second home for thirty years, Gareth headed for his pre-arranged destination.

The consulting room of Patricia Fellowes was always welcoming with its soft lighting, comfortable furniture and flowers to brighten the mood. They had all helped to keep him in the room on his first visit.

Dry-mouthed and nervous as hell about how the encounter was going to develop, Gareth had walked reluctantly into Patricia's office and dropped down into the wing-backed chair she indicated. His mouth felt like sandpaper, and he had been afraid he would be unable to speak. He had poured a glass of water from a jug on the table between them, his hand trembling violently.

"You sounded very upset when you called me the other day," Patricia had said, after he had taken a gulp of cold water. "Can you tell me about that – what it was that compelled you to pick up the phone to me?"

Hesitating, Gareth had studied the woman in front of him. She was about the same age as him, he guessed. Petite, but with an aura of strength and calm, her unwavering gaze had locked onto him from the moment he sat down. Her voice was low and soothing, though the session was almost over before he was able to unclench his fists and relax slightly. His eyeballs had ached from the effort of attempting to hold back tears. Fighting to maintain composure, he looked away from Patricia, fixating on an abstract painting on a wall to her left. Eventually he spoke.

"I didn't want to be here – in this world, I mean."

"You wanted to take your own life?" she asked, gently. He nodded, unable to utter the words.

"But you didn't act on those thoughts?" she asked, her tone level and unhesitating.

He shook his head. "My daughter," he spluttered. "I have to be here for my daughter."

He couldn't really remember what he had said after that, his face dissolving into a mess of tears and mucus as he had reached deep inside himself, beyond even the night of Mel's death, as if dredging silt from a disused well, a dark and frightening place.

Prompted by Patricia's careful questioning, words had come tumbling from him like flood water from an overflowing river carrying all manner of debris in its angry swell. Gareth was embarrassed to think how incoherent and inarticulate he had been, probably making no sense at all.

Waiting patiently for him to finish his spew of dislocated thoughts, Patricia had eventually asked that he come and see her again in a week's time.

"If you feel you'd like to speak sooner, then call me on this number," she had said. "Please don't hesitate to use it, if you feel the need."

In a daze, he had stared at the appointment card she handed him, on which she had written her personal mobile number beside that of her office.

"I think you might benefit from joining an addiction therapy group," Patricia continued. "Not just yet, but maybe in a few weeks. We can talk about it, and I can give you pointers to some local groups."

He had nodded, unsure if he would take up Patricia's suggestions. The hour he had spent with her had been so intense, Gareth had been unsure if he could go through another like it. At the same time, he had walked out of the consulting room feeling as if he had just divested himself of an impossibly heavy overcoat that had been slowing his movements and making it difficult for him to walk.

In that first week, after meeting with Patricia, he must have called her nearly every day. He had felt out of control, scared and unequal to the task in front of him. Every cell in his body had cried out for alcoholic anaesthetic to his pain. It was only his overwhelming desire to be the father Morgan needed, that had kept him away from the booze.

"Come in Gareth. Take a seat." Patricia Fellowes indicated Gareth's usual chair, beside a floor to ceiling window. In the mid-afternoon gloom, streetlights were flickering into life on the pavement below Patricia's office.

"I know we talked about how you might be feeling today, but does the reality match the contemplation?"

Gareth had told Patricia at their first meeting of his imminent retirement from the force. He had known he was going to need help to come to terms with it. "It's worse than I imagined it would be," he responded, after careful thought.

"Go on."

He sighed. Finding the words to describe his troubling thoughts was always difficult and painful, even after several sessions with Patricia. He looked out of the window, trying hard to articulate the myriad emotions raging within him – shame, guilt, embarrassment and a deep sadness.

"I feel such a failure," Gareth said, at length. "I've thrown away my career and a job I loved. There was talk of me becoming Chief Constable, at one time, and look at me now. My superiors have been more than fair, calling it retirement, when we all know it's due to me being a drunk, who's lost his judgement and the respect of his team. Worse than that, I couldn't even find the person who killed my wife – couldn't bring them to justice as I was supposed to do."

He pulled out a handkerchief and blew his nose loudly. Patricia looked on with the calm but penetrating gaze to which he had grown accustomed.

"Most of all," Gareth said, taking a sip of water, "I've failed my daughter – the person I love most in the world. I haven't been there for her, and I've left her to suffer on her own. I will never be able to forgive myself for that."

"Let's just pause there," said Patricia, "because I think you're being very hard on yourself, Gareth. You've told me about the accident and the lack of evidence. That's horribly bad luck for you, but it's not your fault. You've made real progress since you first came to see me, but you have to work on learning to forgive yourself. Try to switch your mind away from recriminations over events that you can't change and over which you have no control."

He nodded, whilst silently acknowledging that was the hardest part of all this therapy. At times, Gareth wondered if he would ever get past the huge psychological boulders standing in his way.

"And then there's Morgan. When did you last see her?"

"A few weeks ago," he replied. "I saw her in the cemetery, on the anniversary of Mel's death, but she didn't want to speak to me. In fact, she ran away as fast as she could. That, and the bender I went on afterwards, are what brought me here in the first place." He took another sip of water, steeling himself against threatening tears.

"I'll never give up," Gareth continued, clearing his throat. "Cards, e-mails, letters even. I'll just keep sending them, even if I never get anything back."

Patricia nodded. "I think that's all you can do, Gareth. You're reaching out to her. She has to decide when she wants to respond. You've come so far in such a short time. Already, you're a different man to the one who came to that first session. When Morgan sees that for herself, she may have a change of heart."

"Maybe."

They talked on until the end of his appointment.

"Where are you going next?" Patricia asked, as he stood to leave.

"Off to the gym," Gareth replied, holding up his sports bag. Patricia nodded her approval, having previously advised he avoid going straight home after his settlement meeting. Don't let yourself be alone after such a stressful experience, she had said.

Walking away from Patricia's office, Gareth recognised the demon voice that called out to him at all times of the day and night.

Just one drink, it whispered to him, to calm you down. God! How he could use a shot of alcohol right now. He fantasised about the relief that a slug of whisky or a large, warmed glass of red would give him. But that would never be the end of it for him, he acknowledged to himself. His was a compulsive, addictive nature, he now recognised, that he barely controlled from day to day.

With a sigh, he jumped into his car and headed directly for the Granton Health and Fitness Centre.

CHAPTER NINETEEN

Glancing at his watch, on leaving Patricia's office, Gareth calculated he had time for a workout in the gym, followed by a swim then a healthy lunch in the café. When he had finished, he would head over to see Eileen, who had just moved into Harley Grange care home. It was hard to believe how rapidly she had deteriorated in a matter of a few weeks. He was no doctor, but he felt sure that the tragic loss of her youngest daughter had played a part in Eileen's swift decline; another consequence of the accident, and his failure to bring anyone to account for it.

His mother-in-law had no idea what was happening to him – her grip on reality was growing weaker by the day. Nevertheless, he found it comforting to sit quietly with her, even if they barely spoke.

The automatic sliding doors of the gym swished open in greeting. He waved to the reception staff, whom he was coming to know well. Since joining, he had visited the gym every day, to still the voice of temptation that was always whispering in his ear. Evenings were usually the worst for him, so to stop himself reaching for a drink, he sweated his way round the exercise machines, finishing up with a swim and sauna. By the time he arrived home again, he was so exhausted that all he wanted to do was flop into bed and sleep.

Having stowed his sports bag in his locker, Gareth walked into the large gym area where the exercise equipment was located. It had become his habit, now, whenever he was in a public place in and around Granton, to wonder if the person responsible for Mel's death was amongst the people around him. It was perfectly possible, he had told himself a million times, but how could he know? To this day, he still had no information as to whether the driver was local to the area, male or female, or anything else that might lead him to the truth. He'd drawn a complete blank, despite exhaustive enquiries. Poor old Ted Dunlop had died from a heart attack before he could remember any details and may have taken valuable knowledge to the grave with him. How many times had he told himself it was hopeless? Yet he would never give up searching as long as he lived.

Gareth grabbed his exercise programme card and walked over to where the static bikes were situated. The place was busy today, he noted, and he could see that all the bikes were occupied. He looked around for an empty piece of equipment.

"Have this one." Gareth turned, to find a woman climbing down from the nearest bike, wiping her face on a towel. "I'm done. Well and truly," she said, breathlessly.

"Are you sure? I can go on something else."

"It's fine. I've been here for an hour already. I think that's quite enough torture for one day."

"That was an impressive speed you had going there," he commented.

"Don't be fooled. I only put it on when I think someone might be watching."

Gareth smiled and the woman returned the smile. She had the most beautiful hazel-green eyes and clear, almost translucent skin, he noticed. He was shocked at himself. When did he last pay attention to an attractive woman? Not once since Mel died. During their marriage, hardly ever. His wife had meant the world to him, so there was never any reason to be interested in anyone else.

Now, though, it felt strange and totally wrong for him to be admiring the woman's slim, athletic figure, as she dismounted the bike to make way for him. To even register another woman's beauty felt disloyal to his dead wife. He thanked the stranger politely, then turned his concentration to setting up the bike for his training programme. He put his head down and began to pedal towards the nirvana of mental and physical exhaustion.

After a vigorous workout and relaxing swim, Gareth headed to the club's café for a quick bite to eat before visiting Eileen. He paid for a salad and a bottle of fruit juice, then looked around for an empty table. The place was packed today, with most of the tables occupied by groups of people gossiping and chatting. He spotted a free place by a window and made his way over. As he drew nearer, he recognised the woman who had been on the exercise bike before him, sitting at the next table. She was gazing intently at a laptop, whilst sipping coffee. Gareth settled himself at the vacant table which caused her to look up.

"Hello again," the woman said warmly, as if she had known him for years.

"Hello. I hope I didn't disturb you."

"Not at all," she said, closing her computer. "I've finished anyway."

"I can't believe how busy it is in here today," Gareth said, for something to say.

"You're not usually here at lunchtime?"

"No. This is the first time. I'm usually here in the evening," he replied. He wouldn't tell her that he chose that time to try and save himself from an alcoholic binge.

They made small talk until the woman, whose name was Petra, she told him, announced that she was running late for an appointment.

"Hope to see you here again some time," she said. He smiled, unsure of how to respond.

"Nice to meet you," he replied, as he watched her gather up her belongings.

Although he tried hard not to, Gareth found himself watching Petra's retreating back as she made her way out of the club. It made him feel guilty and confused. He looked away. Something else to discuss with Patricia, he thought ruefully.

CHAPTER TWENTY

Christmas was in full swing at Harley Grange and had been for some time. From the middle of November, residents had been surrounded by card, paper, glitter and string, as they made cards for their families and decorations for the home. Jim, the maintenance man, had dragged out the artificial trees from the storeroom, together with strands of twinkling fairy lights and glittering baubles of all shapes and sizes, some of which had been brought from the residents' own homes.

Bev, the manager, was a self-confessed Christmas addict. "I just want to give them the best time ever," she protested to her staff. She did not say so, but everyone knew she was thinking that some of the dear souls they cared for might not be with them for another festive season. No-one complained about the extra work.

There was less enthusiasm when it came to agreeing the staff rota for the Christmas period.

"Come on guys. Help me out here," Bev pleaded. "I know you all want to be with your own families, but we have to keep our people safe. Don't make me choose."

All eyes were averted as Bev looked around the staff room. Only Morgan stared directly at her boss, her hand straight up in the air.

"I can do as many shifts as you want," she said. "I'll do nights if that helps. It'll mean I can spend more time with nan."

The truth was, Morgan was desperate to be chosen to work. She dreaded Christmas and all its familial happiness. All she had to look forward to were miserable dark days alone, in a silent empty house.

"Come to us at Christmas, Mo," her Aunt Jess had pleaded, but Morgan had refused the invitation as politely as she could. Having anticipated the kind offer, Morgan had already decided she couldn't face Christmas at her aunt's house. Much as she loved Jess, Charlie and her cousins, she knew that seeing them all goofing around together would simply rub salt into her mental wounds. She would be better off at Harley Grange, she had decided, until the festive season was all over. Bev had said she could stay in the visitor accommodation in return for working some night shifts. That meant she could sleep through the days and only come out after relatives and friends had departed and residents were heading for their rooms. Being on site meant she could also spend every spare moment with Eileen, and that, she told herself, was all she wanted or needed.

Gareth looked around the large, sunny lounge at Harley Grange. His mother-in-law was sitting in the bay window, gazing, without expression, at the leafless trees and withered pot plants in the garden. The feeble light of a mid-winter afternoon was already slipping away into darkness.

Ever since Mel died, Gareth had kept his silent promise, to her spirit, that he would look after Eileen to the end of her days. Mel's mum meant the world to him. She and Derek, his late father-in-law, had been more like parents to him after his own mother and father both died, relatively young.

"Hello Eileen," he said, planting a kiss on her forehead. She smiled sweetly, as she always did, but he wasn't sure she knew who he was any more. He pulled up a chair opposite her. This was his first visit to see his mother-in-law at Harley Grange.

"How are you?" he asked. "You look well." She gave a thumbs up and he laughed. There was still a sense of humour inside that muddled head.

Gareth had argued with his sister-in-law when she suggested Eileen move into Harley Grange after her fall. Eileen is a proud and independent woman, he had maintained; she will absolutely hate giving up the house she called home for most of her life. Surely there must be another way, he had suggested.

Then he had observed the devastating consequences of Eileen's accident, which seemed to rob her of her faculties and her personality almost overnight. Seeing her frail body, barely shaping the covers on her hospital bed, he had been forced to admit that Jess was right. Her mother needed 24-hour care, which she wouldn't be able to receive at home.

Gareth knew of Morgan's offer to look after her grandmother, though he had to hear it from Jess. How typical of his daughter to be so selfless and caring, he had reflected with pride; though at the same time, he was filled with guilt and shame that she hadn't come to him to discuss such important family business. Things had become so bad between them since Morgan had stormed out of her family home almost six months previously, that he had been instructed, through Jess, that he could only visit Eileen on certain days, when Morgan would not be around. How could he have allowed their relationship to deteriorate to such an extent, he questioned himself, with anguish? If it took him the rest of his days, he would make it right between them again, he had vowed.

"I've been down to the gym today," Gareth said to Eileen, trying to make conversation. "I'm getting my six-pack back," he joked, pointing to his flattening belly.

His mother-in-law looked at him and smiled. He wondered if she had any recollection of him telling her that he was going to be leaving the force. Before the fall, Eileen had been one of the few people with whom he felt comfortable to share troubling personal matters. They had spoken a lot about Morgan, and it was from Eileen he had learned about what his daughter was up to, and - more troubling for him - the people with whom she was associating. Now, though, Eileen struggled to put together a coherent sentence. It broke his heart to watch her try.

"I'm back running again and pumping iron. Think I'm getting a bit old for it all, but it's got to be done."

Eileen smiled and clapped her hands, whether at him or in response to some random thought of her own, he had no way of knowing. He continued to chat away to her, staying until her eyelids began to shutter over her eyes and her body beckoned her into sleep.

Driving away from the home, Gareth contemplated the evening ahead of him. It had occurred to him to arrange to meet a friend for dinner, but most of the guys he knew were still in the force and he couldn't face the inevitable questions about his sudden departure. Not everyone knew about his addiction problems, and he preferred to keep it that way. He told himself that if he could make it through tonight without lapsing, it would be a major achievement in his battle for sobriety. He only hoped he was up to the challenge.

CHAPTER TWENTY-ONE

Lying on his bed, scrolling through his social media channels, Todd Hopkins tried to take his mind off the rubbish Christmas he had just had.

This year, his mum and her latest boyfriend of two weeks, Greg, had spent most of their time screaming at each other. Whilst the queen was delivering her annual Christmas message, his mum was throwing a whole bag of frozen roasted potatoes at Greg, one by one. He had ducked, lashed out and caught Shelagh full in the face, leaving her with a black eye which, by Boxing Day, had developed into an expanse of bruising across most of the left side of her face.

After Greg had slammed out, shaking the house to its foundations, Todd had known that was the end of Christmas dinner. What the hell? It was always rubbish anyway. No-one in the house had a clue how to cook, so they had all gorged themselves on cocktail sausages and bags of crisps. Shelagh had sat at the kitchen table, wailing like a banshee, and getting pissed. Today was the day after Boxing Day, and his mum had moved no further than the sofa in the lounge, where she sat now, cradling a bottle of wine and smoking her way through her Christmas supply of fags, seemingly oblivious to the fact that her youngest children seemed intent on killing each other.

"Fuck this!" he muttered as an ear-piercing scream reverberated around the house. Downstairs, the TV was pumping out some stupid kids' Christmas film. His youngest stepbrother and sister were shrieking over the top of it, as usual. If he needed any further motivation to put his plan into action, this was it.

Just as he had done on previous trips to Morgan's house, Todd dressed himself in his uniform black hoodie, jeans and balaclava. From his wardrobe, he took out some pills, a wad of cannabis and all the cash he had secreted inside the pockets of an old coat. Lastly, he slipped the knife he used, when he was out doing business, down the inside of his trainer.

Lurking in the dark corners of Todd's paranoid mind was the suspicion that Morgan had been working on some sort of undercover operation for her dad and his cronies. Maybe she had been using him to learn about the drugs network in Granton, so that she could feed back information to her old man? What if he'd been spotted on CCTV or something and there were eyes on 34 Victoria Terrace, just waiting for him to appear. His nerves were jangling, and his mouth was dry. He popped a couple of tabs to help himself calm down and focus on the job he had to do.

On his way out of the house, he glanced into the living room where his mum was asleep in her chair, head thrown back and mouth open, a cigarette burning away in her fingers. A shout from one of the kids stirred her from her stupor and she looked up, glimpsing Todd in the doorway.

"Where are you going?" she slurred. She'd be making the usual request in a minute – fags or booze, or both.

"Like you care," he replied, taking in her dishevelled appearance as she struggled to focus on him. For a fleeting second, he felt sorry for her. He supposed that in her own sad way, she had tried to be a mother to her many offspring, each of them having a different father. The trouble was, Todd reflected, she was weak and hopelessly dependent on men to look after her and make her feel good. Her problem was, she always chose bastards, most of whom slapped her about then left her with another kid.

His momentary lapse into the softness of pity quickly passed. I'm nothing like her, he told himself. I'm strong and I don't need no-one.

"I'm going to be gone for a while, quite a long while," he said. "I'll ring you," was his parting shot as he made for the front door.

Frowning, and shouting at the kids to turn the TV down, she hoisted herself to the edge of her chair, preparing to try and stand up.

"Todd," she called out, heaving herself to her feet with an almighty effort. "Todd," she shouted again, staggering towards the hallway.

Her words fell into an empty space, for her eldest son was already gone.

CHAPTER TWENTY-TWO

The hustle and bustle of post-Christmas shoppers was overwhelming. Like a sleepwalker, Morgan stumbled through the streets of Granton, tired and slightly disorientated.

Having finished work after lunch, she now had three blissful days off, after a stint of long days and a night shift. Christmas was over, thank God! Now there was only New Year's Eve to survive before life could return to some normality. She'd already planned an early night, so she could blot out all the celebrations, then wake up to another year with its relentless cycle of painful anniversaries and their attendant memories.

Foolishly, Morgan now realised, she had decided to walk down into town to see if she could find a new pair of boots in the sales. Her sleeping pattern was so disrupted after working odd hours and sleeping fitfully at Harley Grange, she was finding it hard to put one foot in front of the other. Exhaustion had sapped all her energy. Worse still, she had failed to anticipate the hordes of eager bargain hunters through whom she was now having to beat a path, as if she were negotiating an untamed forest of unbending trees.

Diving into the last shop on her list, she managed to find the boots she wanted in her size, reduced. Now, she couldn't wait to get home to an early supper, then bed. She decided she couldn't be bothered to walk back to Victoria Terrace. Checking the time on her phone, she saw that there should be a bus leaving the station in about fifteen minutes. She could easily make it. Hastening her pace, she set off in the direction of the bus station, keen to escape the crowds.

The bus terminus was at the end of the main shopping thoroughfare in Granton. Morgan could see that her bus was already there. A long queue of people was slowly shuffling onto the platform. With a bit of luck, she would be able to squeeze onto it and be home in less than an hour.

The prospect of a hot bath and slipping into her PJs loomed tantalisingly before her. She would treat herself to a take-away from the Indian restaurant at the end of the street. She deserved it, after the past few days of difficult and demanding work. Then she would climb into her comfortable bed and stream a film on her computer until she fell asleep. Hopefully sleep would come easily, as she was tired to her bones. Tomorrow she could have a lazy start, then catch up on the course work for her A level resits.

Nearing the front of the bus queue, Morgan could see the seats were filling rapidly, but she should be able to fit in, even if she had to stand, she reckoned. Spurred on by thoughts of the relaxed evening she had planned, Morgan smiled warmly at the bus driver. With a rueful smile in return, he waved her on. Gratefully she heard the doors shut behind her as the bus pulled away.

"Morgan!" Gareth Fairley shouted, watching in frustration as the crowded bus moved off into the evening traffic.

He came to a breathless halt, having sprinted down Barrington Street towards the bus station. He and Petra had hit the Christmas sales, along with hundreds of other shoppers. Each lugged a large carrier packed with bags full of their bargain purchases. After an enjoyable late lunch, they were wending their way back to Gareth's car, parked in the multi-storey car park, near the bus station.

Through the throngs of enthusiastic shoppers, Gareth suddenly spotted his daughter. She had changed her appearance several times since moving out; from scruffy teenager to scary Goth and now, he noted, a casual style of her own, which suited her.

Although she had her back to him, he would recognise Morgan's loping stride anywhere, even amongst a multitude of people. Willing her to turn around, Gareth's heart sank as he watched his daughter squeeze into the bus, seconds before the doors closed behind her. He told himself she couldn't hear him shouting out her name. That was why she hadn't turned round to acknowledge him.

"She couldn't have heard you," said Petra, echoing his thoughts. Having never met his daughter, Petra was not qualified to interpret her behaviour, Gareth reflected, but he kept those thoughts to himself. They were still finding their way into a relationship together, neither of them starting on solid ground.

He had forgotten how heavy with meaning words could be, and how easily they could be misconstrued or misunderstood.

"You're probably right," he said. Privately, he acknowledged that Morgan probably did hear him shout out her name, but chose to ignore him, as she had done for so long. It was no more than he deserved, he told himself. He had let her down badly, but no matter how many times she knocked him back, he would continue to try and make it up to her.

"Well, I don't know about you, but I feel I've done two hours in the gym," said Petra, shifting a large bag stuffed full of purchases from one hand to another. "Shall we go and have a cup of tea and take the weight off our feet?"

Gareth smiled and nodded. He recognised that Petra's suggestion was no throw away remark, no mere suggestion that sprang thoughtlessly to her lips. He was certain that Petra would much prefer a full-bodied glass of red wine, served at a perfect room temperature, or a zesty, sparkling gin and tonic. Either of those would be his preference to a plain old cup of tea, but unlike her, he wouldn't be able to stop at one or two alcoholic drinks.

"Sounds like a brilliant idea," he said, linking his arm through Petra's. It was his way of thanking her for her thoughtfulness. Tender words had never come easily to him.

"I bet you never thought your life would be so exciting when you agreed to come out for dinner with me that first time," he said.

She smiled and patted his hand.

After their first chance meeting at the exercise bikes, Gareth and Petra had bumped into each other at the gym, almost daily. It was Petra who first suggested they have a coffee after their training session, to which Gareth had agreed with some trepidation. Unbelievably, they had talked for hours as other members came and went and were replaced with new cohorts.

Petra had shared a little of her own history. She had left behind a destructive and abusive marriage and a high-pressure job in investment banking in London, to move to Yorkshire and become a potter. Gareth had told her about the accident and Mel's death and about ending his career in the police force. He hadn't told her he was an alcoholic, fearing he might choke on the words as they swelled and stuck in his throat.

At the end of their second coffee session, Gareth had found himself suggesting dinner. Was it a date, he had asked himself afterwards, as he drove away from the gym, worrying that he might have just made a terrible mistake? He wasn't sure what he had done, but he did know that he found Petra utterly engaging and so easy to talk to. He only hoped he would feel the same away from the safe and neutral environment of the gym.

Still nervous about possibly embarking on a new relationship after so long, he had booked a table at a smart new restaurant in Granton, which had been attracting favourable reviews since opening. It hadn't disappointed. The atmosphere was understated and relaxed; lounge music played quietly in the background and there was a gentle hum of conversation, punctuated by the ringing of cutlery on plates and the chink of glasses raised in celebratory toasts.

"This place is lovely," said Petra, "I've been wanting to come here for ages."

Reaching for the wine list, which the waiter had left on the table, she bent her head to examine the selection.

"What sort of wine do you prefer?" she had asked.

Gareth had felt his jaw clench and his mouth become dry. He had been dreading this moment. He took a sip of water before clearing his throat.

"Actually, I don't drink," he had said, rather too firmly, he thought. Petra looked up, questioningly.

"My name's Gareth, and I'm an alcoholic," he said, with a poor attempt at a laugh.

"I'm not sure if that's a bad joke or you're trying to make a serious point," said Petra.

"The latter."

"That's fine," she had said, closing the wine list and placing it on the edge of the table. "Then neither do I."

In that moment, his heart had opened, and Petra swept straight in.

"So, what are you going to do?" Petra asked, pouring tea from a large, white teapot. They had taken refuge from the busy streets of Granton in a quiet corner of a department store café, where the throng of excitedly chattering Christmas shoppers was beginning to dwindle.

"I wish I knew," he said, taking a sip of the scalding hot liquid. "I've tried messaging, emails, telephone calls. I've sent her birthday and Christmas cards, but nothing comes back. Nothing at all. My daughter just doesn't want anything to do with me."

"You could just turn up at her house."

"What, doorstep her you mean?"

"I suppose that's one way of putting it. I just thought she might feel differently if she sees you."

Gareth pictured himself ringing the bell at Eileen's front door and waiting for Morgan to open it. She would slam it in his face at first sight of him, he was sure of it.

With a shudder, Gareth recalled his visit to the cemetery, last month, on the first anniversary of Mel's death. He had been there when the gates opened, so desperate was he to grab a few moments with his daughter. Remembering how she had tried to run away from him, then the look of disgust on her face when he caught up with her, it was hard to imagine she might ever want to spend time with him again.

"Earth to Gareth," said Petra, smiling.

He shook himself back to the present. The journey was always a painful one.

"Maybe you're right," Gareth said. "Maybe I should just pitch up at Eileen's house and see what happens. I have been thinking about it, for some time, but haven't managed to pluck up the courage. I'm scared it might make things worse."

"Could it get much worse?" Petra asked.

He gave a wry smile. She had a point. What more did he have to lose? If he was prepared to incur Morgan's wrath, after all this time, by turning up at her door, perhaps she might begin to understand how much he cared about her, despite his failings as a father?

"I'll do it," Gareth said, draining his teacup. Some Dutch courage would be welcome, right now, he reflected, but that was out of the question. "If you don't mind, Petra, I'll drop you home, then I'll go round there before I lose my nerve."

Petra reached for his hand and squeezed it tightly, a now familiar gesture. He could almost imagine that her strength and resolve was passing, as if by osmosis, into his weaker self.

"Of course, it's alright. I want you to do it. Just let me know how you get on as soon as you can."

CHAPTER TWENTY-THREE

The house was in darkness when Todd arrived at Victoria Terrace. He glanced at his phone. Half past four. According to his calculations, Morgan should be home in about an hour or so. Plenty of time for him to let himself in, quietly, and to chill until she arrived back.

Just as on the previous occasion he had paid a visit, uninvited, Todd found the back gate unlocked and one of the kitchen casement windows open about half an inch. Perfect!

"Rooky mistake, Mo," he would say to her, when he saw her in just a little while. "It's almost like you want me to get in."

It was obvious Morgan's old man didn't come round here very often, which was good news. Todd was pretty sure DCI Fairley would have moved the bin inside the garden and secured the gate, as well as reminding his daughter about shutting and locking all doors and windows.

In seconds, Todd had the window open far enough to haul himself through the gap onto the work surface beneath it. Once inside, he pulled the window almost shut so as not to arouse any suspicions. He didn't want the neighbours looking across to see a window wide open on a bitterly cold winter's day. Like a cat burglar, he jumped lightly down onto the kitchen floor, symbolically dusting off his hands at a job well done.

"So what do we have here?" he said, as he walked from the kitchen into the living room. He couldn't switch on a light for fear of detection, but no matter. Morgan had left the curtains and blinds open, so the rooms were sufficiently illuminated by the bright light of the streetlamp, standing tall in front of the house.

The living room was a decent size, though stuffed full of old-fashioned furniture and knick-knacks. There was a wing-backed chair in the corner nearest the kitchen. He dropped his pack onto it. That's where he would position himself to await Morgan's return. It gave him a decent view of the front door, which opened directly into this room. He could be ready to make a move as soon as he heard Morgan's key in the lock.

A few feet from the front door, a staircase ascended directly to the upper floor. Todd glanced at his phone again. It was almost five o'clock. Still time to check out the top deck before Morgan came back.

He jumped the stairs, two at a time, to a small landing off which there were three closed doors. He opened the first on the right. The smell of Morgan assailed him as he pushed back the door into the bathroom. Her shampoo and shower gel made a nose-twitching, fruit-smelling concoction which he recognised instantly.

Todd remembered a time when he and Morgan were still together. She had just returned from an overnight visit to her nan and the two of them were lying on his bed, checking stuff on their phones. His room had been filled with her fragrance.

"You smell good," he'd said to her, burying his nose in her hair and inhaling the smell of her.

"It's called soap. You should try it," she had responded, slowly peeling off her clothes before offering herself to him. The memory was unbelievably painful - like a sliver of broken glass being plunged into his chest.

Swiftly Todd's melancholy turned to anger. He hated how Morgan still made him feel like this. He had to get a grip and remind himself she'd turned out to be a lying, scheming little bitch. He needed to teach her a lesson. Then he would feel better.

He opened the next door on the landing and peered into the room. Must be the old lady's, he decided. On a chest of drawers, beneath the window, was a cluster of photographs. In several of them he recognised Morgan and women who looked like her, none of them as pretty as she was. There he went again. He must stop thinking this way and get on with what he came to do.

Todd moved on to the third room, which was obviously Morgan's, judging by the Harley Grange uniform hanging from the curtain pole. More photographs of her with people he didn't know. Friends and relatives, he guessed. None of her dad, though, he noted, glancing swiftly around the room.

Overwhelmed by the sense of Morgan all about him, Todd decided to have a quick smoke to steady his nerves and keep himself calm. The pills he took before he came out must be wearing off.

He jogged downstairs and took up position in the corner chair. From inside his backpack, he pulled out a twist of weed, which he slowly rolled into a large spliff. His jitters began to melt away as the drug took effect, and he started to picture the scene when Morgan stepped inside the room and found him there. He wanted her to feel scared and afraid of what he might do to her. Her fear would be his revenge. Bring it on.

CHAPTER TWENTY-FOUR

Morgan stepped down from the crowded bus and inhaled the chill, night air. She had stood for the entirety of her journey, squashed, like soft fruit, between people and their packages.

"Have a seat, love," a woman with several bags of shopping said to her when the seat beside her came free. Even though she was weary to her bones, Morgan thanked the woman but remained standing, allowing older people and women with children to take each vacated place. It meant she spent the whole journey swaying and bracing against the movement of the bus. Still, she was nearly home now, and an aromatherapy oil bath was beckoning her.

What a relief to be returning to her own space, at last. For the past five days, she had been living and working at Harley Grange, filling in for staff on annual leave or off sick. Several residents had become unwell over the Christmas period, and she had accompanied one to the hospital, where she waited for hours until the resident was admitted. Additionally, whilst the home was so short-staffed, she had worked longer hours. When she went to bed, in the Harley Grange visitors' accommodation, she was too tired to sleep, and dozed fitfully through the night, frequently awakened by a resident calling out or pressing one of the emergency bells.

At least she had been able to spend time with Eileen, seeking her out whenever time permitted. They had reminisced over Christmases past, in happier days, though Eileen had been unable to contribute a great deal. Advancing dementia was rubbing out her memories in its cruel onslaught. For her nan's sake, Morgan steeled herself to remain cheerful, though her recollections brought with them as much pain as they did pleasure.

As she approached the welcoming, red-painted door of number thirty-four, Morgan fumbled for her keys in her backpack. They had slipped through the jumble of tissues, charger wire and dregs of makeup to the bottom of her bag, as usual. She grabbed hold of her key ring and selected the correct key for the front door, slotting it into the lock with a sigh of relief.

Morgan knew there was something wrong the minute the door swung open. The distinctive smell of weed seeped out from the living room, wafting about her in a malignant breeze.

Later, she would ask herself why she hadn't slammed the door shut, in that instant of recognition, and run to Jed and Caitlin, her next-door neighbours. Jed was a six foot four, burly security guard who was retired from the army. Not many people were inclined to ignore him, for obvious reasons, although she knew him to be ridiculously kind and soft-hearted. He would certainly have pitched in to help her, in this desperate moment, she was sure of it; but she didn't seek his assistance. Disregarding the inner voice that was screaming at her to run away as fast as she could, she pushed the door open and stepped inside the house.

In the same moment that she reached to flick the light switch on the wall to her left, Morgan was seized by her right arm and twisted around so that she had her back to her captor, who kicked the door shut, cutting off her means of escape. From her left side, a gloved hand snaked round in front of her face, clamping her mouth shut and almost suffocating her.

It took several seconds for Morgan to process what was happening. When she realised the danger she was in, she tried to call out, but it was hopeless. The hand, pressed so tightly over her mouth, prevented her from making any sound. Like a terrified animal caught in a vicious trap, Morgan fought to wriggle free, but it was as if she had iron bands wrapped firmly around her upper body. Her assailant had rendered her paralysed, unable to move or make a sound.

"Hello Morgan. Good to see you again. It's been a while."

Of course, she had known who was inside the house the instant she smelled the drugs. It was no random, opportunistic crime she had unfortunately stumbled into, but a premeditated, carefully planned assault.

Subconsciously, Morgan had always known that Todd would come for her one day. With his character and history, he wasn't going to let her walk out on him and live her life as if they had never met. In his crazy world, rules were for suckers, crime was the only career choice and life was all about taking what you believed to be due to you. She knew he would think she had dissed him by taking the drugs he freely gave her and walking out on what he thought was a 'relationship'. What a joke. Neither he nor anyone else in his dysfunctional family knew the first thing about relationships. Still, on his reckoning, she owed him, and he wasn't one to forget it.

Several minutes passed in which they remained standing behind the front door, where layers of coats hung from pegs on the wall, narrowing the space around them. The foot of the stairs was about three feet away. Morgan's heart was pounding violently in her chest and her mind was whirring over possibilities for escape, desperately seeking the one that offered the most chance of success.

What if she tried to grab one of the coats to throw it over him? Would that give her time to open the front door and run out into the street, where she could scream for help and hammer on Jed and Cait's door? Hopefully, they would be at home or, if not, someone else might hear her cries.

Nearly petrified by terror, Morgan forced herself to focus on how she might surprise Todd for long enough to make her escape. Once out in the street, she would scream until her voice gave out, to attract attention from passers-by or neighbours. Surely someone would hear her and come to her aid.

Just as she was preparing to bite the hand tightly held over her mouth, Todd suddenly relaxed his grip on her left arm. Before she had time to pull away from him, in the dim light that penetrated the frosted glass panes in the front door, Morgan detected the unmistakeable glint of a kitchen knife in the hand that had just released her.

Swiftly, Todd brought the ice-cold steel of the blade to rest on the skin of her neck. Morgan knew that if she moved, even slightly, the knife would slice into her, as if she were no more than a piece of meat on a cold slab.

"So, I thought I'd make a surprise visit, as you haven't bothered to look me up since you left. Come to think of it, you never actually said goodbye, as I remember it. We've got some catching up to do, Morgan Fairley, haven't we?"

She flinched at the use of her real name.

"What's the matter? Surprised I've found out who you really are?"

Morgan's stomach churned at the stink of Todd's fetid breath. His face was so close to hers that, with his every utterance, drops of saliva landed on her skin. Turning her head slightly away from him, she felt the knife's blade shiver against her neck, it's sharpness lightly tracing an imprint on her skin.

Fear and panic were creeping into every cell of her body. How the hell did he know so much about her – her real name and where she lived? Wracking her brain, Morgan tried to remember if she had ever given away any clues as to her identity. She didn't think so. When she lived with Todd, she had been meticulous about revealing as little of her personal history as possible. She spun him a story about her dad being a policeman and running away from home because he was strict, and she hated his guts. That, at least, was partly true. The rest she lied about, including her surname.

He must have been following her to find out where she lived. There was no other explanation she could think of. That really creeped her out. It meant she hadn't been imagining it when she'd sensed there was someone shadowing her wherever she went.

Standing frozen with terror, like an ice statue, Morgan struggled to figure out how Todd had managed to gain access to the house. Had she unwittingly left keys at Todd's place and that's how he got in? Worse thought still, had he been in the house at times when she was there? The idea that Todd might have been lurking around her whilst she was sleeping, horrified her. With her mind racing over multiple possibilities, she was unable to lock onto any sense or reason.

Mulling over Todd's possible plans for her, the sickening realisation came that no-one knew she was going to be at home, alone, for her three whole days off work. Josie was on holiday herself, and had gone to stay with her mum, in Derbyshire; and Bev, her manager, knew that she was going to be away from work for a few days, but hadn't asked about her plans. That left only Eileen, who had no clue what was going on from one day to the next.

There wasn't a soul in the world who was expecting to see or hear from her for several days. No-one would think it unusual for her to be out of touch; so, unless she could somehow attract the attention of her neighbours or a passer-by on the street outside, then she was completely at Todd's mercy. God alone knew what he was capable of doing when he was fired up with anger and resentment like this, but Morgan was afraid that she was about to find out.

CHAPTER TWENTY-FIVE

Snow had begun to fall on the moors behind Petra's cottage. Flakes like roughly torn pieces of paper, floated towards the windscreen of Gareth's car. With a wave, he pulled off the gravelled drive, glancing in his rear-view mirror at Petra standing at the front door.

Driving away from Cragview Cottage towards Granton, after dropping Petra off, was like descending from a magical moorland eyrie to a different planet. The snow metamorphosised into rain and the empty landscape gradually filled with bricks and glass.

Gareth recalled the childish wonder he experienced on his first visit to Petra's home. He vaguely remembered the moor from outings when Morgan was a child, but he hadn't been up there for years. Criminals were disinclined to travel that far, since the terrain offered few places to hide out. He found it hard to believe he'd disregarded so much beauty.

Accepting Petra's invitation to lunch at Cragview had marked a new development in their relationship - more significant, even, than their dinner date. Arriving at the cottage, he had walked up the stone-flagged path to the entrance; but before he could lift the burnished brass knocker, sitting proudly in the centre of the large, wide front door, it had swung open to reveal Petra, standing before him, framed in the doorway. Behind her, a flash of blinding sunshine had suddenly broken through the wintry clouds, illuminating the space around her. Momentarily, she had appeared cloaked in celestial light, her face softly illuminated like a figure in a Michelangelo frieze.

For a moment, Gareth had believed himself to have stumbled into a mysterious, parallel universe in which Petra was a spiritual being, not mortal. Only when she'd smiled and ushered him into the warmth of the cottage, had the strangeness dissipated and the spell been broken.

"Welcome to Cragview Cottage," she had said, gesturing for him to step inside.

Gareth crossed the threshold, and as he did so, the light had dimmed slightly, allowing him to take in the open plan interior.

Instantly his eyes had been drawn to the windows and patio doors in the back wall. Each of them framed what he could only have described as a living picture of moor and heath, in which the colour was constantly changing with every mercurial movement of the weather.

"This is stunning," Gareth said, unable to take his eyes from the view at the back of the property. "I've lived in Granton for years, but I've hardly ever been up here. I had no idea there was anything like this on my doorstep. And this view you have...." His voice had tailed away as he struggled to find the words to express his appreciation.

"It is rather special, isn't it?"

Gareth had lost all sense of time, on that first visit. A leisurely lunch had been followed by a brisk walk on the moor in the fading light, with Scruff, Petra's border terrier, dancing at their feet. They shared a little more of themselves and Gareth had learned that Petra, too, had suffered trauma in her life.

After suffering a miscarriage, due, Petra believed, to the stress of her job in finance, she had craved a simpler, more meaningful life. Her husband did not share her aspiration, and they had divorced, acrimoniously. When the divorce was finalised, Petra had given up her job to pursue a long-held dream to take up pottery. After a week's residential course in the Yorkshire Dales, she had fallen in love with the area and set herself up in business, succeeding to the point at which she now received commissions from all over the world. She had stumbled upon Cragview Cottage during a walk on the moors, she told Gareth, and she had been entranced by it instantly - renting at first, then buying when the elderly owner had passed away. Now she divided her time between creating and teaching. She had never been happier, she had said, with conviction.

"You're welcome to stay," she had said, placing her hand over his, as they had sat before the log burner, sharing their stories. "But I'll understand if you don't."

He could easily have driven that night, since he hadn't touched a drop of alcohol. Nor had Petra, for that matter, out of consideration for him, he knew.

He had nodded, and without speaking, had followed her up the stairs. Wordlessly, she had pushed him back onto her soft, inviting bed, with its plumped pillows and colourful quilt. They had undressed each other slowly, in the light of a candle, which Petra had carried up the stairs like a character out of a nineteenth century romantic novel.

In those moments, as they had explored each other's bodies, for the first time, it was as if he had entered another world and time in which there were only the two of them, the wind moaning at the window and the flickering light of the candle throwing eery shadows on the walls. He had felt strangely disconnected from his daily life, even from his memories of Mel, losing himself in the magic of the moor and the beautiful owner of Cragview.

Thinking about it as he negotiated the busy traffic in Granton town centre, Gareth marvelled at how quickly his relationship with Petra had progressed, from that first conversation in the gym. Petra was such an easy person to be with; she was warm and engaging - not to mention beautiful – and he felt completely at ease with her. Sure, he had made comparisons with Mel, who would forever occupy an unreachable place, deep in his heart; yet that had not stopped him from wanting to continue seeing Petra.

After that memorable lunch at Petra's delightful home, Gareth had remained at Cragview, spending the whole of Christmas there. He had gone home only to collect clean clothes and other essential items. Since there were no near neighbours to call upon, and no family for either of them to accommodate – Petra's parents having elected to sail off on a world cruise - they had indulged themselves in selfish solitude for the entire festive period.

Descending into Granton for the shopping expedition, earlier that day, had come as a total shock to Gareth's system. Finding himself encircled by chattering crowds of excited shoppers had been a brutal return to reality. So many people and so much noise.

Then he had spied Morgan, squeezing herself onto the platform of a bus, filled to the brim with travellers. The sight of her had sent a shockwave through his system as well as the familiar sensation of guilt. He was certain she must have heard him calling her name and had ignored him, which must mean that her resolve to dissociate herself was as strong as ever.

As he drew closer to the centre of Granton, Gareth was dragged from his reflections by the sight of a long line of car brake lights illuminating one by one, in front of him, as if in an orchestrated show. He sighed impatiently, thumping his hand on the wheel in frustration. Eileen's house was on the other side of the city, and it looked as if it was going to be a slow crawl through the centre.

His ring tone suddenly filled the car. It was Petra. He pressed the hands-free receiver button.

"Hi, love," he said.

"How are you getting on?"

"Not good. The traffic's horrendous through the centre. I've hit the rush hour and all the bargain hunters, like us, making their way home. I'm afraid Morgan might have gone out for the evening by the time I get there."

"Can't you find some clever route along the side roads?" Petra asked. "You must have done some high-speed chases all around the highways and by-ways of Granton at various times in your career?"

"I was just thinking along those lines myself. I think I can find another way to Eileen's, but it will literally be all around the houses."

"Go for it, darling. You can't give up now."

"I know, though I'm sure I'll find the house empty when I get there. Morgan was in town today, so she might be going out tonight. It's probably going to be a wasted journey."

"No matter. You've got to see it through now you've made your mind up to try and see her. If she's out, you can shove a note through the letter box. At least she'll know you tried."

"You're absolutely right, as usual. Thanks so much for your support, Petra. I can't tell you how much it means to me."

"I just want to be able to help you, darling," said Petra, before ringing off.

CHAPTER TWENTY-SIX

Gareth arrived in front of 34 Victoria Terrace a little after five-thirty. The journey from Cragview had taken much longer than usual, but he had managed to find a route through quiet residential streets, avoiding the town centre.

The terrace was lined with cars, as usual, since few of the old houses had garages. He passed number thirty-four, on his right, whilst scanning the road for a space to park. Glancing across, he saw that Morgan's house was in total darkness, with no signs of life. His heart sank. Maybe this was going to be a wasted mission after all, as he had feared.

Deciding to call at the house anyway, he parked a few hundred yards up the road and walked back down. In contrast to the glowing windows of the neighbouring property, number 34 stood in disconsolate darkness.

He cursed himself for advising Eileen to seal up her door letterbox and replace it with a wall-mounted box, for security. It meant he was unable to look through the flap to see if there was any evidence of Morgan being home. He had to content himself with peering through the living room window, but it was hopeless. Eileen's thick lace curtains obscured the interior.

He pressed the front door bell several times and stood back to look up at the first-floor windows, but there was no sign of life. It really did look as if Morgan was out. Gareth sighed, bemoaning yet another failed attempt to reach out to his daughter. Time was passing them by, and she was a grown woman now. Years and memories were being lost in a fog of misunderstanding.

He shrugged up his collar against the cold that was seeping through his jacket and gnawing at his fingertips and headed back up the street towards his car.

Hang on a minute, he said to himself, coming to a sudden stop. There was the alleyway behind Eileen's house. He should check round the back to see if he could see anything from there. If there were no lights and the curtains were closed across Morgan's bedroom window, then the chances were she was out, and he should go away and leave her in peace.

Gareth walked briskly round to the back of the house, into the alley. To his surprise and concern, he found the gate was ajar a couple of inches. Fat lot of good it was taking out letterboxes and installing an alarm system – not that Eileen had ever used it – if the gate was left open for all and sundry. This dark alleyway would be a godsend to any would-be burglar, particularly if the occupier left them a perfect means of access. He must warn Morgan about all this, no matter how unwelcome his advice might be.

He pushed the gate open wide enough to step inside the garden. It had become untidy and overgrown, with weeds springing up between the paved path to the back door. Eileen and Derek had been so proud of this space, tending it faithfully when they were younger and fitter. Eileen would be devastated to see it now, in such a state of neglect. He knew that Morgan had never taken much of an interest in horticulture, so she wouldn't bother with it. He must pop round one day with a mower and some shears to tidy it up a bit, if she would ever let him.

From the gateway, Gareth peered down the garden towards the house and for a split second, thought he saw some movement in there. He stood stock still. It had been no more than a shift of the light, but he could swear he saw someone move across the doorway between the kitchen and living room.

Slowly, quietly, he advanced towards the house, keeping to the shadows, as much as he could. He was almost at the back door that led into the utility room, when he heard a crash from the direction of the lounge. It had to be an object falling to the floor, he figured. If so, then there must be someone in there, creeping about in the dark. Surely Morgan wouldn't go to such lengths to avoid him?

Gareth pulled out his phone from his jacket pocket and dialled Morgan's number. From his vantage point, behind the kitchen extension, he could hear her ring tone singing out from inside the house. He recognised it as one of her favourite pop songs. His skin tingled as adrenaline began to pump around his body. Instinct borne of years of policing told him something was very wrong here.

He scanned the back of the house. The curtains to the upper windows appeared to be open, so he didn't think Morgan was in bed, asleep. Having heard her phone ring inside, he was pretty sure she was in there. She may have forgotten her phone or left it behind when she went to work. That was most unlikely, he reasoned. In common with most young people today, she never went anywhere without it. So, what was going on in there?

Gareth peered closely at the windows and door. There was no sign of a forced entry, as far as he could tell. Except - wait a minute - one of the kitchen windows was open a couple of inches. An experienced burglar could easily have wedged it open wide enough to shimmy through onto the work surface inside. He might be getting carried away, but his gut told him an intruder had gained access to the property through this window and was still in there, with his daughter. Even if he was ridiculously wrong about that, he didn't care. He was going to find a way in somehow, to check that Morgan was alright.

He forced himself not to panic as he considered the possible repercussions if someone had, indeed, managed to force an entry and, at this very moment, might be contemplating some harm to his daughter. He needed to concentrate and think clearly about the best way he could help Morgan.

Gareth knew if he simply smashed into the property, like a bull in a china shop, he would probably spook whoever was in there. That might lead to Morgan being injured, or worse; he daren't even think about it, right now. Grabbing his phone again, he called up Pete Ryburn, a former colleague who owed him a favour.

"Pete, it's Gareth", he whispered down the phone.

"Gareth? Is that you mate?" came the puzzled response.

"No time to chat, Pete, sorry. I'm at my daughter's house and I'm pretty sure there's an intruder in there. It looks like he got in through an open window, as far as I can tell. I think Morgan may be in there as well, and I'm scared to death, mate. I'm ready to go in but I'm afraid something will go wrong if I try and handle it on my own. Can you get a squad car down here and I'll try and contain the situation until it gets here?"

"No problem, mate. I'm on it now. Do what you can, but don't try any heroics. We'll be there soon as."

"Thanks Pete. And please hurry."

CHAPTER TWENTY-SEVEN

In, out. In, out. Morgan attempted to calm the rising panic which was threatening to stifle her breathing.

Besides the rope Todd had now tied tightly around her wrists, after yanking her arms behind her back, Morgan now had a filthy, stinking scarf stuffed into her mouth. It made her retch as Todd ordered her to bite on it, before he wrapped it roughly around the back of her head, so tightly she could hardly turn her head without it cutting into her cheeks. She could still feel the threatening pressure of the knife blade held against her back. One wrong move by her, if she tried to escape, might prove fatal.

Whilst he concentrated on tying her hands and covering her mouth, Todd mumbled and muttered under his breath, his words barely audible. She guessed he had taken or smoked something, judging by his incoherent rambling.

The gist of what he was saying, as far as she could tell, was that he was going to make her pay for lying to him about her real identity and scrounging off him, as he saw it. Clearly, he was incensed that she had dumped him, after all he thought he had done for her. Repeatedly he called her a lying bitch, and worse, all the while building himself into a frenzy of rage. He looked and sounded insane.

Whatever else Todd had done when she was with him, he had never hurt her physically. At times, she might even say he'd shown tenderness towards her when she'd been drunk or coming down from some substance or other. The way he was behaving now, he was in a completely different zone, pumped up with a toxic mix of drugs and adrenaline. In this state, she feared there was no limit to what he might do to her.

"OK bitch," he spat out at her, globs of frothy saliva hitting her cheek. "Listen carefully to what you're going to do." Morgan strained every sinew to try and understand Todd's garbled instructions.

"You and me are going to take a walk down to the cashpoint," he continued. "When we get there, you're going to give me all the money in your bank account. And don't try telling me any more lies. I know exactly how much you've got in there and I know you lied through your fuckin' teeth the whole time you bummed off me."

Questions flew at Morgan like flaming darts, though her brain was so fogged with terror, she couldn't work anything out. How did he know what was in her bank account? Was he bluffing? He seemed to have devised some sort of plan for dealing with her and her money. She had to escape before he was able to take it any further.

"Before we go," said Todd, his face so close it was nearly touching hers, "you're going to give me a guided tour of this little place and you're going to show me where all the old lady's money is hidden away. And don't try telling me there's nothing here. I know you're Gareth Fairley's daughter. Your family's stinking rich – the old woman, too, I'll bet. Just tell me where the treasure is, no messing me about, and you might avoid me sinking this blade between your ribs. Understand?"

Morgan's mind was racing again. What would he do when he discovered there was no cash in the house, except perhaps, a few stray coins? She knew he didn't have a bank account of his own and had only ever dealt in cash. Did he not know there was a limit on daily withdrawals? In his drugged-up state, had he forgotten how the system worked? It was entirely possible. When she last looked, there was just over three thousand pounds in her account. No way could she take all that out at once. What would happen when he realised?

Morgan tried to speak, to explain, but it was hopeless. The gag held the lower part of her face, like a vice. She shook her head, as he was issuing his instructions, which he took to be her refusal to do as he ordered. He became incensed and moved the knife up to her neck, drawing blood as he nicked the skin just below her ear.

Roughly he pushed her towards the stairs. She stumbled and tripped up the first step, causing Todd to spit out a torrent of incomprehensible cursing and verbal abuse. She felt sick with fear as she began to climb the stairs, conscious of the proximity of the knife blade to the vulnerable, exposed flesh of her neck.

Upstairs, still holding the knife to her throat, Todd pulled out every drawer and searched every cupboard and wardrobe, in the process discovering only a couple of pounds in loose change. He was becoming increasingly incoherent, eventually gesticulating for her to go back downstairs. With the knife shifted to her back again, she tried to hold herself as rigidly as possible. Nevertheless, she felt pin pricks of pain as the blade connected with her body through the layers of her clothes.

As she descended the stairs, Morgan remembered there was money in an old biscuit tin, in one of the cupboards. Eileen had been a great one for hiding cash around the house "just in case", she used to say. Morgan had handed most of it over to the home for Eileen's spending money but retained about fifty pounds. Like her nan, she contemplated possible emergencies that might demand ready money. This was certainly an emergency, though not one she had foreseen.

Morgan tried to nod her head towards the kitchen, but her movement was restricted. Unable to understand, Todd shook her, like a rag doll, all the while screaming in her ear. He was completely losing control. Shuffling one foot in front of the other, Morgan managed to convey that she was attempting to reach the kitchen. Still gripping her arm and keeping the knife to her back, Todd measured his step to hers as they processed into the kitchen like mourners in a solemn funeral procession.

Leading Todd slowly towards a set of open shelves on the far wall, she stopped in front of the brightly coloured biscuit tin where the emergency cash was kept.

Releasing her arm, but moving the knife up to her neck again, with his free hand, Todd lifted the tin down and swiftly levered off the lid to reveal its contents. It was immediately obvious that it contained only a small number of notes and a few coins. His expression darkened.

"There's fuck all in there," he said. "You don't seem to understand, you silly bitch. If you keep lying to me, I'll stick you with this fucking knife and you're dead."

Every word he threw at her was emphasised by a look of pure hatred on his face. His intention was frighteningly clear.

Whilst Todd was peering into the biscuit tin and stuffing its meagre contents into his jacket pocket, Morgan glanced around the kitchen to see if there was anything she could use against him. Although her hands and mouth were tied, it would be useful to know where there was something she might grab as a weapon.

On the sink drainer were an upturned mug and cereal bowl, which she had washed up and left to dry before she left for work, several days ago. Neither of those would do much; but if she threw them, they might startle Todd long enough for her to make a break for the door.

"I'll be back to do a proper search later," said Todd, "so don't think you've got away with anything." Spinning her round, he steered her back towards the living room.

"What's gonna happen next is, I'm gonna free up your hands and mouth and you and me are gonna take a walk down to the bank. I'm going to be holding on to you real tight, arm in arm, like, and we'll be taking this with us."

Standing in the kitchen doorway, Todd waved the knife in front of Morgan's face, bringing the blade to rest on her cheek. She hardly dared breathe for fear of injury.

"One stupid move from you and I'll slice that pretty face of yours until no-one will recognise you." He laughed hysterically, like a hyena baying in the wild.

Unable to nod, she moved compliantly towards the front door, her mind once again racing over the possibilities for escape. From where she stood, she could see an umbrella hanging from a row of pegs beside the front door, next to a large bunch of keys. Maybe, if Todd released her hands as he said he would, she might be able to grab either or both of those when they reached the door. If she could hit him hard enough, that might buy her time to free herself and escape.

As Morgan was mulling her options, she was startled rigid by the sound of the front doorbell ringing out into the room. The sweetly chiming introduction to one of Eileen's favourite songs was an incongruous accompaniment to the drama unfolding within the walls of the house.

Twice more the bell rang and for longer each time. Whoever was on the other side of that door was determined to be heard. It was excruciating to think that a potential rescuer was standing a few feet away from her, separated only by a piece of wood, yet he or she was ignorant of the danger lurking within the house. If she could only cry out or somehow attract their attention, this nightmare might end. She could weep with frustration but dared not make a move.

As if reading her mind, Todd shifted the knife to her neck, once again. With his eyes, he warned her not to do anything which might advertise their presence in the house to whoever was standing outside.

The ringing on the doorbell ceased after a while. For what seemed like an age, but was probably only a few minutes, they stood, as if petrified, listening for sound on the other side of the door. Morgan's hope of rescue rapidly flipped to despair as she heard footsteps walking away from the house, and down the street. Whoever it was had given up. She was on her own and must redirect her thoughts, now, towards identifying the first possible opportunity for escape from this terrifying situation.

Slowly, like two zombies, Todd and Morgan shuffled towards the front of the house. When they were almost at the front door, Morgan's backpack, which she had dropped on entering, suddenly jumped, startlingly, into life as her phone rang out. Now it was her favourite music that repeatedly played into the silent room. Was it the same person who had just rung the doorbell, she wondered? She fervently hoped so, as it meant there must be someone outside the house intent on seeing her. She strained to listen for any audible clues as to who it might be but could hear only the voices of people walking by on the pavement and the hum of cars carrying their passengers home from work.

Hardly daring to breathe, Morgan waited for Todd's reaction. She guessed that he was making the same calculations as her.

"Who the fuck's that?" he asked her, apparently forgetting that the awful mouth gag he had tied on her was preventing her from uttering a sound. What the stinking rag could not do, however, was to disguise the reek of fear emanating from every pore of Todd's skin. Standing still as a statue, in the centre of her nan's living room, Morgan felt a rush of adrenaline coursing through her whole body.

CHAPTER TWENTY-EIGHT

Second by second, Morgan grew calmer. She was going to get out of this, she told herself. Keeping her head perfectly still, so as not to disturb the blade, her eyes darted around the living room in search of a means to distract her captor.

Todd was standing behind her and closest to the front door, still gripping her right arm with one hand as he held the knife to her neck with the other. On her right, positioned beneath the front window, was a small coffee table standing barely a foot away from her. A heavy, cut-glass ashtray, which Eileen had retained from her husband's smoking days, sat tantalisingly close to the edge of the table.

As Todd pulled her away from the door, probably calculating it was not safe to exit that way, Morgan managed to stumble against one of the skinny legs of the coffee table, causing it to wobble perilously. The ashtray slithered off the edge of the table onto the sanded wooden floorboards. With a surprisingly loud crack, it shattered into several pieces. Silently, Morgan gave thanks that her nan had never chosen wall to wall carpet for this room, electing instead for polished boards and her prize Axminster rug.

"Stupid bitch," Todd muttered in her ear, his eyes darting to the window.

Recognising that Todd was rattled by this unexpected turn of events, she swiftly calculated how she might overpower him and make her escape. Years ago, her security conscious father taught her self-defence techniques as a means of protection in case she found herself in a dangerous situation. Thank God he overcame her mum's protests that she was too young for such activity.

Even as she thought about it, some of the techniques she had been taught came flooding back to her. If Todd freed her wrists, as he said he would, she felt reasonably certain she could execute a couple of manoeuvres that would bring him to the ground. That would buy her time to get out of the house and onto the street, where she would scream for help from her neighbours or any passer-by. She hoped against hope that the person who had rung

113

the doorbell, a few moments ago, would still be outside, and might be able to help her to escape.

The more she thought about her plan, the braver and more confident she became. I can do this, she told herself. I *must* do this.

In the back garden, Gareth Fairley had been quietly scouting around, looking for a means of forcing entry to the house.

Behind the kitchen extension was a collection of terracotta plant pots, the contents of which had long since withered and died. Several of them stood off the ground on bricks left over from the construction of the kitchen extension.

If necessary, he could use one of the bricks to smash a pane in the back door so he could reach in and use the key he hoped would be hanging in the lock. Eileen always used to leave it there, despite his remonstrations. He guessed that Morgan did the same. He would prefer to wait, before taking any action, until Pete or one of his officers arrived on the scene, so they could cover back and front between them. At the same time, he needed to be prepared in case it all kicked off inside the house. For all he knew, someone in there was carrying a gun or a knife which might be turned on Morgan at any moment. The thought made his blood turn to ice.

Gareth glanced at his watch. The station was about twenty minutes away so Pete should be here soon, with backup. Please God, don't let anything happen to Morgan before they arrive, he prayed silently. He couldn't lose his daughter as well as his wife. It would finish him, once and for all. Morgan must survive this ordeal and he must do whatever it took to keep her alive.

Morgan could clearly see that Todd's drug-dulled brain was struggling to figure out his next move. Momentarily, he seemed to forget that he was holding a weapon, though his hold on her arm remained as tight as ever. His hand, gripping the knife, fell to his side as he dragged her back towards the kitchen.

There was no time to think. Seizing her opportunity, with all the strength she possessed, she turned towards Todd and thrust her right knee hard into his groin, with all the force she could summon up.

Instantly, he dropped the knife and staggered backwards, hands covering his crotch as he cried out like a baby. Morgan stamped on the knife, preparing to kick out to keep him down until she could make a run for the back door. Caught up as she was in the moment, her sub-conscious nevertheless registered the sound of glass shattering. Before she had time to think about it, her dad loomed up in the kitchen doorway, almost filling it with his strong, solid frame.

Was it really him, she asked herself, or was it wishful thinking playing tricks with her mind?

"Come to me," he yelled at her, in the deep authoritative voice that had always made her jump to obey him whenever he used it on her as a child. She dashed towards him, just as Todd plucked the knife from the floor and lunged at her, having recovered himself sufficiently to go on the attack. The blade caught her right arm, slashing through the sleeve of her coat and connecting with her upper arm. There was the sensation of her skin being sliced by the knife and the pulsating flow of blood to the wound. It barely registered with her as she took shelter behind her father's broad back.

"Drop the knife," Gareth ordered, his voice steady and firm and his eyes locked on to Todd, who was prowling around the living room, like a hunted animal, judging the right moment in which to pounce on its enemy.

Todd shook his head. "No way Fairley," he said. "I don't take no orders from you. It's me calling the shots this time. You'd better take a good look at your precious little daughter, because she ain't gonna look like that for much longer."

He was whipping the knife wildly around him with such force, Morgan felt a flutter of air on her cheek. She watched over her father's shoulder, barely breathing, her eyes fixated on Todd's every move.

"Drop the knife," Gareth repeated. "Armed police are on their way. They'll be here any minute."

Todd gave a hysterical shriek of laughter, all the while continuing to pace around the room, brandishing the knife as if he were slashing an imaginary opponent.

"D'ya take me for a fucking idiot, Fairley? It's just you and me and your lying little bitch of a daughter here." He made a feint at Gareth as if he were fencing, bursting into crazed laughter as Gareth leaned away from him.

"Now here's what we're gonna do," he said, an intense look on his face. Watching Todd from behind her father's back, Morgan was transfixed by the madness blazing from his eyes. He was high as a kite and completely out of control.

"You two are gonna give me all your cards with their pin numbers. Then I'm gonna tie you both up tight, whilst I pop down to the cashpoint and help myself to all your dosh. And don't bother about comin' after me, 'cos I'll be long gone by the time you get loose."

As Todd paced around the living room, there was a sudden loud hammering on the door that made them all jump.

"POLICE! OPEN UP".

Todd's body became rigid. He looked at Gareth and Morgan in disbelief.

"What the fuck kind of little joke's this then, Gareth? Got someone to play cops and robbers with you, eh?"

He leaned towards the window and flicked back the curtain. Instantaneously, the room was illuminated with flashing blue light, turning its occupants ghostly pale.

"Give it up, Todd," said Gareth, holding out his hand. "Give me the knife."

"I ain't doing nothing you say." Todd replied, taking a step towards the kitchen, where Gareth was still blocking the doorway. "Get out of my way, or you'll feel this blade in your gut. Then your little princess can watch her old man die as well."

Gareth slowly raised his hands above his head and stepped into the sitting room., motioning for Morgan to follow behind him. They moved together, Morgan shadowing her father at every step. As soon as they had cleared the kitchen doorway, Todd made to dart past them, still waving the knife. The second he drew level with Gareth, the older man grabbed at Todd, attempting to disarm him. Younger and nimbler, Todd was able to dodge out of his way, but Gareth didn't give up so easily. He threw himself on Todd, grasping hold of his clothing. Todd wriggled and pulled like a young dog, eager to escape its leash.

Morgan watched intently, desperately looking for an opportunity to help her father, despite having her wrists still

116

tightly bound. Todd was unzipping his hoodie, preparing to shrug it off and break free from her father's grasp. At that moment, there was a terrific crash as the front door was slammed open with a battering ram.

"Armed police!" a voice shouted as two uniformed and one plain clothed officer piled in through the door. Dressed in bulky protective gear and clutching a range of weapons, they seemed to shrink the room in an instant.

The first police officer, his arms held rigidly at shoulder height and with a handgun clasped in his two hands, instantly trained the weapon on the two figures, wrestling each other in the kitchen.

"Hold it right there and don't move," the plain-clothed officer shouted, as he shadowed a colleague, advancing towards the kitchen.

Suddenly Gareth doubled up, clutching his stomach. Morgan screamed in horror as she watched blood oozing between her dad's fingers and dribbling down the back of his hands. In the shock and disturbance of the police entry, Todd had stolen a second to swiftly thrust the knife into his opponent's belly. Instantly, Gareth released his hands to hold them protectively over the wound. Todd escaped from his stranglehold and fled through the open kitchen door through which, moments ago, Gareth had forced his entry.

Gareth's face contorted with pain, but he found the strength to issue instructions. "Pete," he yelled to his former colleague, "there's a gate at the end of the garden, leading into an alleyway. You need to get round there."

"Already taken care of, boss. I sent two uniforms back there before we came in. They'll get the bastard, don't you worry."

Even before he had finished speaking, there was the sound of raised voices outside. Morgan could hear Todd shouting obscenities, answered by the stern responses of the police officers who held him captive. Inside the living room, Pete freed Morgan's hands and she rushed over to her father, who had slumped into a chair, still clutching the wound.

"Are you ok, dad?" Morgan cried, grasping her dad's arm. Gareth nodded. "It's not as bad as it looks," he said, though

Morgan didn't believe him. His skin was bleached of colour, and she could see the pain etched in his face.

Pete came over and put an arm around her.

"Try not to worry, Morgan. An ambulance will be here any minute. Keep applying pressure, boss. The paramedics will be here soon."

"What about your arm, love?" Gareth asked, staring at the circular crimson stain expanding like a mushroom cloud across his daughter's coat sleeve.

Morgan glanced down at her arm and was shocked to see how much blood she had lost. The drama and heightened tension of the past half an hour had numbed the pain and made her forget her own injury. Remembering how Todd had sliced her with the knife, her knees suddenly went weak, and she felt a dull ache spreading down her arm.

"Grab her," Gareth commanded, as Morgan swooned and appeared on the point of fainting. A uniformed officer sprang forward and shepherded Morgan to the stairs, where she flopped down.

In the same moment, the sound of an ambulance siren filled the room. Paramedics poured through the gaping front door and began working on Morgan and her father.

Despite the loss of blood, Morgan's injury was judged superficial, and the paramedics were able to patch her up, without the need for further treatment. Gareth's wound was assessed to be more serious, and he was quickly bundled into the ambulance to be transported to hospital.

Seeing her father slumped in the chair, clutching his belly, had sent Morgan's mind into turmoil. Everything had happened so quickly, and she hadn't been able to process any of it. Strangely, as if the past year had never happened, her heart was filled with love for her father. She knew she couldn't bear it if anything dreadful were to happen. Insisting that she accompany him to hospital, she clambered into the back of the ambulance.

"Come on, dad," she said. "You've got this." She took his left hand, which hung limply by his side and held it tightly in her own. As he looked at her, there was no mistaking the fierce love shining in his eyes. She held his hand to her cheek and for the first time since her mother died, Morgan allowed her tears to flow freely. She sobbed, quietly and relentlessly, until the ambulance doors were thrown open again and her dad was trolleyed into the Emergency Department of Granton District Hospital.

CHAPTER TWENTY-NINE

January 2016

"Remind me never to upset you", said Josie, as she bit into her bacon roll. "You and your Kung-Fu kicks."

Morgan gave a wry smile. She was sitting in the staff room at Harley Grange with several of her colleagues, attempting to eat her lunch in peace and quiet. The others were having none of it, however, quizzing her relentlessly about the facts of her recent ordeal.

"Seriously, Mo, I'm so proud of you." Josie continued. "We all are. You really kicked ass with that scumbag, Todd Hopkins. The streets will be a better place when he's locked away."

"I'll drink to that," said Sunita, raising her bottle of orange juice. "You could be on the news, you know, Morgan."

Morgan shook her head vigorously and shuddered.

"No way," she said.

The memory of being pursued by news hungry reporters still haunted Morgan. She could see them now, hanging around her home and school, desperate to get her and Gareth's story on her mum's accident. When she had been in the darkest place possible, and trying to process her mother's death, the press pack made her feel like a defenceless animal, relentlessly pursued.

Then there had been the social media trollers who had posted vile stuff, including comments about her mum deserving to die because she was married to a cop. It had driven her to despair and prompted her decision to adopt her mother's maiden name to try and regain some anonymity – that and the desire to disassociate herself from her father. Eventually, the interest in her story had waned, then ceased altogether; but for as long as her mum's killer remained at large, Morgan feared her story might resurface and she might once again become caught up in the relentless quest for newsworthy print.

Only Morgan's friend Josie and her manager, Bev, knew the whole truth. To the rest of her colleagues, she was Morgan Garrett, Eileen's granddaughter. Morgan's mother - Eileen's daughter-in-law - had died some years earlier, Morgan had told them. As for her father, he worked for long periods abroad and Morgan rarely saw him. Since her mum died, Morgan had been living with her nan. The man who visited Eileen regularly was merely a friend of the family. In his increasingly dishevelled and unkempt state, no-one seemed to recognise him from his appearances on various news channels. If they did, they didn't say anything.

It was her aunt Jess who had helped Morgan to devise a story behind which she might conceal difficult facts.

"I'm scared in case anyone figures out who I am and starts poking around our life again," Morgan had said to her aunt, when they had been discussing her job offer from Harley Grange. "I couldn't bear all that, all over again."

"Don't worry, love," Jess had said. "I'll concoct something close to the truth, and I'll speak to your dad, to make sure he's on board with it all."

Morgan had bristled at the suggestion that her dad should be consulted, but finally accepted that he needed to agree to the messaging. When it came to Eileen, Morgan and her aunt reflected with sadness, she was unlikely to present a problem. The combined effects of the accident and her fall had robbed her of memory and reason. If she ever did contradict the fabricated story, Morgan and Jess agreed, it was most unlikely that anyone would be able to make any sense of what she was saying.

It had helped that Bev insisted Morgan take a week's sick leave after the Todd incident. For once Morgan did not object, happy to be out of reach of her colleagues' curiosity. Again, only Bev and Josie knew the whole truth, including Gareth's part in the incident. They agreed to keep that to themselves, which meant no-one else at Harley Grange was aware of Gareth's involvement, though they were told of Morgan's bravery. That had seemed to satisfy everyone's desire for details of the drama in which Morgan had found herself caught up.

Crucially, from Morgan and Gareth's point of view, there had been no link to Melissa's death, as far as they had been able to tell, so no re-opening of that story.

"I want to try and keep a lid on all this," Morgan's dad had said to her in the ambulance on the way to hospital, after the stabbing. "We don't want people, especially the press, crawling all over our private business, again." Despite bleeding profusely from the stab wound inflicted by Morgan's ex-boyfriend, and clearly in a great deal of pain, he had only wanted to talk about Morgan's protection, ignoring all her attempts to keep him quiet and calm.

"You should carry on using your mother's maiden name," Gareth had insisted. "I totally understand why you wanted to do that, and I think you were right. I'm sure it's helped to keep the media at bay."

He hadn't known it, but with those words and his selfless act of putting himself between Morgan and the sinister blade of Todd's knife, Gareth had just taken enormous strides towards reconciliation with his daughter.

"How's your dad doing now?" Josie asked, out of hearing of the others.

"Mm? What? Sorry, I was miles away," said Morgan when she realised Josie was talking to her. "He's good, thanks. The doctors say the knife didn't damage any vital organs, but he had a deep wound which needed internal stitching. He'll be in hospital for another week or so, for observation and to check the wound is healing."

Morgan was interrupted by Joseph, another of the carers, who popped his head around the door, calling her name.

"There's someone out here who would like to speak to you," he said, winking and looking mysterious.

"It's not a reporter, is it?" Morgan asked, fear tightening her throat.

"Nope. It's someone you know," said Joseph, a huge grin splitting his face from ear to ear. "I think you should come out."

Warily, Morgan stepped into the corridor. There, standing patiently waiting, his face almost obscured by an enormous bunch of flowers, was Dominic Cooper.

CHAPTER THIRTY

It was a little after 8.30pm when Morgan walked through the doors of The George pub, her heart pounding and stomach churning. Strangers' faces swam in front of her as she looked around for Dom. The din of talk and laughter was like a sudden deluge of water hitting her eardrums with tremendous force.

When Dom had appeared at the staff room door, his face barely visible above an enormous bunch of flowers, Morgan had been at a loss for words.

"These are for you.....obviously," he said, a faint blush colouring his cheeks. "I just wanted you to know how much I admire what you did. Phyllis told me about you defending yourself against that bloke that broke into your house, and....well...I'm in awe. I'm certain I would not have been so brave."

Then it had been Morgan's turn to blush. She hated being the object of attention.

"Thanks," she said, taking the flowers that had been thrust at her.

She and Dom had talked briefly about the incident, then he surprised her by asking if she fancied joining him and some of his friends at a gig at The George on Friday night. One of their mates was in the band, and it might cheer her up, he had suggested, after all she had been through.

"The band have only just got together, and they could use the support, so it would be an act of charity if you came along."

Taken aback by the unexpected suggestion, Morgan's first instinct had been to think of an excuse for refusing. The only person she ever went out with was Josie, who knew her story and didn't try to poke around in her business. If she accepted Dom's invitation, there would be him and all his friends asking questions all night long. She wouldn't be able to relax and enjoy herself for fear of giving away her most carefully guarded secrets.

"Er….I'm not sure what I'm doing on Friday. Can I let you know?"

"Of course," he said. "Can I give you my number so you can message me if you're coming, and I can look out for you?"

"Sure." Morgan handed Dom her phone so he could input his number.

"Hope to see you Friday," Dom said, returning the phone.

Morgan smiled, in a non-committal way. "I'd better get back to work. I've got heaps to do."

"No problem. Have a good day."

"Thanks," she said, turning away. "And thanks again for the flowers."

Morgan had slithered back inside the staff room, pulling an agonised face at Josie and the others, who were waiting, with eager anticipation, to hear what had happened.

"Fabulous flowers," said Joseph.

"Just go," Josie had said, when Morgan had finished telling her about the conversation with Dom. "You can always make an excuse and leave, if you feel uncomfortable," she went on. "You never know, you might even enjoy yourself. He's pretty hot," she teased, nudging Morgan on the arm. "How about if I turn up at the pub and pretend it was a coincidence? That way, you could come and join me if it all gets too much for you."

"Thanks Jo, that's really kind of you, but I think I've got to do this on my own. Either I take a chance and go, or I stay away and give Dom the brush-off when I next see him."

"Your call, girlfriend".

All day that Friday, Morgan had been in an agony of indecision. Now she was here, standing in a crowded pub, and all she could see were complete strangers. Perhaps Dom had changed his mind, even though she had messaged to say she was coming. In one second, she told herself, I am reversing through these doors and on my way home.

"Morgan!" a voice called out to her from one corner of the crowded pub.

She looked round and saw Dom walking towards her, a beaming smile on his face. Her shoulders relaxed as relief washed over her.

"I'm so glad you came," Dom said, guiding her towards two tables, pushed together, around which about six or seven people were already seated, talking animatedly to each other. A mix of male and female, they all looked around her age, she guessed, as she scanned the group.

"Guys – this is Morgan," Dom announced. Heads turned, briefly, towards her; a couple of the guys gave her a wave.

"Hey Morgan", the two girls responded. They all shuffled up together so that Morgan could sit on one end, with Dom beside her. He leaned into her slightly, to be heard over the general hubbub, as he went round the table, introducing each one.

"That there is Odette," he indicated towards a petite blonde sitting beside another girl. "She and I met on our first day of school, and I haven't been able to shake her off since."

"Don't listen to him, Morgan. Just feel sorry for me," Odette joked.

Dom rolled his eyes, before continuing. "Then we have Phoebe, her boyfriend Taylor, and another couple of schoolfriends, Fin and Haydn." Each person gave her a wave, as they were introduced. Morgan waved back.

"Adam's the friend who's in the band, and I'm Dom, as you know," he said, "though I get called a lot worse by this lot."

Morgan laughed, picking up on the good vibe between the group of friends. Already she felt relaxed in their company and privately congratulated herself on having plucked up the courage to come out. Drinks flowed freely, though no-one would allow her to buy one. Having left herself insufficient time to eat before she came out, she soon began to feel fuzzy headed. Better slow down, she warned herself. I don't want to blow it by getting pissed.

Half an hour later than billed, the band filed into a corner of the pub, which had been set up for their session. They were met with well-intentioned heckling and joshing from Dom and his friends. Undeterred, the band struck up their first chords and soon found their rhythm, capturing the attention of the room with their clever blend of genres.

"They're really good," said Morgan, leaning closer to Dom, to make herself heard. He inclined his head towards her, at the same time, resting an arm lightly across her shoulders. She was acutely aware of their bodies touching, however lightly. Could he feel the heat exuding from her every pore, she wondered anxiously?

"Are you glad you came?" Dom asked. She hesitated for a moment, considering his question.

"I really am," she replied, smiling broadly.

Attraction sparked between them like a lightning storm.

At the end of the evening, Dom offered to walk her home. She politely declined, knowing she would be unable to resist him and, inevitably, they would fall into bed. Much as she wanted that - and she really did want it - in a perverse way, she needed to deprive herself of that satisfaction. If Dom was going to be her next boyfriend, she so wanted things to be different from her sordid affair with Todd.

"Are you free tomorrow?" Dom asked, as everyone was leaving the pub at closing time. "I go back to uni on Sunday, and I'd really like to see you again before I go, if that's alright with you."

She smiled. "That would be great," she said.

"Do you like Thai food?" he asked.

"I love it."

"Let's meet here again at 7. The restaurant's only a few blocks away."

"See you then," said Morgan, trying to sound much cooler than she felt.

CHAPTER THIRTY-ONE

Morgan had barely had time to stow her bag in her locker before Josie came bouncing into the staff room, like an excited child.

"So how did it go then?" she asked, peering at Morgan as she tried to read her expression. Try as she might, Morgan could not restrain a broad grin breaking out across her face.

"Good," said Morgan, unwilling to jinx herself by saying too much. The truth was, she could hardly believe Dom might be interested in her. It seemed too good to be true.

"Please don't ask me too much," she said. "I'm seeing him again tonight and I'll tell you more when I'm ready."

Josie wrapped her arms around Morgan, giving her a huge hug. "My friend is happier than I've seen her in ages. That's more than enough for me."

How she made it through the day, Morgan didn't know. Excitement and nerves competed for her mind and thoughts.

By the time evening came, she was feeling extremely anxious. She even contemplated messaging Dom to cancel, but decided she must face up to her fears. Her life would never improve if she continued to back away from challenges.

She dithered over what to wear for a while, finally deciding on her torn black jeans, black vest top and a black, slouchy jumper, with a wide neck, that Josie bought her for Christmas. Not her usual style, but Josie had begged her to wear it on the date and she had promised to do so.

That'll have to do, she told herself as she grabbed her parka and backpack and set off for The George.

She was a few minutes late to the pub and found Dom already at the bar, chatting to one of the bartenders. The place was filling up with people queuing for drinks and gathered at tables. Dom looked up as she entered and waved at her smiling. Josie was right. He really was extremely hot.

She joined Dom at the bar, offering her cheek as he leaned in to kiss her. She loved the shower-clean smell of him.

"What'll you have?" he asked.

"A small lager, please. Shall I find somewhere to sit?"

"You can try. I'll bring the drinks over."

Morgan bagged the last table in the bar area, which was packed with Saturday evening revellers. She looked around at couples chatting amiably, some holding hands across the table. There were groups of girls and gatherings of guys preparing to go on to a restaurant or maybe a club. A normal Saturday night. It felt so good to be part of it.

In a snap of realisation, Morgan decided she didn't want this to be a confessional, "tell-all" kind of evening. She didn't want to trample the fragile, tender shoots of this relationship – if that's what it was – by loading it with her sad story. After all, she hardly knew this guy. A few snatched conversations and a quick snog the night before were all that lay between them. No, there would come a moment, maybe in a few weeks, maybe a few months – if they were still together - when it would be the right time to be completely honest with him. Until then, she would continue to live as Morgan Garrett, keeping it vague and simply enjoying having a special someone in her life for however long it lasted.

"Good find," said Dom, setting the drinks down on the table.

"Cheers!" Morgan replied, raising her glass.

Dom and Morgan laughed and chatted, discussing favourite films, books and music. They had much in common but argued agreeably about their differences of opinion.

Does this guy have any faults, Morgan wondered? He was interesting and funny, regaling her with stories of the antics he used to get up to with the friends she had met the evening before. He was also clearly passionate about his studies and becoming a doctor so that he could help to save lives. She loved that.

"God, I'm doing all the talking," Dom said, returning from the bar with another couple of drinks. "It's time for you to get a word in," he joked. "Who is Morgan Garrett?"

She faked a smile, though inside she was shrinking and tightening against the anticipated assault of curiosity and questioning.

"Not much to tell," Morgan replied with fake nonchalance. "I messed up my A levels, so didn't go to uni, as planned. I bummed around for a while, doing odd jobs here and there, not very well. Then my nan had a bad fall. I moved into her house to look after her, but she needed more care, so that's how she came to be in Harley Grange. I spent a lot of time with her there and got offered a job as a care assistant. That's about it, really."

More partial truths, spoken in a light tone to discourage any deeper interest. She had become proficient at lying and dissembling to keep people at arms' length.

"I've watched you at the home – you're brilliant at your job. Everyone loves you, it's obvious. Phyllis never stops going on about you."

"Phyllis is fabulous, she's such a character," she spoke enthusiastically, feeling they had moved to more solid ground.

"Your parents must be really proud of what you do," said Dom.

It was a surprising remark, but one with which Morgan didn't want to engage. She smiled but didn't respond.

"Do you know what, I'm starving! Shall we go and eat now?"

Dom drained his glass and banged it down on the table. "Excellent idea," he said. "Let's go before it gets too busy."

CHAPTER THIRTY-TWO

"That was an amazing meal," said Morgan, as she sat back, holding her stomach. "I've eaten far too much."

"I think that means it's time for the bill," said Dom, summoning the waiter over to their table.

"Crikey," said Morgan, looking around. "Where did everybody go?"

The busy restaurant they entered had emptied, except for them and one other couple. The waiters, no doubt keen to finish their shifts, were discreetly tidying and setting up tables for the following day.

To Morgan's relief, the conversation in the restaurant had veered away from personal matters onto more neutral ground. Dom was so easy to talk to that Morgan hadn't noticed the time.

There was an awkward silence as they exited the restaurant, standing in the doorway, whilst fastening their coats.

"Walk you home?" he asked. She nodded and they strolled back to Victoria Terrace, hand in hand. It was a short distance and soon they were standing in front of the house. Morgan put the key in the lock and threw open the door. Wordlessly, she held out her hand, beckoning Dom inside. He followed meekly. When the door shut behind them, he bent his head to kiss her. She responded eagerly, throwing off her coat and pulling at Dom's. Taking his hand again, she led him up the stairs.

"Are you sure?" he asked. She nodded, laying a finger on his lips, to indicate he should follow her in silence. Her resolutions about taking things gradually flew out of the window as she led Dom into her bedroom.

In the darkness of the small room, they tore off each other's clothes, laughing as they fumbled with zips and buttons. The room was chilly, and they jumped into Morgan's single bed, burying themselves under the duvet and clinging together for warmth. Morgan felt Dom harden against the softness of her belly. She rubbed herself against him, feeling the heat suddenly explode from his body and her own as the intensity of their desire grew. Unable to wait any longer, she guided him inside her, and they both cried out as they climaxed together, gazing at each other in wonder at the intensity of their passion.

It was late when they finally fell asleep, exhausted from exploring each other's body. Every inch of Morgan's skin found its perfect place against Dom's as tiredness overwhelmed her, and she slipped into a blissful, relaxed sleep.

Morgan awoke to the pale winter light creeping into her bedroom from around the curtains. Glancing at her phone, she saw she had slept for almost nine hours. She hadn't done that since her mother died.

Instantly aware of the person beside her, she snuggled to fit herself into his sleeping form. Waking beside another warm body made Morgan sigh with contentment. Today was a day off and she could happily stay curled up here, with Dom, for the rest of the day. They could have a leisurely breakfast, maybe go for a walk, she figured. She didn't mind what she did, as long as it was with him.

Then, with a jolt, she suddenly remembered what she had planned for the day. Before arranging last night's date with Dom, she had promised to visit her dad in hospital. Morgan had been shocked beyond measure to see her father looking so pale and weak, as he lay in the ambulance, with paramedics working on him continuously. It had made her realise that her love for him was undiminished, and she had visited him every day since her ex-boyfriend had almost killed him.

Today being a Sunday, she needed to catch the only morning bus at eleven, which left her with only a couple of hours. Time enough to get ready, but not long to spend with Dom.

Dom stirred and reached for her again, running his hand lightly along the side of her body, grazing her breast. She moaned quietly, with desire and frustration. No time, she told herself, with agonising self-discipline. She couldn't put off her dad, after all he'd been through for her sake, and if she didn't catch that bus at eleven, there wasn't another until the afternoon.

She pulled away from Dom's eager embrace. "I'm really sorry, Dom," she said. "My dad's home for a while, and I forgot I'm having lunch with him. I need to shower and get ready, then head out for the bus. I wish we could stay here all day, but I've promised my dad. I haven't seen him for ages."

Except for Josie and Bev, Dom knew no more than Morgan's work colleagues about her personal life. For the moment, at least, she wanted to keep it that way, and so she had told Dom the well-rehearsed story, concocted by her aunt Jess, behind which she had been hiding ever since she started work at Harley Grange.

Dom planted another kiss on her neck, then let her go. "Of course. I understand. You must go and see your dad, though I don't want to let you out of my sight."

A warm glow radiated throughout Morgan's body at Dom's words. She had been thinking the same about him, so to hear it from his lips was all the reassurance she needed after the intimacy of the night before. Better still, as Dom pulled on his clothes and prepared to leave, he spoke about her coming over to stay with him at his student house in Manchester.

"I'm not far away, so you can come and stay when you're not working, and I'll be home often," he told her. "What do you think?"

What did she think? She thought those were the best words she'd ever heard. Clearly, he saw a future for them together, even when he was back at university.

"Of course I'll come over and see you, whenever I can," she replied, her heart fluttering with happiness. She could catch a bus from Granton to Manchester, she calculated, or get the train. It would be an easy journey for her, though she'd do it, even if she had to catch ten trains to see him. Better not tell him that, though; she didn't want to blow it by seeming too keen, too soon.

"I'll be home again next weekend," said Dom. "See you then?"

She nodded, pressing her finger to her lips, then laying it lightly on his.

"Until next weekend," she said.

CHAPTER THIRTY-THREE

The bus engine juddered into life and pulled slowly out of the station. There were only six other passengers on board, Morgan noted. She settled her ear pods in place and scrolled through to one of her favourite playlists. With time on her hands and music in her ears, she let herself replay the past couple of nights with Dom, daring to dream about what the future might hold for them.

She must have fallen asleep, because it seemed like hardly any time had passed before the driver was calling out her stop. Morgan made a quick dash into the hospital shop to buy her dad's favourite chocolates and a car magazine. He had been complaining of being bored, which she found reassuring. It must mean he was getting better, she told herself.

Arriving at his private room, she found the door shut. She threw it open and burst in, all eagerness to see him. With her mouth open, ready to speak, she came to a screeching halt on finding a strange woman sitting beside her father, holding hands across the bed. Seconds too late, the stranger withdrew her hand, but Morgan had seen the connection and instantly recognised what she was witnessing. Her dad had a girlfriend.

"Morgan!" said Gareth with a nervous smile. "I wasn't expecting you today."

"Obviously," she said sharply.

"Morgan love, let me introduce you to Petra. I've been wanting to tell you about her, but well……" his voice trailed away in embarrassment. He cleared his throat. "Petra and I have been seeing each other for a few weeks now. We met at the gym, before Todd Hopkins tried to skewer me with a kitchen knife."

Morgan looked from her dad to the woman, and back. Her mind was racing. She was totally unprepared for this new development and hadn't given any thought to the possibility of her dad having a girlfriend. She looked across at the woman, trying to assess what she was being confronted with.

"Petra, this is my daughter, Morgan," said Gareth.

"Hello Morgan," said Petra, smiling.

"Hello," Morgan replied.

"I'd better go, love," said the stranger. "I'm teaching at the studio in a couple of hours. The traffic's bound to be awful, so I should be on my way. I'll be in again tomorrow."

Don't kiss him, Morgan thought to herself, I won't be able to stand it. Thankfully Petra gathered up her coat and bag and left, lightly brushing Gareth's arm with her hand.

"Bye darling," said Gareth, watching Petra out of the room. He turned to Morgan.

"I'm so sorry, love. I really didn't want you two to meet that way. I've been trying to figure out how to tell you about Petra, but there never seemed to be a right moment. I can imagine how hard that must have been for you."

"I don't think you can, dad," Morgan replied, flopping down on to the chair which Petra had vacated.

"Believe me, I wasn't looking to meet anyone – hadn't even thought about it. I joined the gym to try and get fit and keep off the booze." Her father had told her of his fall from grace at work and his battle with addiction. He had also admitted to her that he was an alcoholic. It came as no surprise to Morgan. She had left home, in large part, because of his drinking.

"I seemed to keep bumping into her," Gareth continued. "We got talking, had coffee, then dinner and...well..." His voice tailed off as he struggled to find the right words.

Morgan sighed. "It's ok dad. I don't expect you to be a monk for the rest of your life, but this was......a shock."

"I realise that, and it's been a shock to me too, love. Your mum was everything to me. I never imagined being with anyone else, but Petra is such a lovely person – caring, kind and...."

"She's very beautiful, dad. I can see that. It's just...."

"What, love?"

"I feel like you're rubbing mum out of your life – my life too, for that matter. I don't ever want to forget any little thing about her. I want to believe that she's gone away and might come back any time." Morgan was fighting back tears as she tried to explain to her father how affecting this new situation was for her.

"Come here, love." Gareth patted the bed beside him. He took his daughter's hand in his as she perched on the edge of the bed.

"Your mum is locked into our hearts forever, in different ways. I won't let you forget your mother, and you won't let me forget my wife. We'll talk about her to the end of my days, remember her birthday and other special days together. She'll always be with us."

Morgan nodded, leaning over to rest her cheek on her dad's chest as she mourned her mum for a few moments. Their lives were moving on inexorably – her's and her dad's - and there was nothing she could do to stop that.

"Are those chocolates for me?" Gareth asked, breaking the intensity of the moment with a cheeky smile.

"Sure are," said Morgan. "Fill your boots." She handed him the box of mini-chocolate bars she had bought and the magazine.

They chatted, ate chocolates, and played a silly game of I-Spy, with hardly any objects to choose in the sparsely furnished room. There was no more talk of Petra, and Morgan decided it was too soon to mention Dom. Right now, she decided, she just wanted to get back on track with her dad.

CHAPTER THIRTY-FOUR

Morgan watched her father walk around the front of his car to settle himself into the passenger seat beside her. His posture was unusually stooped, she noted, and he flinched as he fastened the seatbelt. He had only been out of hospital a few days after a stay of several weeks. There was no question that the Todd drama, as Morgan and her father had come to call it, had aged him. Morgan caught her breath as she foresaw the old man her father would become.

"Are you sure you're up to this, dad? I'm worried about you."

"I'm fine, love. It's you we need to worry about. Now, when you're ready."

After making all her checks, Morgan started up the engine of her father's car and pulled away from the kerb outside Eileen's house.

During Morgan's regular visits to her father in hospital, the pair had confessed their fears during and after the knife attack. Morgan admitted to being totally creeped out by the realisation that Todd had been stalking her for weeks, before attempting to take her captive and steal all her money. Her father admitted he felt the same.

"It worries me sick thinking of you walking out in Granton, late at night, and hanging around waiting for buses," Gareth had responded. They agreed that the answer, for them both, was that Morgan should learn to drive and buy a car so that she would have the security of her own transport.

Despite Morgan's protestations, her dad had insisted on paying for a course of lessons and offered to supervise her practice as soon as he was discharged from hospital.

"That would be great, dad," she had said, giving him a big hug, which made him wince with pain. "Sorry, sorry dad. I keep forgetting."

True to his word, Gareth had presented himself at Victoria Terrace on Morgan's day off, so she could practice what she had been learning in her lessons.

"I thought we'd drive first around town to practice being in busy traffic, then take a spin out to the countryside," said Gareth. What do you think?"

"Sounds good."

Gareth patiently directed Morgan through the late morning traffic, then out of town towards the moors above Granton. Spring was still weeks away and the trees were bare of leaves, their buds waiting to be enticed into their annual appearance. The greyness of winter was hanging in the air and the roads were damp from a light drizzle.

"I don't think I've ever been out here before," said Morgan, as they drew away from the busy streets of Granton.

"You've probably forgotten that your mum and I brought you out here when you were little, but then we got out of the habit of it."

"It's wild, but wonderful," said Morgan.

Gareth cleared his throat. "Actually," he said. "I have a confession to make."

"What sort of confession?"

"In five minutes or so, we'll be arriving at Petra's place – Cragview Cottage."

"What?" Morgan slammed on the brakes, then stared her dad straight in the face.

"Morgan! For Christ's sake, you can't just stop like that." Gareth peered anxiously in the wing mirror to check for following traffic. Fortunately, there were no cars behind them.

"And you can't just pull a stunt like tricking me into turning up at Petra's cottage with no prior warning," said Morgan, glaring at her father.

"She is expecting you," said Gareth, "and she really wants to meet you properly, rather than across a hospital bed. Now, can we at least move off. We can't sit in the middle of the road like this. If you feel strongly about it, we'll turn around and go back."

Morgan pulled away, slowly. She was furious. Although she had met Petra several times since their first encounter, they had exchanged only a few words before Petra had made an excuse to leave each time.

"I was afraid if I asked you to come out here, you'd say no," said Gareth.

"Well, I would like to have been given the option, thanks very much."

Gareth sighed and rubbed his forehead. "I'm sorry, love. I've messed up again. It's just that Petra's so keen to have you for lunch. She keeps on to me about it."

"Where is Cragview then?" Morgan asked.

"Just up the road here, about half a mile away. We're almost there."

"Ok. If Petra's expecting me, I don't want to appear rude. But please don't pull a stunt like that on me again. I hate surprises."

"I won't love. I promise."

Gareth had not oversold Cragview Cottage, when he'd described it to her, Morgan later acknowledged. The minute it came into view, she could see it was special. Set back from the road, on rising ground, it looked forwards towards the modernity of Granton and back to the timeless, empty moorland that hadn't changed in centuries. Constructed of solid stone blocks and slate, its appearance was softened by a pretty front garden edged with sturdy shrubs, heathers and a variety of ferns. Weaving a procession through the borders was a generous display of snowdrops heralding the approach of spring.

Morgan pulled into a small car parking area in front of a wooden, black-stained outbuilding. Beside a set of double doors, a grey slate sign read 'Petra Lang Pottery'.

"Petra's studio," said Gareth.

"Wow!" said Morgan, sounding seriously impressed. "This is all quite something."

From the car park, three generous stone steps led to a flagged path running in front of the cottage. Gareth opened a waist high, wrought iron gate at the top of the steps, leading Morgan to the wide, grey-painted front door. At the creak of the gate, a volley of excited barking could be heard inside the property.

"That's Petra's dog, Scruff," said Gareth. "He's the cutest little fella, but he can get a bit over-excited."

The front door swung open as Gareth reached for the heavy brass knocker at its centre. Petra stood in the doorway, holding a small dog, which appeared determined to wriggle out of her arms.

"Welcome to Cragview," said Petra, smiling. "I'm so glad you could make it."

Morgan looked back at the garden and down the hill to the sprawl of Granton. "This place is amazing," she said. "You have a beautiful home." Stepping through the front door, she looked around at her father, following behind her, giving him an encouraging thumbs-up of approval.

CHAPTER THIRTY-FIVE

April 2016

The spring days were lengthening towards summer, drawing people out to sit or to stroll in the sunshine, instead of scurrying to take refuge from the harsh winter weather. Whilst everyone around her seemed to be rejoicing in the sensation of having more daytime to enjoy, Morgan felt she had never been so short of time.

"I don't have enough hours in my day," she complained to Josie, whilst helping her friend to serve lunch to the residents of Harley Grange.

"I'm not surprised," said Josie. "Apart from working here, you're doing all your studying, not to mention finding time for dishy Dom Cooper."

Morgan poked her friend in the ribs with a playful grimace on her face.

"Enough of that," she said. "At least I don't have to spend hours on public transport now that I have the car."

"That's true. I'm so jealous of your little car. Wish my dad would buy me a brand-new Fiat 500, but there's no chance of that."

Morgan had passed her driving test at the first attempt, to her own and Gareth's delight. Planning to save for her first old banger, she almost fainted when her dad turned up at Victoria Terrace, a week after her test, dangling the keys to a new car.

"Your mum and I always intended to buy you your first car when you passed your test. You've done that, with flying colours, so I know she'd approve."

There had been tears and hugs as Morgan expressed her gratitude, and both she and her dad spoke of how much they wished Mel were with them to share another milestone in Morgan's life. It had been an overwhelmingly emotional moment for them both.

"It came as a complete shock to me," Morgan told Josie. "I never imagined myself having a new car, but it's made such a difference to my life, I can't begin to tell you."

"Bet Dom likes having a designated driver to take him to the pub these days," Josie joked.

"Actually, he's been really weird about it – and about me learning to drive."

"How do you mean?" Josie asked.

"Well, when I told him I was learning to drive, all he said was – what's wrong with public transport? Then when I passed my test and got the car, he just said he thought it was a bit excessive. He really burst my bubble and I was pissed with him for quite a while. I think he realised what he'd done, and he was all apologetic afterwards, but I still don't get why he was like that."

"Maybe he's jealous because he doesn't drive?" Josie suggested.

"Possibly," Morgan replied, though she wasn't convinced. Dom had been nothing but supportive to her since they first met. Many a time she had contemplated giving up on her dream of university, and several times she had been on the point of abandoning her A level re-sit course, but Dom had encouraged her and made her feel she could do anything. That's why his attitude to her learning to drive didn't make sense. She wasn't going to worry about it, though. After all, she was still keeping secrets from him and telling half-truths about who she was. She could hardly challenge his behaviour when her own was far from perfect. Besides, they were making exciting plans for the future, and Morgan didn't want to do anything which might prejudice their next few months together.

At the end of her shift for the day, Morgan jumped into her car and headed for Cragview, as she did most evenings after work.

Ever since her terrifying ordeal with Todd, Morgan had felt uneasy staying on her own in Victoria Terrace. Each time she stepped through the front door, her mind flashed back to Todd's hand over her mouth, stifling her screams. She could almost sense the cold steel of the knife against her neck and the slice of the blade across her flesh.

At night, when she lay in bed, she heard cracks and creaks in the old house which she had never noticed before. She imagined an intruder creeping up the stairs, exploring each room before coming to her, alone and defenceless in her bed. Sleep lapped at the edge of her consciousness but refused to settle with her. Only when Dom was staying in the house with her, did Morgan feel safe.

"I'll make up a room for you here, at the cottage," Petra had said, when Morgan confided her fears over supper at Cragview, one evening. "I'll give you a key, and you can come and go as you please."

It was an offer she couldn't refuse, and it proved to be the answer to her fears. Once inside the solid stone walls of the cottage, she felt safe and secure, with Petra and her dad. More than that, she loved the drive to and from Cragview and the slow reveal of the changing seasons. On this glorious spring evening, as she drove away from the confines of Granton after work, the enormous sky billowed all around her. April would soon give way to May and the moors were now flushed with the fresh colours of pink and white heathers and lime green ferns. By the time she reached the cottage, all Morgan's cares and worries seemed to have evaporated, absorbed into the age-old peat of the endless moor.

Morgan found her father and Petra sitting at the end of the rear garden of Cragview, gazing out across the landscape. Petra was sipping a glass of white wine and her father a zero-alcohol beer. They turned at her approach.

"Hello love. Come and join us?" said Gareth.

"Don't mind if I do," said Morgan, pulling out a chair and gratefully accepting the glass of wine which Petra poured for her. "What a lovely evening."

"Isn't it though?" Petra responded. "We were just appreciating the warmth of the sun on our faces."

"Talking of sun," said Morgan, "I have some news."

Both Gareth and Petra turned to look at her. "Oh?" said her father.

"Dom and I are planning a holiday together – after our exams. We're hoping to get down to the south of Spain and I'm going to drive us there," Morgan announced.

Her father's expression wasn't quite what she had been hoping for. His expectant smile turned to a quizzical frown, which instantly made her hackles rise. Petra was looking at her thoughtfully.

"This is the boyfriend we haven't met yet," Gareth stated, in a tone of mild disapproval.

"No, because I haven't yet told him I'm Morgan Fairley, not Morgan Garrett," said Morgan, with unconcealed irritation. "He knows you as a friend of the family only, just like everyone else at Harley Grange, except for Josie and Bev. I don't want to tell all until I'm good and ready."

"And when do you feel that will be?" Petra asked.

"I'm not sure, but maybe on this holiday….if it goes well."

"I'm sorry love, I don't want to rain on your parade," said Gareth. "You deserve a boyfriend who loves you and treats you well. It's just, after Todd……"

"I know dad. I understand how you feel, but Dom is nothing like Todd. They're barely of the same species. I'm sure you'll like him when you meet, but I'm just not ready for all that means, yet."

"Ok, love. You can handle yourself, I know. I've seen that for myself. I have to stop being the overbearing father and let you live your life. When do you think you'll go?"

"We both finish our exams at the end of May, so as soon as possible after that."

"Well, I hope you have a wonderful holiday and a well-earned rest. You truly deserve it."

"I'll drink to that," said Morgan, raising her glass.

CHAPTER THIRTY-SIX

June 2016 - Europe

Morgan glanced across at Dom's sleeping form beside her. Legs outstretched, head thrown back on the cushioned head rest and with a gentle snore escaping from between his parted lips, he was the picture of rest and relaxation. If only she could say the same of herself.

After finishing their exams, Dom and Morgan had booked the first available ferry to take them from Dover to Calais. They set off from Granton one morning in early June, with the vague aim of heading for the south of Spain, but with little idea of when and where they would stop. They would be spontaneous, they agreed, stopping to camp when and where the fancy took them. Morgan would be the driver and Dom, her navigator and organiser of accommodation.

It had all sounded so exciting and the perfect antidote to the stress of exams and revision. Right now, though, the reality was not quite measuring up to the anticipation, Morgan reflected. After two long days of driving, she was tired and irritable, and wishing that Dom could take a turn at the wheel, so that she could nap and relax, just as he was.

Glancing at the satnav on her phone she saw she still had 75 kilometres to go, so about another hour of driving before they reached their destination for the night. She cracked open the window a couple of inches, relishing the warm breeze on her cheek. Reaching for her water bottle, she took a couple of sips, then shook some droplets onto her face to freshen herself up.

"Wake up, Dom!" she said gently, shaking him lightly.

"What?" he exclaimed, anxiously blinking and looking around him. "What's up?"

"Nothing's up," Morgan replied, "but I'm knackered. I need you to help me find the campsite and if the place is ok, I want a day off tomorrow."

"No problem," Dom said, hurriedly, sliding himself back into an upright position. "We can stay there for the rest of the holiday if you want. I'm not bothered about getting down to the south of Spain. It was always a bit ambitious anyway."

"I still want to make it into Spain," she replied, "but maybe just head straight for the nearest coast and leave it at that. If we stay around the north-east area, we could probably get a train into Barcelona one day."

"Sounds good to me," said Dom, leaning across to give her a kiss. "Now, let me have a look at this map and my satnav and I'll help you find our home for the night."

Opening the tent flap to inspect the day, Morgan's senses were assailed by the sight and smell of the sparkling waters of the Bay of Biscay.

They had pitched their tent in a farmer's field the night before. It was late when they arrived and Morgan was so tired, she didn't care where she was. She just wanted to curl up and go to sleep.

This morning, it was a different story. She had slept deeply and undisturbed until the bright morning sunlight beckoned her to wake up and enjoy the day. Yawning and stretching, Morgan registered the plaintive cry of seabirds and the rush of seawater splashing the shore.

The campsite was on a terraced slope, she noted, about five hundred yards from the beach. From her vantage point, Morgan watched, as the gentle waves lazily unfurled themselves into long fingers reaching and pointing up the beach. All her tension and irritation of the previous evening had melted away, now forgotten. Her mind was focused on capturing every detail of the spectacular scene before her. She would store it in her memory, to revisit on dark, damp days at home.

"Breakfast is served, mademoiselle."

Dom appeared before her carrying two takeout coffees and a bag of croissants and fresh fruit. She hadn't even heard him leave the tent. Her stomach rumbled at the sight and smell of the food and drink. It had been hours since she last ate anything substantial.

"That coffee smells amazing," Morgan said, grabbing a cup and taking a sip of the strong, hot liquid.

"We're in a small village here. Just the farm and a handful of houses. But they have a fabulous boulangerie serving fresh coffee and amazing pastries. Unbelievable!"

"Mm, this croissant is delicious. Best I've ever tasted," said Morgan, licking the crumbs of light, buttery pastry from her fingers.

Over breakfast, Morgan and Dom discussed their next stopover.

"I've had a look at the maps and done a bit of research on the internet and I think we should head for the Bay of Roses, in northeast Spain," said Dom. "There are beautiful beaches and coves there, and we might even hire a sailing boat for the day."

"Wait! Hire a sailing boat? I've never sailed in my life."

"It's ok. I know how to sail. One of the few good things my rubbish father did for me and my brother was to teach us to sail. When we were young, most of our holidays were spent in and around water, though mum hated it."

Morgan was surprised to hear Dom speak of his father, since he rarely ever mentioned him and changed the subject whenever his name came up. It was from Phyllis she'd learned details of Dom's parents' messy divorce, it being a favourite pastime of Harley Grange's liveliest resident to indulge in gossip.

Morgan hadn't asked too many questions, being sensitive to her own complex and difficult relationship with her father, which she had no wish to share with Phyllis. She wondered, though, if it was part of Dom's attraction that he had endured a fractured family life, just as she had.

"I never knew you could sail," said Morgan, with surprise. She hadn't regarded him as an outdoorsy type. "What other secrets are you hiding from me?"

"What do you mean?" Dom asked, abruptly, looking at her with a strange intensity that made her feel uncomfortable.

"Just joking, Dom," Morgan replied, giving Dom a playful punch on the arm. It appeared she had hit a raw nerve for some reason she couldn't fathom. Better not dig any deeper, she cautioned herself.

"Sorry," he said, seconds later, shaking himself like a dog shakes water from sodden fur. "I was a million miles away then."

"Well can you bring yourself a bit closer to home and help plan out a route to this Bay of Roses place?" Morgan said, keen to move the conversation away from whatever uncomfortable thoughts had been troubling her boyfriend.

"I'm on it," Dom said, flapping out the road map in front of the tent. Surreptitiously, Morgan studied his face, noting the sudden shift from light to darkness and back again, like black clouds passing over the sun, then drifting away on the wind.

Lurking at the fringes of her mind was the fear that Dom might already be tiring of her. They had been seeing each other for almost six months now, since Christmas. Perhaps that was enough for him, Morgan reflected. Insecurity caused a twist of anxiety in her chest as she scrutinised Dom tracing a route across the road atlas map with his finger. Maybe the mental drift she had just observed was him being irritated with her and contemplating when to dump her?

Stop with such negativity, Morgan cautioned herself, leaning over Dom's shoulder to look at the map he had spread out on the ground. Just because life has gone wrong in the past doesn't mean it'll always be that way, or so her father continually assured her.

Morgan listened as Dom reeled off a list of places he wanted to visit, which he thought she might like. Hearing him read aloud descriptions of the various locations they might visit, re-kindled her excitement. This holiday was going to be amazing, she told herself, and she was going to enjoy every minute of it.

CHAPTER THIRTY-SEVEN

Over breakfast, Dom and Morgan agreed to hit the road again, since Dom had devised an easier, shorter drive for Morgan that day. He quickly packed up the tent and stowed away their belongings in the car. Arguing about whose music choice was best, whilst streaming their favourite tracks, made the time fly. Before she knew it, Morgan was pulling into the entrance to their next destination, all her misgivings of the previous day, forgotten.

Dom had chosen a campsite with a marina and harbour complex on one side and a stretch of soft, golden sand on the other.

"This is paradise," Morgan said, her eyes shining in rapt delight. "Let's pitch the tent later and go and explore."

Dom readily agreed. They parked up to take a stroll, hand in hand, down to the harbour. The heat of the day was still intense, though a slight breeze, wafting in from the sea, created a perfect temperature. A sudden swell of joy almost took Morgan's breath away. She hadn't experienced such happiness for as long as she could remember.

"You've found us the perfect spot," she said, kissing Dom lightly on the cheek.

A fifteen-minute walk brought them down to the harbour, where they bought ice-creams and sat on the sun-warmed stone wall, to watch the activity of the marina.

Set within a huge concrete and stone circle, broken only by the harbour entrance, the marina was home to hundreds of boats. Morgan watched, transfixed, as elegant yachts moved serenely from their moorings towards the harbour gateway before having their sails unfurled to welcome the gentle wind blowing in from the Mediterranean.

At first, Morgan noted, there was an alarming bobbing and rocking motion, as the boats passed through the harbour entrance and caught the wind; then came the magical moment when the sails sucked in the full strength of the wind and the boats heeled over, their hulls lightly kissing the water. Those boats with an expert at the wheel skimmed over the waves, as light as pebbles thrown across the surface. Others, less skilfully operated, languished aimlessly, their sails flapping angrily, as the skipper battled to align correctly with the wind. Morgan imagined herself out there, wrestling with equipment she didn't understand and the natural elements over which she had no control. A shiver of nervousness rippled through her.

"Shall we ask about hiring a boat tomorrow?" Dom asked, as they sat dangling their legs over the edge of the harbour wall.

Morgan had imagined a lazy day on the beach - swimming, finding some good food and relaxing, after their long journey. She glanced at Dom, noting his fascination with the boating activity below them. It was obvious he was itching to join in.

"Ok, let's do it. But I have to warn you, I really do know absolutely nothing about boats, and I'll probably be more useless than you can possibly imagine."

Dom leaned over and kissed her full on the lips. "You won't be useless. You'll soon pick it up. I have every confidence in you," he said, leaning towards her and licking ice cream off her lips, before kissing her with a tenderness that set her heart pounding.

Walking back from the harbour, they decided to stop off at a bar, on the edge of the marina complex, for a drink and some food. It was already buzzing with people chatting and laughing about voyages they had made or were about to make. Dom's ears were twitching like antennae, as he listened in to the nautical conversations. He really was extremely excited, Morgan observed, just like a kid before Christmas.

The manager of the bar was an English guy, called Jake, with whom they quickly struck up conversation, as he took their order. When Dom enquired if Jake knew of any place they could hire a sailing boat for the day, he was stunned to receive the offer of Jake's own boat, free of charge.

"You'll be doing me a favour," Jake said. "I bought the boat a couple of seasons ago, but then took the job here. Since then, I've hardly been out on her. I'm afraid she's not looking her best because I haven't had time to go down and clean her up, so you'll

149

need to do a bit of work before you start. If you're ok with that, then meet me at the mooring tomorrow morning at 10. I'll give you the keys and talk you through everything. As far as I'm concerned, you can use her for as long as you're here."

Dom was beside himself. It was obvious to Morgan that he'd been passionate about sailing as a child. To have unlimited, free use of a boat, on the Mediterranean, for the duration of their stay, was beyond his wildest dreams.

"See, it's fate," said Dom, as Morgan watched him dance a jig on their way back from the bar. "We're meant to go sailing, you and I, and it's going to be brilliant," he said, grabbing her round the waist and lifting her off the ground.

"You're mad!" Morgan shouted as he swung her around, ignoring the quizzical expressions on the faces of passers-by.

Dom's excitement was infectious, temporarily overcoming Morgan's trepidation at being out on the wide, open sea. This was the start of their holiday proper, she told herself, after the hours of driving to get here. With Dom's arm draped across her shoulders, she turned to watch the sun sink steadily below the horizon, the pavement still radiating heat onto her bare skin. As the sea slapped gently against the harbour wall and the halyards of the sailing boats played their tinkling tunes, she experienced a sensation of happiness she hadn't felt for the longest time. Dom's enthusiasm was contagious, and now she too couldn't wait for her sailing debut to begin.

CHAPTER THIRTY-EIGHT

"Here she is!" Dom announced, having successfully negotiated his way through a maze of boats and pontoons to where Jake's boat was moored.

Gypsy Queen, they discovered, was a twenty-six-foot sailboat which, by Jake's own admission, had seen better days. The peeling paintwork, the veil of spiders' webs around every porthole and the overpowering smell of damp and diesel fuel all pointed to neglect and a lack of care. Jake assured them, though, that despite her shabby appearance, the boat was completely seaworthy and safe. Morgan glanced across at Dom, who was oozing excitement from every pore. No trace of concern on his face, she noted, deciding to take that as a positive sign.

"She just needs a bit of a clean and she'll be fine," Dom assured Morgan, after Jake had shown him over the boat. "It won't take long and there isn't much tide here, so we should still be able to go out in an hour or so."

Morgan located a bucket, brush and some cleaning materials. Washing portholes and sweeping up an army of dead spiders wasn't what she had imagined for the first proper day of her holiday, but there was no way she was making her maiden voyage in the company of so many insects. She set to cleaning, with vigour, whilst Dom fiddled with the ropes and sails. Bobbing gently on her mooring, Morgan could almost imagine the Gypsy Queen was as excited to be on her way as were her new sailing companions.

"I think that should do it," Dom announced, an hour later. "Let's grab some lunch and be on our way."

Jake had provided a picnic of olives, crusty bread and Manchego cheese, together with a selection of fresh fruit, which they fell upon like a couple of castaways finding food on a desert island. They were both starving hungry after their intensive bout of cleaning and tidying.

"Time to set sail," said Dom, when barely a crumb of food remained.

Soon they were motoring past the solid walls of the harbour mouth, leaving behind the shelter of the marina. Morgan's stomach flipped at the sight of the wide-open sea on which they were about to embark. Between the fathomless waters below her and the infinite blue space above, she suddenly realised what an insignificant speck of humanity she was within the vastness of the universe. It was a deeply humbling thought.

"Can you just hold her steady, whilst I get the sail up?" Dom asked.

"What me?" Morgan responded, panicking as she pictured the boat capsizing when she took the helm.

"It'll be fine. I won't take a minute and then we'll be sailing. I'll watch you and shout instructions."

Timidly at first, then with increasing confidence, she succeeded in maintaining the boat in a straight line whilst Dom hauled on the sail ropes. Morgan watched as the thick, white canvas sheet crawled up the mast until it was fully extended and secured.

"Perfect!" said Dom, planting a light kiss on her forehead. "We need to keep the boat just off the wind so the sail will catch it and then we should be able to cut the engine."

Morgan looked on in amazement as, with a whooshing sound, the sail suddenly billowed outwards, holding the wind in a canvas cradle as the boat leaned perilously to one side. She gripped a guard rail, believing the boat was about to deposit its two passengers into the sea.

"Don't worry, Mo. It's supposed to do that," Dom reassured her. "I'm going to cut the engine and away we go."

Morgan anticipated the boat would come to a dead halt, without the motor driving it forward, but without mechanical assistance, the Gypsy Queen continued to glide steadily through the waves at surprising speed. Having lost the background din of the chugging and spluttering of the engine, she immediately appreciated the quality of the peace and quiet that descended upon the little boat. Only the plaintive call of sea birds and the soporific sound of boat slicing through waves disturbed the silence.

"This is wonderful," said Morgan, stripping off to her bikini top and skimpy shorts.

"Whoa! Have a care for the skipper," Dom joked, as his eyes feasted on Morgan's slender figure and smooth, pale skin. "I need to concentrate."

Morgan gave him a playful punch as she took up position on the bow, whilst massaging sunscreen into her gently warming skin.

I will never forget these moments, Morgan thought to herself, as she gazed at the contrasting blues of the sky and the water, whilst trailing her fingers through the brilliant white curl of the waves. Her nose twitched with the exhilarating freshness of the breeze and the churning water.

She watched as Dom expertly trimmed the sails to track the best course across the bay, one hand lightly resting on the wheel.

"You can have a go at sailing now, if you like," Dom said. "Just keep the nose slightly off the wind. You won't need to make much adjustment."

Nervously Morgan took the wheel, feeling it move through her hands. She yanked it in the opposite direction, to bring it back on course, or so she thought, but the little boat suddenly swung out to starboard, the sails flapping wildly.

"What have I done wrong?" she asked, panicking.

Dom laughed. "Don't worry," he said. "You've oversteered a bit. You hardly need to move the wheel at all. Look, I'll show you."

Dom stood behind her, enveloping her with his arms and placing his hands over hers.

"Just take it gently. Feel the strength of the breeze and the movement of the boat beneath your feet," he said. "And just maintain her on the compass reading I gave you. That's all there is to it."

Morgan tried to do as she was told, despite being distracted by the proximity of Dom's body, pressed against hers.

For the first time in her life, Morgan felt truly alive. It was extraordinary to be relying only on the wind, the sails and a compass to propel the small boat towards its destination. Although they were not far out to sea, the land they had left behind looked colourless and unremarkable in comparison to the blue vastness of the sky and water.

Dom had moved away to sit beside her. Morgan looked at him and smiled, serenely. She could not find the words to aptly describe how she felt in this moment, so remained silent. As if he were in tune with her thoughts, Dom returned her smile, wordlessly. The space between them was heavy with unspoken declarations that would follow later, she felt sure.

"Would you like to do what Jake's done?" Morgan asked. She and Dom were sunbathing on the forward deck of the Gypsy Queen, after an invigorating swim off the boat.

They had sailed for a little over two hours until they discovered a small cove, within striking distance of the beach, where they dropped anchor. Half a dozen other yachts had done the same, their occupants lazily distributed between the sea, the beach and the decks of their boats. Not quite a remote paradise, Morgan reflected, but as close as she imagined she would ever get.

"How do you mean?" Dom asked, rolling onto his side to face her.

"Just upping and offing and going where you want, on a whim?"

Jake had revealed a little of his life story whilst he'd showed them over the boat, that morning. He'd had a lucrative job in IT, working for an investment firm in London, he told them. Despite the financial rewards, though, he grew increasingly bored and frustrated with his life and was constantly on the lookout for something more exciting. When his girlfriend dumped him, he decided it was time for a change, so he sold his expensive apartment in Docklands, bought a campervan and surfboard and headed for Europe.

"I spent a season bumming around on the surf in Portugal. There are people there chasing waves until they're almost too old to stand up anymore," Jake had told them. "There was one guy I met who was nearly seventy, still following his passion. He'd only ever worked for long enough to finance his lifestyle, doing seasonal jobs and anything that paid. It got me thinking I could do the same."

"So you just walked away from your life?" Dom asked, barely disguising the envy in his voice.

154

"Pretty much. I go home about once a year and family and friends come to visit. I still have money left over from selling the flat, so I work just enough to fund the basics and the rest of the time I please myself. I came here to sail, then got offered Gypsy Queen for a knock down price, so I bought her. I took a job in the bar as a regular waiter, to earn some pocket money, then got promoted to manager after the last one left. The job's taken up more time than I intended, but it's been fun. I'll stay for as long as it suits, then move on," Jake shrugged. "I'll be heading for the slopes when this place closes for the winter, then I'll be back for Gypsy Queen next year. So you see, she needs some exercise, poor girl."

Dom and Morgan had listened open-mouthed, imagining what it might be like to live for the moment, like Jake, instead of focussing all their energy on pursuing ambitions and careers.

Dom considered Morgan's question for a moment, then turned his gaze to the turquoise sea, sighing heavily. "If you're asking me whether I'd like to walk away from exams, years of training, hard work and responsibility so that I can indulge my passions and follow my dreams? No, of course not," he said, in a heavily ironic tone. He looked at her and rolled his eyes. "Of course I bloody would. I envy Jake like hell, the lucky bastard."

"Don't you think it's a bit selfish?" Morgan persisted.

"Why so? If you don't have anyone depending on you – even if you do - shouldn't you be able to be a bit irresponsible for a while, when you're young?"

Morgan detected a profound longing in Dom's tone. She suspected she had hit upon a sensitive subject.

"Is this about Eliza? Do you feel responsible for her?"

"A bit," he replied. "After dad left, she fell apart. It was scary - horrible to watch. Kids expect their parents to be strong, to be there for them. It felt like there was suddenly no one there for me. My older brother, Will, was off at uni, at the time, so he was out of it all and didn't see what was really happening. I just wanted everything to be back to normal again, so I could have the life I had before, but it soon became obvious that wasn't going to happen."

"So you stepped up to your dad's role – to fill the gap?"

"Something like that." Dom sighed heavily, his whole demeanour suddenly changing. There was a terrible sadness about him, as if remembering the past caused him great pain.

Morgan turned over onto her side, to face Dom. This was the most he had revealed about himself and his life. It meant a lot to her that he felt comfortable to be so open, and it encouraged her to be more honest herself, no matter how difficult that might prove to be. Delicately, she planted kisses all over Dom's face, light as the brush of a butterfly's wings, finishing with a generous kiss on the lips.

"I think you're amazing," Morgan said, wriggling her body into his.

"Do you?" Dom asked her, suddenly pulling away. "Do you really?"

"Of course, I do," she said, giving him a reassuring kiss. For a few moments Dom looked at her, with intensity, as if he was searching for verification in her face. Did he doubt her sincerity, she wondered?

Then, just as quickly as it came, his serious expression lifted, and his features relaxed. He leaned across and kissed her full on the lips. Taking her hand, he led her down to the cabin below. She allowed him to steer her onto the bunk in the bow of the boat, falling backwards onto the bare mattress.

Her skin tingled from head to toe, as he unfastened her skimpy bikini top and lightly cupped one breast in his hand. Her senses were overpowered by the smell of sunscreen, the golden glow of their lightly tanned bodies and the sensation of bare skin on skin. She noticed the sound of the sea gently splashing against the hull, the call of sea birds overhead and the gentle tilting of the boat from side to side as it was rocked by the waves. She was helpless to resist Dom as he undid the ties on her bikini bottoms and swiftly entered her. Arching her back, she cried out with pleasure as he climaxed inside her.

No sooner had they caught their breath than they were reaching hungrily for each other again, consumed by mutual desire. Only when they were exhausted by their passion, did they fall apart, gasping for breath and struggling to return to the moment. Dom took Morgan's hand in his and lightly squeezed it. "I love you, Morgan," he whispered.

For a few seconds, Morgan lay still, allowing his words to reverberate around her head, like a peel of bells ringing out joyful news. She could hardly breathe, as if her heart had swollen and squashed the breath from her lungs.

"And I love you, my darling Dom" she said, after the briefest pause. The words felt strange on her lips, though she had never been more certain of anything in her life.

On the return voyage, Gypsy Queen was like a wild, unbroken horse, giddy with freedom after being restrained.

A brisk, warm breeze had blown up during the afternoon. It filled the sails and sent the boat skittering across the water. Sitting on the deck, with her legs swinging over the side, Morgan relished the wind's cooling effect on her hot, suntanned skin.

As the marina honed into view and Gypsy Queen nosed back towards the harbour, Morgan marvelled that, less than a week ago, she had been living an uneventful life in a northern English town. Her days had rotated through a cycle of work, study and spending time with her family, whilst eagerly anticipating the next time she was to see Dom. An ordinary life, really.

Now, with the wind fanning her hair and the deep blue sea beneath her, she was an adventurer, with a future that looked exciting and full of possibility. She would have that gap year of travel and exploration, as she had planned, except it would be with Dom by her side instead of Brady Forrester. Just as Jake had, the two of them would go where the fancy took them, until their money ran out.

Morgan went to stand behind Dom, at the helm, wrapping her arms about his waist. Neither of them spoke as they gazed ahead, each lost in their own thoughts.

CHAPTER THIRTY-NINE

June 2016

Wiping droplets of sweat from his forehead, as they trickled in salty rivulets down his face, Gareth dismounted the running machine which he had been pounding for the past thirty minutes. Having exercised his way around the gym, he paused to catch his breath and check his vital signs on the digital watch he was wearing – a birthday present from Petra.

Although his body felt tired and his limbs were aching, his mind was running as fast as ever, continuously spinning out troubling and unwelcome thoughts.

It had been a month now since he started his new job, he reflected, and it was proving more challenging than he had anticipated. The role involved working with persistent young offenders to try and guide them away from repeat offending. It was work he had been passionate about, when he was in the force, so he had been delighted and flattered when he was head-hunted by Marlon Franklin, a former offender himself.

Marlon was Chief Executive of a charity called the Young Offenders Partnership. He and Gareth had crossed paths on numerous occasions, over the years, sharing a platform together at several high-level conferences about youth crime. Their views coincided on the importance of rehabilitative work at early-stage offending, so when Marlon called to offer him a consultative position, Gareth didn't take long to accept. He had been struggling to adapt to life outside the force and to decide what he wanted to do next.

"Are you sure it's going to be the right fit for you?" Petra had asked him, when he came off the initial contact call, flushed with surprise and gratification that someone out there thought he still had something to offer. "I mean, you've spent most of your working life dealing with crime and punishment and all that heavy stuff. Wouldn't you like to do something completely different?" she had asked, slight worry lines wrinkling her brow.

"Such as?" Gareth had demanded. "I don't know anything else – can't do anything else. You can't teach an old dog new tricks, love." Petra had sighed and disappeared into her studio.

He had known what she was thinking because he'd had the same thoughts. She was worried that going back into his old world, albeit in a completely different role, would lead him back to his bad old habits. He was worried too but having recovered from his Todd-inflicted knife wound, he had found himself with time weighing heavily in his hands, which allowed his mind to meander through a forest of dark and negative thoughts.

"It was alright immediately after I left the force," he had told Patricia, at an emergency session he requested, when he realised he had two feet at the top of a slippery slope to disaster. "In fact, I was almost relieved to go. It meant I didn't have to pretend, anymore, that I was doing the job, when it was clear to everyone around me that I wasn't. Then I met Petra, which was the best thing that's happened to me since Mel died – that and getting my daughter back. For a while, it felt like everything was going my way."

"What changed?" Patricia enquired.

Gareth hadn't been able to come up with an answer to Patricia's question, except to say that despite all this new-found happiness, the old demons were threatening him again, like a swarm of pestilential insects, buzzing loudly around his head the instant he awoke and when he tried to sleep at night.

"You're a washed-up nothing, is all I could hear inside my head," he had told Patricia. "No-one wants to hear from you anymore. Why would they? You have nothing to offer, and no-one cares what you think. You're finished. You're over." He'd knocked the knuckles of his right hand forcefully against his right temple.

"Have you had a drink?" Patricia had asked, gently.

He sucked in air, giving himself time to answer the question.

"Yes," he had replied, looking down at his hands. "Petra was away on a course for a couple of days, and I didn't want to bother Morgan with my stupid issues, so I slipped into the pub and got hammered. Same old story – I'll just have a couple, I told myself, but once I started, I couldn't stop. The landlord had to take my keys off me and get me a taxi home."

He had hung his head, unable to look Patricia in the eye, as he listened to her gentle admonition that he should think of calling her or his sponsor at the addiction group whenever he had these negative thoughts. Gareth nodded, they had spoken for a while longer, but he had left with a clutch of doubt in his chest. Having lost confidence in himself again, the road ahead had loomed up before him, as rocky and bumpy as ever.

Then Marlon had called, and after two challenging interviews, in which he and Marlon had bounced around their ideas for change, Marlon offered him the job. He had tried not to sound too eager, but when he came off the phone, he had jumped around Cragview like an excited toddler - ignoring Petra's more muted reaction - so pumped up had he been with this unexpected boost to his self-confidence. It mattered more than he could explain that someone valued his experience and believed he had a contribution to make in such a critical area of society.

After only a few weeks, however, he began to realise that his mind was firmly set towards catching criminals and bringing them to justice and accountability. His new job required him to work towards rehabilitating and supporting convicted offenders and he was finding it difficult to manage the change of direction.

Then there was the whole Morgan thing.

"Gareth Fairley!" a voice behind him called out, as Gareth made his way to the gym changing rooms. He flipped out of his train of thought and turned to find himself looking at a familiar face, but one he couldn't immediately place.

"Si Thompson," the man said. "We were at Granton HQ together."

"Silo!" Gareth responded, recognising the features of his former colleague, and remembering his nickname from so long ago. "It must be ten years since I last saw you, when you left the force. How are you doing?"

"Well, the hair's falling out and I've gained a bit of weight since then, but I'm doing alright I think, though the Doc says I've got to get rid of this." With a rueful grimace, the other man clutched a roll of fat, like a life ring, sitting around his belly.

Gareth recalled that Si "Silo" Thompson earned his nickname because of his daily consumption of food. Pies, pasties, bacon rolls, doughnuts and packets of crisps – all disappeared in a matter of minutes, seemingly without any effect on his weight or health. Everyone joked that his gourmand lifestyle would catch up with him one day. Looking at him, Gareth noted, that day had obviously arrived.

"I heard you've left as well," said Si, wiping his neck with a small exercise towel, sweat appearing to ooze from his every pore.

Bad news travels fast, Gareth reflected, recalling that Si had been a bit of a gossip. "That's right," he said. "I retired at the end of last year." It wasn't strictly true, of course, and Si Thompson probably knew the full story from his various contacts still working at Granton HQ, but he wasn't in the mood for confidences.

"You got time for a semi-skimmed, sugar-free decaff coffee, mate?" Si asked, with a grin. "I need a shower something rotten, as you've probably clocked. See you in the café in fifteen?"

Gareth wasn't in the mood but didn't want to appear churlish towards his former colleague. He'd grab a quick drink with him, then be on his way.

"Ok," he said. "A swift one. I've got a meeting this afternoon."

"Magic. See you in a bit."

"So what are you up to these days?" Si asked, toying with a bowl of fresh fruit and natural yoghurt. "A gentleman of leisure, is it?"

"Not quite. I've taken up a position with YOP – Young Offenders' Partnership. Been there about a month, now."

"Oh yeah! I've heard of them. Marlon Franklin's in charge, isn't he? I remember him – a proper hard nut. I always wonder about guys like that. Can a leopard really change its spots?" Si Thompson shrugged, as if by way of answering his own question. Gareth decided not to engage, as he didn't want to get drawn into an argument.

"Sounds interesting, though," Si continued. "Poacher turned gamekeeper now for you, eh? What is it you're doing there?"

Briefly Gareth outlined his role.

"How about you?" Gareth asked, when he had finished describing his new employment. "What are you up to these days?"

"Oh, I've tried my hand at quite a few things since I gave up being a copper. Been a driving instructor for the past five years or so. I can't say I've achieved the height of my ambition with it, but I'm more or less my own boss and the hours suit. Touch wood, no-one's killed me yet."

It was the kind of remark Gareth was used to hearing in his former workplace, but it landed badly with him, and he couldn't hide it. He bristled at Si's words and looked down at his coffee cup.

"Shit, mate. That was bad. My mouth is as big as my belly, as my wife's always telling me. I heard about Mel and the accident. I'm so sorry, mate. She was a lovely lady and the kids loved her when she taught them."

"They threw away the mould, Si. What can I say? It's been tough without her."

"You never caught the person that did it, did you? That must really hurt."

There it was – the thump in the solar plexus. The failing he would never be able to forget. Si Thompson couldn't ever imagine, thought Gareth, just how much pain and grief he had suffered, and still suffered, over the greatest failure in his career. God knows, he didn't need Si, or anyone else, to highlight the irony of the situation and his own utter uselessness.

"I haven't given up," Gareth responded defiantly. "It's not over for me. One of these days, you know how it is, that person, whoever they are, will make a mistake, let something slip or some snippet of information will turn up – a lead of some kind - and I'll be on it."

He didn't reveal to his former colleague - in fact he hadn't yet told anyone - how his mind had been working overtime since he took this new job. He hadn't been expecting it, was surprised how it had crept up on him, but with every kid he spoke to, he was asking himself the same question. Could it have been this one?

Instead of scrutinising the responses to his carefully prepared, professional queries to enable him to draw out information and evidence for his reports to Marlon, he was searching for clues as to Mel's killer. It was messing with his head and affecting his ability to do the job properly. No amount of strenuous exercise and distraction techniques had helped. Perhaps Petra had been right after all; perhaps he should have looked for something completely different to fill the rest of his working life.

"How's your daughter doing?" Si enquired, pushing his half-eaten bowl of fruit and yoghurt aside. "She must be grown up now?"

"She'll be twenty this year," Gareth replied, reflecting on the passage of time that had brought him a young woman as his daughter, no longer a child. "She had a really rough time of it, losing her mum at such a vulnerable age. She went off the rails a bit, I think it's fair to say, but then so did I. She's good now – working at Harley Grange, the old people's home, whilst she does her re-sits. Hopefully, she'll be off to university in September."

"Amazing!" Si responded. "You must be so proud of her."

"I am that – proud and worried, of course. She's driving round Europe on holiday, at the moment, with her new boyfriend. I haven't met him yet, so I don't know what she's got herself into. The last one was a thoroughly bad lot, so I hope her taste's improved." He didn't go into detail about Todd Hopkins, hoping that he and Morgan had successfully contained that particular story.

"I've got a photo of her here," said Gareth, pulling out his phone. "Her and the new chap on a beach somewhere in Spain. He looks alright, but as you and I know only too well, you can never tell."

Si took the phone from him and peered at the screen, a puzzled expression on his face. He used his thumb and forefinger to enlarge the image.

"What's his name – the boyfriend?" Si asked.

"Dominic. Dominic Cooper," Gareth replied.

"I know him," Si said. "I taught him to drive a couple of years ago." He handed the phone back to Gareth.

"No, mate. That can't be right. This Dominic doesn't drive, so Morgan's having to do it all herself. It's worrying me sick, I don't mind telling you. She's only just passed her test."

"I swear it's the same lad," said Si, taking the phone again to stare at the photograph. "The reason I remember him so well is because he passed first time after only six lessons. Not many do that, I can tell you."

"But if it's the same guy, why would he lie, and let his girlfriend drive for hours every day without helping out?" Gareth wondered aloud.

"No idea, mate," said Si.

A cold chill was beginning to seep into Gareth's veins, travelling slowly, but steadily towards his heart. He drained his cup and grabbed his coat and sports bag. He needed to contact Morgan, without delay.

"Sorry Si. I have to dash. You couldn't do me a favour could you?" Si looked at him quizzically.

"You couldn't just check your records to see where the lad you taught lived? I know I shouldn't ask but….."

"No worries, I understand. Anyway, I don't need to check. I can't remember the number, but I picked him up at Osterley Gardens. It's near the Sports stadium. I remember because his mum used to answer the door, most times. She was such a meek and mild little thing, but the boy was ….." he paused, clearly searching for the right word.

"Was what?"

"Angry," said Si. "He was never rude or anything like that, but he just had this air of simmering rage. Typical teenager I suppose. I don't know whether he and his mum argued a lot, though I didn't think that at the time. She looked like she wouldn't say boo to a goose."

"Right," said Gareth, the hair rising on his neck and the smell of fear in his nostrils. "I've got to go. Thanks for that, Si. I appreciate it." Gareth held out his hand and the other man grasped it tightly.

"Good luck mate," said Si. He went to give Gareth a friendly pat on the arm, but the other man was already halfway to the exit.

CHAPTER FORTY

"That was possibly the most exhilarating ride of my life," Morgan said, after leaping down from Gypsy Queen to take mooring ropes, as Dom had instructed her.

"Well, I think, Miss Garrett, that we have earned ourselves a long, cold beer at Jake's Place," said Dom, as he made final adjustments to the fenders and checked the boat was firmly secured for the night.

Morgan winced slightly at hearing her assumed name. During the return journey, as she sat on the deck, enjoying the sensation of having her legs showered by cooling sea spray and staring at the endless blue sea and sky, she had resolved to tell Dom everything about herself.

For this relationship to progress, she recognised, she must be completely honest with him, as he had been with her, that afternoon. So far, he didn't really know the person he was going out with, only the version of herself she chose to present to him. It was time to talk about the accident and her mother's death and how that had catapulted her out of the life she once led. She would be honest about dropping out of school and getting into drugs, which led to her eventually becoming involved in the disastrous relationship with Todd and the knife incident in Victoria Terrace.

"The perfect end to a perfect day," Morgan said, planting a light kiss on his lips. She hoped and prayed he would understand and forgive her for lying to him the entire time he had known her.

They strolled, hand in hand, to Jake's bar. Morgan's skin tingled from the embrace of sun, wind and salt water. The blush of a light tan was beginning to appear all over her body.

The bar was packed with a sailing crowd, when they arrived, but Jake managed to free a table for them.

"How did it go today?" he asked, after depositing two glasses of chilled St Miguel in front of them. Dom took a long, steady drink before replying.

"Fantastic, mate," he said, wiping beer froth from his upper lip. "She's a little beauty. Handles perfectly. We can't thank you enough for letting us go out on her."

"No worries," Jake responded. "Like I told you, she needs the exercise and she's not going to get it from me this summer. Use her all you can."

Dom and Morgan each raised their glass in a show of gratitude, as Jake weaved his way back to the bar.

"So, you enjoyed your debut sailing trip?" Dom asked, reaching across the table to take Morgan's hand. "I think you have all the makings of a sailor, if I may say so."

Morgan laughed. "Well, I don't know about that. I didn't really do anything, but I did enjoy it," she said. "I'd love to go out again."

"Does that mean you're happy to stay here or do you still want to go to Barcelona? I know it was on your wish list."

"I'm definitely up for staying here," said Morgan. "This is such an incredible adventure for me, learning about sailing and getting around by boat. We're not going to get another chance like this any time soon. We can go to Barcelona another year."

Dom grinned. "I was so hoping you would say that. Let's buy some charts from the marina chandlery tomorrow and decide where else we can go. I'm sure there are quite a few places we can manage to sail to from here."

"Great idea. In the meantime, let's get something to eat. I'm absolutely starving." Morgan opened up the menu which Jake had set down on their table and began to study it carefully.

Draining his glass, Dom gave a sigh of satisfaction. "I'll order us another couple of drinks on my way to the loo, whilst you decide what you want to eat. Be back in two ticks."

"Aye, aye, skipper." Morgan replied, as Dom set off to wrestle through the throng of people gathered around the bar.

She studied the menu carefully, finally deciding on a selection of tapas to share with Dom. As she looked up, she noticed that he had left his card wallet on the table. She glanced up but couldn't see him anywhere amongst the layers of people surrounding the bar. Hopefully, he could put the drinks on a tab with the food, she thought.

Without thinking, she reached across and picked up the small leather wallet. She opened it and flicked through the individual cards.

Why did she do that, she asked herself, much later? What was it that compelled her to look inside Dom's wallet? Was it some sense of foreboding that had clung to her like a malign mist ever since she met him? Despite her profound happiness at being with Dom, she had been secretly expecting some disaster to befall her, because it always did.

Furtively looking up to check that Dom wasn't on his way back, Morgan studied the cards, one by one. She knew it was wrong, a bit deranged even, but she couldn't stop herself.

On one side of the wallet, there were the usual payment cards, each one tucked into a small pocket. On the other side, a pass key – probably to Dom's student accommodation – and some other essentials of daily life. Amongst these, her eyes were drawn to the pink and blue tip of a card she thought she recognised as a driving licence. That couldn't be right, she said to herself, as she tentatively pulled the palm-sized piece of plastic from its pocket inside the wallet, glancing up again to see that Dom was talking to Jake, at the bar. She gasped with astonishment to find herself looking at a photograph of her boyfriend – his face devoid of expression as required by officialdom - staring back at her on the front of a UK driving licence.

Frowning, she checked the name and address on the card, thinking perhaps it belonged to Dom's brother and they looked alike. *Cooper, Dominic James,* it read. The address given: *12 Osterley Gardens.* That, as she well knew, was Dom's home address.

Glancing at the date of issue, she saw that the licence was already two years old, having been issued in April 2014. He had passed his test before she had. So, why, then, had he repeatedly told her that he didn't drive? Why had he let her reach the point where she was exhausted and almost falling asleep at the wheel, without offering to help? Her head was swirling with possible explanations, none of which made any sense.

"What are you doing?" She jumped as Dom's hand slammed down on the table, covering the wallet with his hand. The gold signet ring on his little finger glinted dangerously at her, illuminated by the lights strung around the terrace.

"You left your wallet on the table," Morgan said, hearing the guilt in her voice. "I thought you might need it to pay for the drinks."

"But why are you looking through it?" Dom persisted, grabbing the small case and stuffing it in his shorts pocket. His face was stern, and he was talking to her as her father might to a suspected criminal whom he was interrogating.

"Hey, I'm not the one who needs to explain anything here," Morgan's voice raised a few decibels. "Why don't you tell me what the fuck you're doing with a driving licence when you told me you couldn't drive?" she demanded. His mouth dropped open, as if there were words he was about to speak, but his lips wouldn't shape around them.

"Can we carry on this conversation away from here?" Dom said, looking pained. "I'll explain everything, I promise."

She jumped up from the table, knocking over her chair, which fell backwards onto the stone floor. Leaving Dom to take care of the bill, she ran away from the restaurant as if she were trying to escape a fire raging out of control. Those sitting immediately around her fell silent as they looked on at the drama playing out in front of them, a hint of schadenfreude rippling through their midst.

Without thinking where she was going, she ran towards the harbour, stopping eventually to slump down onto the still-warm, solid concrete wall which encircled it. Panting for breath, she lifted her face to the evening breeze, allowing the fading rays of the sun to dry the tears that had been streaming down her cheeks as she stormed away from the bar. The sight and sound of the sea calmed her slightly.

Although darkness was creeping over the horizon, boats were still returning to the marina, after a day's sailing. Morgan could hear their occupants laughing and joking as they looked forward to supper and a chilled beer. Less than two hours ago, that had been her, as she eagerly anticipated a relaxed supper with Dom, discussing the highlights of the day. Now her evening and, probably, her relationship, lay in tatters.

After a couple of minutes, Dom caught her up and came to sit beside her. She couldn't look at him. It was if her whole body was held in a brace to prevent it from breaking and falling apart. She heard him breathe a heavy sigh into the night air.

"I've been wanting to tell you for so long," Dom said.

"Tell me what, exactly?"

Although she had no idea what he was going to say next, she knew it wasn't going to be good. It seemed she wasn't the only one being untruthful.

"I don't really know where to start," Dom said, biting his lip and staring into the far distance as if he was unable to look at her.

Morgan allowed herself to steal a glance at Dom. His face was a picture of misery and defeat, as if he had lost an internal battle that had been raging within him for a long time.

"Why did you tell me you couldn't drive?" she repeated, angrily.

"I never actually said I couldn't drive. I only said I *didn't* drive."

"Oh, for fuck's sake!" Morgan responded. "You let me believe you couldn't. What's the difference? Either way, you let me drive the whole way, even though you knew I was finding it really tiring. What was that about?"

"Please, Morgan, let me try and explain." Dom reached for her hand, but she pulled it away from him. He sighed and turned to stare into the distance, as he spoke.

"Ok, so I told you about my dad – how he took me and my brother sailing and other adventure stuff. When I was a kid, he was my absolute hero. I adored him. He always had loads of time for me and Will – playing with us, teaching us different sports, encouraging us in whatever we did. He was.....just great. I admired him and I wanted to be him."

"What's that got to do with you lying about being able to drive?" Morgan demanded, with irritation.

It was obvious Dom was struggling to find the words to explain himself as his mind replayed long-gone happy days from his childhood. From her own experience, Morgan knew exactly how painful that could be.

"When he left us, I just couldn't believe it. My dad would never do that, I told myself, because he cared about us too much

– me and my brother. I blamed my mum at first, thinking she had driven him away. I was wrong, of course. He was an egotistical bastard, my father, I know that now. He left mum for a younger woman who made him feel like some young stud again. It was all such a sickening cliché of the middle-aged man having his selfish mid-life crisis. The realisation shattered my world. Everything I knew and believed to be true, turned out to be false."

Morgan took a sharp intake of breath. These could be her words, she reflected. It was uncanny. Dom was describing exactly how she had felt, watching her dad retreat into himself, whilst seemingly forgetting her existence.

"He's got a whole new family now," said Dom, with bitterness, "and I haven't seen him since the day he left. He tried to make contact once or twice, but I didn't want to know. I think my brother's seen him a few times, but I've never asked him about it. Will was away at uni when it all blew up, so he didn't see the worst of it, didn't have to suddenly turn into the big man and look after mum."

She waited, without speaking, for Dom to recover himself. She could tell that the scars left by his family's breakup were still livid and unhealed.

"Mum fell apart when he left – she had a nervous breakdown, I suppose. She still isn't coping and pathetically clings to the hope he'll come back one day, even though they're divorced now. She'd have him back tomorrow, I think, if he turned up on the doorstep and smiled at her. I hate it." Dom almost spat the words.

"As for me," he continued. "I just went off the rails. Turned out the world was nothing like I thought it was going to be, so why should I be the good, studious kid I'd always been?" He turned to look at her, as if by way of an appeal, but she continued to stare straight ahead. It was almost as if he was telling her story, but it still didn't explain why he had lied to her all this time.

"I had a mate, Mikey, whose dad owned a garage near where we lived. He worked for his dad, and planned to take over the business, one day." Dom paused, chewing his lip and tapping his fingers on the wall, a study in agitation.

"Contrary to what I told you, or, rather, led you to believe, I did learn to drive. In fact, I had my first lesson the day after my

170

seventeenth birthday. I needed to pass my test so I could get myself around, and mum as well, because she hated driving. It made her nervous. I had six lessons and passed first time."

As she listened, Morgan had the sense that there was a tsunami of information rolling her way from which she couldn't escape. It was tracking relentlessly towards her with every second that passed.

"One day, I was hanging out at the garage, with Mikey. A new BMW had just come in for service – a beautiful car, sleek and gleaming."

The tsunami wall was towering above her now, the rush of its passage almost deafening her. She was about to be consumed by it, buffeted and tossed around like a broken tree trunk.

"You can give it a whirl, if you want, Mikey said. My dad's on holiday in Australia for a couple of months, so he won't know anything about it. It's a great car, he said. It almost drives itself."

She could have stopped him there, held up her hand like Moses holding back the Red Sea. But she didn't. She had to hear him out, even though she knew, now, what he was going to say next.

"So I took it out, without thinking. I remember that I kind of relished the illegality of it, me who never broke a rule in his life. Prefect, model student and all that shit. I got in that car, and I drove it out of Granton and along the country roads towards Flintby, feeling like a pop star, or a celebrity or something. It sounds so totally pathetic when I talk about it now."

He took a deep breath, as if he needed to prepare himself for what he was going to say next.

"Mikey was right. The car drove like a dream, positively purred along. The sound system was spectacular. The whole experience was a blast."

"Until you killed my mother," Morgan interrupted, her tone flat, expressionless.

Dom stared at her, his mouth half open, as if she had, literally, snatched the words he was about to say.

"What did you say?" he asked, at last, his eyes wide and unbelieving.

"Funnily enough," Morgan said, her tone heavy with irony as she fought back tears, "I decided, when we were out on the boat,

171

today, that I was going to tell you all about stuff I haven't mentioned, because it was just too big a deal. I felt I'd reached the point where I could trust you with my truth. I thought we were going somewhere, you and I, so I wanted you to know everything about me – the accident, me losing the plot and getting into drugs and dad becoming an alcoholic. It's quite a story," she said, adopting a mock lightness in her voice.

Diverting her gaze from the evening activity of the marina and the people sitting out on deck in the cool of the evening, toasting a successful day at sea, she turned to look directly at Dom.

"My real name is Morgan Fairley," she said, watching the recognition slowly dawn behind his eyes. "Garrett was my mum's maiden name. I started using it after the accident, partly to help me hide from the world and partly to disassociate myself from my dad. He and I had a major bust-up, after mum died. You know how it is," she said, her eyes flashing anger at him.

"You…it was your mum….your dad is the police officer? Jesus Christ! This is unreal. Morgan, god, I'm so sorry. I don't have the words for this," Dom said, his voice tailing off, his face slack with shock and disbelief.

"Well try, Dominic. I've read all the official stuff and the crap on social media, but I'd like to hear it from the horse's mouth, from the person who broke nearly every bone in my mum's body, then drove off into the night, leaving her slowly dying, but then never coming forward to admit what he had done."

Her anger was bubbling like volcanic lava, now, threatening to explode and spew out its molten mass over all those in its path.

"Can you tell me why you did that, Dom, because God knows, me and my dad have been wondering about that one for a long time? Can you tell me why you ignored all the appeals for information, including from my dad personally, putting his grief on show in a desperate attempt to find out what happened? Why have you allowed me and my family to suffer so much, so fucking much, I can't even begin to tell you…"

Tears burned her cheeks, and her head was pounding from the shock of her discovery and the building rage that threatened to explode her into a million pieces of flesh and bone. She jumped to her feet, spitting out her words over Dom's head. He flinched as droplets of her saliva sprayed his face. He hung his head as if bowed by the weight of his guilt.

"This is a fucking nightmare," Dom said, running his hands through his hair and looking around frantically, as if he might find answers to his own questions in the empty space around him. "I can't believe it. How can this be happening?"

Even in the fading light, Morgan could see how pale Dom was, underneath his light tan. For a second, she contemplated pushing him off the wall and into the water below, darkening now from turquoise to black as the light gradually faded.

Perhaps he would bang his head on the harbour wall as he slipped, inexorably, into the invisible depths, sinking towards his death as she walked away, never to admit what she'd done, just like him. Her thoughts were insane, she knew, but she couldn't stop them flooding her brain. She must be going mad - stark, staring mad.

"I was so fucking scared when it happened," Dom said. "I just couldn't believe what I'd done. Just like now, it felt completely surreal, like I was watching a movie or something outside myself. It couldn't be that I had just hit a person, I told myself, over and over again, as I sat there, immediately afterwards just trying to take it all in. I remember seeing the dog up ahead of me, trotting along, oblivious, in the middle of the road and the old man, the dog's owner, along the grass verge."

Dom paused for a few seconds, staring into the far distance, as if searching there for a complete memory of that dreadful night.

"I remember I took my foot off the accelerator and was preparing to brake when your mum appeared from nowhere, right in front of me," he continued. "Suddenly, there she was, in the headlights, like she'd dropped out of the sky or something. It was so dark, down by the school, and she was in a dark coat, with the hood pulled up. There was no time to stop, nothing I could do. I slammed on the brakes but couldn't stop in time. The sound......it will stay with me for the rest of my life."

Morgan sensed that there was more Dom could say about the moment of impact and the gut-wrenching sight of her shattered body lying motionless on the road, but he was trying to spare her.

There was no need for that. She had all the devastating details firmly locked in her brain.

"I saw the old man walking slowly towards the car," Dom continued. "I panicked, all sorts of shit zooming round my head. Would I be sent to prison? If I was, what would happen to mum if she was left all on her own? I couldn't think straight, but some instinct pressed my foot hard down on that accelerator and I took off."

Morgan leapt up from the wall, her face a picture of anger, like an enraged beast preparing to fight.

"You left her to die, you fucking coward. If it hadn't been for that old man, who stayed to comfort her, she would have died, all alone, on that cold, hard road. Have you any idea what it feels like for me and my dad to have to think about that? She wasn't even worthy of a few minutes of your time to see if she was still alive, if she could be saved…"

Evening strollers turned their heads as her angry words reverberated across the still night air. As she marched off, Dom ran after her, pleading for her to sit down and talk.

"Please Morgan, it wasn't like that. Just let me explain."

Morgan stopped and spun on her heel, coming face-to-face with Dom.

"You're a piece of shit Dominic Cooper, and I never want to see you again."

"Morgan, please…." Dom's face was contorted, a study in pain and anguish.

"Don't even think about coming back to the tent tonight," Morgan yelled over her shoulder, as she walked away. "You can sleep on the beach for all I care. I'm leaving tomorrow, without you. You can make your own sorry way home, and don't ever contact me or my family again. I never want to see your face again, you absolute fucking coward."

Dom watched as Morgan stormed off, following her with his eyes until she disappeared from view. He felt sick to his stomach, not knowing where to go or what to do next. It was almost worse than the night of the accident.

Thrusting his hands in his pockets, Dom turned towards the sea, as if searching infinity for answers. All that came back to him was the sound of water splashing against the harbour wall and the mournful cry of scavenging sea birds searching hungrily for their supper.

CHAPTER FORTY-ONE

With Si Thompson's worrying words ringing in his ears, Gareth raced back to Cragview, his mind running faster than the car's engine.

He should have insisted on meeting this Dominic character, he berated himself. He might have gained a sense of him – whether he was trustworthy, or another lowlife like Todd Hopkins, except with a posher accent. It didn't sound much, the deception about him not driving, but his detective's instinct, honed by years of experience, was flashing him a warning he could not ignore.

Why would this guy lie about the fact that he had passed his test and was qualified to drive, he asked himself? Si had said the kid passed first time, after only six lessons. He must be an excellent and confident driver, so what was his problem? It made no sense to Gareth's forensic brain. More importantly, if he had lied about that, what else might this Dominic be concealing?

As he sped home to Cragview, Gareth tried repeatedly to call Morgan.

"Please pick up, love," he silently begged. "Please just answer your phone." It rang to voice mail, and he left another desperate message.

It really scared him that Morgan wasn't answering. The last time that had happened, she was being held captive by a half-crazed drug dealer. Every nerve ending in his body was sending messages to his brain that his daughter was once again in some kind of trouble. What could it be, he asked himself, turning over wilder and wilder possibilities in his mind?

Arriving at Cragview, his car screeched onto the drive, sending gravel flying in all directions. Even before he had climbed out, Petra emerged from her studio, a concerned expression on her face. Scruff followed shortly afterwards, taking up a place of safety behind her legs from where he peered round at Gareth.

"Is everything alright?" Petra asked, making her way down the path towards the drive.

"I'm not sure love, but I've got a bad feeling that it might not be. Can we go inside?"

Petra nodded and followed him into the living room, listening carefully as he proceeded to recount his meeting with Si and to share all the information he had gleaned from his former colleague.

"That's certainly puzzling," said Petra. "Why would Dominic lie about something like that?"

"Exactly what I was wondering, and I can't think of a good explanation. I've got a bad feeling about this, Petra, after all that business with Todd. If I can't get through to Morgan in the next hour, I'm driving down there. I know it's a bit extreme, but I can't sit here doing nothing except worry that something awful has happened to her. If I get through to her along the way and everything's alright, then I'll turn back, and she'll be none the wiser. She doesn't need to know I'm on her case. Thank God, she gave me the co-ordinates of the campsite she's staying at, like I asked her to."

"Well, if that's what you want to do, darling, I'm coming with you, as long as I can find someone to look after Scruff. Give me half an hour and I should be ready."

177

CHAPTER FORTY-TWO

With tears streaming down her face, Morgan clung to the car steering wheel, as if her life depended on it.

Blinking hard, she peered through the windscreen, as if searching for a route in a snowstorm. Tears blurred her vision and distorted streetlights, which leaned towards her like illuminated daggers suspended over the road.

The clock on the car dashboard told her it was almost midnight. She couldn't believe how late it was. Should she even be driving after several beers and such an exhausting evening? At that moment, she didn't care. All she knew was, she had to put distance between herself and Dom.

Following his devastating revelation, she had run back to the campsite, without pausing for breath. Panting, and with her heart pounding in her chest, she had crammed all her possessions into her backpack, rolled up her mat and sleeping bag, and flung everything into the car. Without a backward glance, she pulled away from the pitch, pressing her foot hard on the accelerator as soon as she exited the site.

Desperate to leave behind the horror of the evening, Morgan sped through the emptying streets of the small town in which they had been staying, with barely a thought as to where she was going. Fearful of another confrontation with Dom, she had not even taken the time to programme her satnav. Instead, she followed road signs which she hoped would take her in a northerly direction.

Forty-five minutes into the drive, Morgan felt a wave of exhaustion roll over her. Her day at sea and the tumult of the evening were beginning to catch up with her. She was passing through yet another small town, where there were few lights to suggest that anyone else was awake apart from her. She pulled over to the side of the road so that she could try and figure out where she might safely stop to grab a couple of hours' sleep.

Morgan leaned her head on the steering wheel and would have allowed herself to drift into sleep, right there, had she not been startled by a sudden knocking on her driver window.

A male face peered in at her, separated only by the glass of the window. Shocked, she let out a scream, instantly checking that her door lock was activated. Gripped by terror that she was about to be attacked on this deserted street, in an unknown town, she reached for the ignition to start up and pull away. As she did so, the man held up his hand, palm facing her, to indicate she should not move.

"Sorry, sorry," the stranger shouted at the closed window. "Sorry to frighten you. I was thinking maybe your car is broken and you need help?" The man spoke good English, with only the hint of an accent.

Morgan shook her head. "The car is fine. I'm fine, thank you," she said.

"If you have a problem, I am walking to my sister's hotel, a short distance from here." The man pointed up the road in front of them to where a white painted building stood, slightly set back from the road. Morgan could just make out an illuminated sign overhanging the pavement, advertising the name of a hotel.

"If you need a place to stay tonight, my sister has some empty rooms. It is up to you. I only wish to help you. My name is Felippe, and my sister is Juanita. I will walk on, now, to the hotel. You can follow me if you like."

Morgan pictured a neat, freshly made bed in a quiet room where she could sink into oblivion for a few hours. The prospect almost made her faint as she realised how tired she was.

Just as he said he would, the stranger set off walking slowly up the road, towards the hotel building. He was in his thirties, she guessed, slightly built and, from what she could tell, genuinely concerned to find her alone, parked up on an empty street. But what if he was just preying on her vulnerability and about to lure her into a horrible trap? It was the sort of thing she read about on social media all the time. Added to that, her dad had drummed into her, from her earliest years, that she should never go off with a stranger.

But what are my options, she asked herself, biting her lip? For sure, she was not going back to the campsite. She didn't want to see Dom again now, or ever. Of that much, at least, she was certain.

Morgan's eyes were scratchy with tiredness which seemed to sit on her eyelids, almost forcing them to close. She knew she had to sleep before continuing her journey. In her distress, she had left the campsite without even considering her route. Then there was her return ferry – she would need to rearrange that, but it was too late to do it now. She desperately needed to sleep before tackling all of that.

Full of misgivings about following the stranger, Morgan pulled away from the kerb, driving slowly behind him, as he walked up the hill to the hotel. There were no other vehicles or pedestrians around, she noted.

In front of her, Felippe maintained a calm, unhurried stride, without looking back. Surely, if he was planning any kind of move on her, he would manifest some level of agitation or threatening behaviour, Morgan asked herself? That was how Todd behaved when he took her hostage. With him, she had been able to smell the fear and sweat exuding from his every pore as he held her in his iron grip, that terrible day. Morgan recalled his wild, staring eyes, the pupils enlarged from being high. She wasn't picking up any tell-tale signs of danger from this guy, though she was terribly aware that she could easily be mistaken.

Eventually, after what seemed like an age, but was only a few minutes, Morgan drew level with the hotel and stopped the car. The building was a large old house, with a modern extension to one side. Troughs of geraniums hung beneath every window facing the road. It looked safe and welcoming, as far as she could tell.

She pulled into the car park and watched as Felippe let himself into the hotel building through tall wooden double doors. As they swung open, Morgan glimpsed a softly lit reception area. There was a large, ornate desk at the rear of the space, with a table lamp casting a warm glow onto wooden wall panelling and a gleaming, tiled floor.

Behind the desk sat a woman, whom Morgan guessed to be Juanita. From a distance, she looked to be a few years older than her brother, of heavier build, but with the same thick, curly hair tumbling over her shoulders. A beaming smile broke over her face the minute Felippe walked through the door, and she jumped up from behind the desk to greet him, warmly, with kisses on each cheek.

Felippe and the woman began to talk, animatedly – she guessed about her –as they both looked round in her direction. The woman's smile slowly faded as she listened intently to what she was being told. Whatever her brother was saying, she appeared to agree with him, nodding occasionally. Morgan remained in the car, uncertain how to proceed.

After a few moments, Felippe and the woman emerged from the hotel and walked out to where she was parked. Morgan tensed, ready to make a bolt for it. The woman leaned in towards the car, whilst keeping her distance. Morgan cracked the window open a couple of inches.

"I'm Nita," the woman said. "This is my brother, Felippe. He told me you may need somewhere to stay tonight. I have rooms available, if you would like to come in and look around before you decide."

The thought of that comfortable bed loomed even larger now that Morgan was so close. Grabbing some rest was an imperative, and she couldn't sleep in the car. That would be completely unsafe. She glanced, again, at the welcoming façade of the hotel and then at the concerned, friendly faces of the two people looking in at her.

"That would be great. Thank you," Morgan said. She pulled into the car park, checked that she had her phone and passport in her backpack and followed Nita and her brother into the hotel.

After completing the formalities of registration, Juanita showed Morgan to a room on the first floor, at the back of the building. The rate was ridiculously cheap, and Morgan suspected the sister was giving her a discount out of sympathy for her sorry predicament. She would have to find a way to repay this kindness when she was able to do so.

"This is perfect," Morgan said. "Thank you so much."

"Would you like anything to eat, senorita?" said Juanita. "A little bread and cheese perhaps?"

Morgan shook her head.

"Thank you, but I'd like to go straight to bed, if that's alright."

"Of course. As you wish," said Juanita. "Breakfast is served in the restaurant from 7 o'clock in the morning until 9.30. Please, join us when you can."

As soon as Juanita shut the bedroom door behind her, Morgan ripped off her clothes and fell into bed. Though she was bone-weary, her mind was still racing. She laid her head on the soft pillow, picturing Dom still only a few miles away. She hadn't checked her phone but guessed he had been trying to call her. Thank goodness she had thought to block his number before leaving the campsite.

Though her body craved sleep, Morgan's mind bombarded her with questions. How could this be happening to her, after all she had been through? Why did she have to meet and fall in love with the very person who killed her mother and caused her family so much pain? The unfairness of it all was more than she would ever comprehend.

In the solitary darkness of the strange room, away from everything and everyone she knew, Morgan buried her head in the pillow to try and disguise the sound of her uncontrollable weeping. She didn't care if she was being self-pitying. How much more did she have to take, and how many more times must she find a way to pick herself up from rock bottom? Morgan let her tears flow until there was nothing left.

Eventually, when she felt desiccated, like a shrivelled, dry piece of fruit, Morgan turned onto her back and lay staring at the ceiling. The hotel was quiet, so Felippe and his sister must have gone to bed, she figured. The only sounds were of insects and nightlife foraging and exploring the garden below. It reminded her of the heavy silence of the encircling night at Cragview, broken only by the movement of nocturnal creatures.

Holding that thought, Morgan reached for her phone and switched it on. There were loads of messages and missed calls from her dad. How bloody typical that she had decided to leave her phone behind when she and Dom went out on the boat because she had been terrified that she might lose it overboard. She had stuffed it inside her PJs, in the bottom of her sleeping bag, which meant her dad hadn't been able to reach her, nor she, him.

Now, Morgan was desperate to speak to her father and to hear his reassuring voice. She had held off from calling, until now, because she just needed to get as far away from Dom as possible before stopping to take stock. Having stumbled on this place for the night, where Dom would never find her, she couldn't wait any longer. Scrolling through her contacts, she tapped on her dad's number, praying he would answer despite the lateness of the hour.

After a couple of rings, Gareth picked up.

"Morgan, love. Is everything alright? I've been so worried about you. Where are you?" At the sound of his voice, Morgan started sobbing again. It was such a relief to hear him.

"I'm sorry, dad. I didn't have my phone otherwise I'd have called you earlier. I know you've been trying to reach me." The effort of trying to swallow her tears brought a painful lump to her throat, making it difficult to speak.

"Ok, love. Don't worry about that. We're talking now. Is it about Dom?" Gareth asked, an edge in his voice.

"How did you know?" Morgan replied, astonished.

"I've found out some things about him which I don't like the sound of. I won't beat about the bush, love, because there's stuff you should know. He passed his driving test years ago – first attempt after only six lessons - so he's been lying to you about not driving. I'm worried about him."

"Dad!" said Morgan, realising that he didn't know the full story. "It's him. He's the one who killed mum. Dom did it."

A gasp of shock on the other end of the phone, then silence. "Dad, are you there? Can you hear me?"

"I'm here love. I just.....I don't know what to say, what to think......Where are you now? Is he there with you?"

"No, dad. I left the campsite as soon as I found out. I'm in a hotel, about an hour or so from the site. It's a long story, dad, and I'm really tired, but I just wanted to talk to you."

"That's alright, love. You did the right thing by calling. Have you driven there all by yourself?"

"Yes," Morgan said, a sob escaping from her as she realised the enormity of her predicament.

"Right," said Gareth, in a decisive tone. "I haven't been able to reach you to let you know what we're doing. We're on our way to you, love – Petra's here with me."

"What do you mean?" asked Morgan, confused.

"When I found out about Dom and then I couldn't reach you to tell you about it, I couldn't just sit around worrying. Petra and I discussed it, and we left home a few hours ago. Petra's managed to book us onto the first ferry over to Calais this morning, so if you're in northern Spain, we should reach you late this evening."

"You can't do that, Dad. It's much too far for you. Now that we've spoken, I'll be alright, as long as I get a good night's sleep."

"I won't hear of it, Morgan. You can't drive all that way back on your own, after all that's happened. We can share the driving between us and talk about all this stuff with Dom on the way, or when we get safely home. I can't take it in at the moment. After all this time we find out who was in that car, and he turns out to be your boyfriend. It's incredible, absolutely incredible."

"I know Dad. I can't take it in either. I keep thinking I'm having another horrible nightmare and I'll wake up and everything will be normal again, or as normal as it ever gets for me."

They talked briefly about arrangements until Gareth made Morgan promise she would ring off and get some much-needed sleep. She agreed, relieved, despite her protestations, to hand over responsibility to her dad.

The phone call with Gareth proved to be the perfect sleep inducer. As soon as Morgan had finished speaking to him, she laid her head on the pillow and fell into a deep and dreamless sleep. Sharing the incredible news about Dom had given her some desperately needed inner calm after a day of tumultuous emotion.

When Morgan awoke, it took several seconds for her to ground herself in the unfamiliar surroundings. All too soon, the dreadful revelations of the previous evening came flooding back to her, though she did wonder, at first, if it had all been a spectacularly bad dream.

From the ground floor, Morgan could hear voices and activity. Glancing at her phone, she saw it was almost 9.30am. She had slept, without waking, for more than eight hours. The mind-numbing tiredness had left her, and her head was clearer, but the grumble of her stomach reminded her she was hungry. Perhaps she could nip downstairs and see if there was anything left to eat.

Pulling on her shorts and T-shirt, she opened the door to her room. At her feet was a tray, covered with a chequered cotton napkin. A small note, with her name on it, lay on top of the tray. She opened and read it:

"Dear Senorita Morgan
We didn't want to disturb your rest, so have left you some food from breakfast.
We hope you slept well.

Felippe and Juanita

How kind of the brother and sister to think of her in this way. They really had been guardian angels, it seemed. If she hadn't encountered Felippe when she did, goodness knows what she would have done.

Morgan peered under the napkin and saw that slices of warm bread, cooked meat and cheese had been laid out, together with fresh fruit and a small jar of honey. The smell of strong coffee from a small cafetière wafted up, making her almost swoon. She took the tray into her room and instantly fell upon the food as if she hadn't eaten in days.

When she had consumed her fill of breakfast, Morgan jumped into the shower, relishing the pounding of the water on her skin. After briskly drying herself with the soft, white bath sheet hanging from the towel rail, she felt re-energised and ready to face whatever the day might throw at her.

Before she did anything else, however, she must phone her dad to check on his progress.

In the light of day, Morgan felt horribly guilty that her father and Petra had set off to drive hundreds of miles, in the middle of the night to come to her aid. What if they were in an accident due to tiredness? It would be all her fault.

Morgan glanced at her phone. No message from either of them. Should she call? Maybe they were resting somewhere. Just as she was pondering whether to book another night at the hotel, her phone jumped into life and began to ring. Petra's name appeared on the screen. Morgan eagerly pressed the receiver button.

"Hi! Where are you?" she asked, breathlessly.

"We're making good time, darling," said Petra. "We caught the first ferry this morning and your dad's been putting his advanced driver skills to good use, so we've been zipping along. I put in the address you gave me, and the satnav says we're about five hours away. With a couple of stops along the way, we think we'll be with you this evening.

"That's great. I can't wait to see you, but are you sure you don't want an overnight rest before you get here? You must be absolutely exhausted," said.

"We're fine. Completely hyper on coffee, but apart from that, we're good. We've taken it in turns to drive and had a power nap along the way."

"I'll go down to reception, as soon as we finish, and check there's a room for you," said Morgan. "It doesn't seem particularly busy here, but it's a wonderful place. The owner and her brother have been so unbelievably kind to me. I'm sure they'll fit you in."

"Sounds perfect. Go and check, then phone us back," said Petra.

Juanita expressed herself delighted to offer accommodation to Gareth and Petra. They could arrive any time, she told Morgan, and there would be a room ready for them and food, if they wanted it.

"That's great," said Petra, when Morgan reported back. "I'm looking forward to a shower already."

"I can't wait to see you both," said Morgan, her voice wobbling with emotion.

"Just hang on a few more hours, love," said Gareth. "We'll be with you just as soon as we can."

CHAPTER FORTY-THREE

To calm her agitation, and to pass the time until her dad and Petra arrived, Morgan decided to walk into the nearest village, taking directions from Juanita.

When she arrived, a small food market was in full swing, bustling with shoppers and browsers. In other circumstances, Morgan would have loved to wander down the narrow avenues between the rows of stalls and counters, accepting the votive offerings of the sellers promoting their produce and tempting her to buy. She would have sampled, questioned, then inevitably purchased some local cheese or a selection of cooked meats and freshly baked bread.

Today, although her stomach was responding hopefully to the sights and smells of spice and sweetness, perfectly cooked meat and fresh fish, she wasn't in the mood to linger. The heat of the day was building, and shoppers were beginning to take refuge in the dark, cool depths of the bars and cafés that lined the four sides of the market square. Morgan bought only a large bottle of water and some fruit before re-tracing her steps to the hotel.

The heat was becoming oppressive to her, so after making a booking for Gareth and Petra, she returned to her room, grateful that the bed had been made, the windows thrown open and the curtains drawn to keep the heat at bay.

The hotel was quiet and peaceful, other residents having gone out for the day Morgan presumed. Flopping down onto the bed, she began scrolling through her phone, searching for information about Dom on social media. Had he been keeping any other dreadful secrets from her, she wondered?

It wasn't long before drowsiness overtook her, pulling her eyelids shut no matter how hard she tried to resist. It was only when the sound of increasingly insistent knocking at her bedroom door penetrated her deep sleep, that she woke with a start. Briefly, Morgan struggled to orientate herself in time and space. It was the familiar voice at the door that eventually reminded her where she was, and why.

"Morgan. It's me love." Before the knocking was repeated, she leapt to the door, throwing it open wide.

At the sight of her father and Petra standing in the corridor, their tired and anxious faces scanning her own, Morgan threw her arms around them both.

"Thank you," she said. "Thank you so much for coming. I can't tell you how glad I am to see you both."

"Come in," she said, ushering the weary travellers into her room. "I have so much to tell you."

Not until Gareth and Petra had heard the full story of Morgan's discovery about Dom could they be persuaded to go to their rooms to shower and freshen up. They soon returned to join her for dinner in the hotel restaurant.

"After all this time and all that searching, he walks into our lives," said Gareth. "I can't believe it."

"I know," said Morgan. "Sometimes, I think we're living in a parallel universe, and we've accidentally fallen out of the real world that everyone else inhabits."

"At least we *know*," said Gareth, staring into the distance as if he were looking back down the years of torment during which he had used every skill, every contact, every effort to bring to justice the person who had snuffed out the life of his beloved Mel. Looking at him, Morgan could see a physical change in her father already. He held his head and shoulders higher, as if the deadweight of his failure had been lifted and put aside.

"What are we going to do, dad? Are we going to tell the police?" Morgan asked.

"I think we have to, love. Dom may not have been able to avoid the collision, but he sure as hell should have reported the accident and faced the music. He committed an offence."

"Will he go to prison?" Morgan asked, the enormity of Dom's situation gradually becoming apparent to her.

"He may do. I'm not sure. Depends on whether he gets himself a good lawyer."

Morgan pictured Dom standing in a courtroom, head bowed in shame and disgrace, Eliza looking on, a picture of anxiety. She

188

felt conflicted. Even if it was just an accident which he couldn't have avoided, his actions meant she would never again see her mum's goofy smile of pride at her achievements. Never again would she be able to reach out for her mother's guidance and wisdom, always so lightly delivered. For the rest of her life, she would watch friends celebrate and commiserate with their mothers, knowing that could never happen for her. She hated Dom for slinking away from what he'd done, leaving so much hurt and pain behind him.

Yet, at the same time, she couldn't help sympathising with the angry young man Dom had been, railing against the hand that fate had dealt him. She had been in a similar place, not so long ago, and she had broken the law also.

"I can't help feeling a bit sorry for him," Morgan said, pushing her food around her plate.

"What makes you say that?" Petra asked, gazing at Morgan intently.

"He had a really hard time over his dad leaving and his mum becoming dependent on him. When all his mates were out living the carefree life, he was having to take the place of his dad. He did a stupid, stupid thing but then I've done some stupid things. You have too, dad," Morgan said, looking pointedly at her father.

Gareth didn't respond, clearly pondering what Morgan had just said.

"I can see what you're saying, and I think that's very fair of you," he said, eventually. "The trouble is, my vision has been clouded by anger for such a long time – all I've wanted, since your mum died, is to find the person who smashed up our lives, so that I could make them accountable for their actions. That's how my mind works after thirty years in the police force. But I'm learning – from you and from the young men I talk to at Granton Prison. People make mistakes – terrible mistakes sometimes – but that doesn't have to define who they are for the rest of their lives. When the dust is settled, we should talk to Dom, all of us, and have it out with him.

"Reconciliation, you mean," said Morgan.

"Maybe, just maybe, we'll get to that," Gareth replied.

CHAPTER FORTY-FOUR

Dom watched Morgan's rapidly disappearing figure until it had been swallowed up by the throngs of people heading to bars and restaurants for the evening. No point trying to follow her, he acknowledged, after all that had just passed.

Standing stock still and directionless, he pictured Morgan lying alone, in the tent, tossing and turning as she churned the bombshell news that her boyfriend killed her mother and drove off into the night, leaving her for dead. How must she be feeling at hearing such unimaginable news?

He was desperate to be able to explain to her all that had happened that night, excluding the haunting recollection of the sound of flesh and bone being struck by tonnes of metal travelling at speed and the pitiful cry which shattered the quiet calm of the winter evening. That must be his awful memory to carry, not hers.

As so often happened, Dom's mind turned to the repository of his darkest memories. He pictured himself arriving back at Mikey's dad's garage. Not knowing what else to do, he had driven straight there, after the accident. His friend had completely freaked out when he saw the damage to the car and heard what had happened.

"What the fuck, Dom?" Mikey had repeated several times, as he clutched his hair in his hands and paced up and down the garage, staring at the front bumper for a few seconds, then resuming his pacing, all the while muttering to himself.

"I should go to the police," Dom had replied, "tell them what happened. The person – a woman, I think - just ran out straight in front of me, without looking my way. I had no chance to brake or avoid her. I think she's dead."

Dom hadn't been sure Mikey had heard the last part as he had spoken it so quietly – afraid to utter the awful words.

"No!" Mikey had grabbed him by the collar of his Puffer jacket, thrusting his face into Dom's. "You do not go to the police," he said, slowly and emphatically. "You wait and see if anything comes out about it. If the woman's dead and the old boy didn't see anything, you're in the clear. I should be able to sort this out," Mikey said, pointing to the damage across the front of the BMW. "I've got a mate who owes me a favour. He'll help me with it, before my dad gets back. If we put it through the insurance, dad will get to know all about it, and the shit will really hit the fan. I'm not even sure it's covered anyway."

Dom had tasted the bile rising from his stomach and filling his mouth. He retched and vomited onto the garage floor until there was nothing left inside him. He had just killed someone - he was pretty sure of that. Taking another's life was the worst thing you could possibly do, even if you didn't mean to. He could never be the same person again, after tonight.

He should own up to what he'd done, without delay. He should present himself at the police station and confess everything, regardless of what Mikey said. The woman ran right out in front of him before he had chance to stop. It was an accident, he would say, a horrible, tragic accident. He was deeply, deeply sorry.

But he hadn't turned himself in to the police. He'd walked home from Mikey's garage, his thoughts colliding, then spinning out of control around his brain.

If he confessed, would he have to go to prison, he had asked himself? How would his mother cope if that happened? She was already fragile, having suffered a devastating divorce from his father. He had worried that it might break her completely to discover her son was a convicted criminal, responsible for an innocent woman's death.

"I watched every news bulletin, national and local," Dom would have told Morgan if she were still here with him. "I scanned all the main social media channels, every few minutes, hoping and praying I'd read that your mum had survived. It was all I could think about."

At that she would have exploded, he knew. "Don't give me that," she would have yelled at him, not caring who heard. "All you cared about was saving your own sorry skin."

She would have been right to say that, of course; she who was so brave and caring. He didn't deserve to be with her, and she didn't deserve someone as weak and cowardly as him.

It was on the morning after the accident that he had learned the shattering truth about what he had done. On the strapline of the local news, which ran continuously across the bottom of the screen, carrying breaking and major stories, he had read the following:-

"Local headteacher and wife of senior police officer killed in hit and run accident outside school."

He had listened to the reporter describing Melissa Fairley, his expression solemn, listing her achievements and her success as head teacher at St Mark's Primary. She was married to Detective Chief Inspector Gareth Fairley of Granton Police, the male presenter had recounted, and the couple had one teenage daughter, no name mentioned. Little was known about the driver of the car involved in the collision, and police were appealing for information about a possible stolen vehicle, believed to be extensively damaged at the front.

"Fuck!" Dom had slapped his forehead several times, as if doing so might help him to order his chaotic thoughts. His conscience had screamed at him to go to the police station and confess to what had happened, but his growing fear and paranoia meant he wasn't listening.

The bulletin had shifted to a clip from a press conference in which Morgan's dad had appeared, wearing his police uniform. Describing the circumstances of the accident, DCI Fairley had then confirmed that the victim was declared dead by the paramedics who attended the scene. His voice cracking with grief, he had been forced to pause and look away from the camera, as he wrestled to compose himself sufficiently to finish his appeal. Anyone with any information at all, he struggled to say, should please come forward and contact his colleagues immediately to help the police identify the heartless criminal who had callously driven away from the scene.

Dom had watched, in horrified fascination, as Morgan's dad had been helped from the interview table by an anonymous person of whom only a sympathetic arm could be seen on the screen. It was obvious he was a broken man. Pain was etched on his face and reflected in his whole demeanour, and he, Dominic Cooper, was the cause of it. He simply could not absorb the enormity of what he had done.

Incredibly, in a matter of days, the story had been consigned to a short piece in the local online paper, ranking after the report of a house fire in Denley and an advertisement for an upcoming Christmas Fair.

From an article in his news feed, Dom had learned that Ted Dunlop, the elderly gentleman whom he had passed on the Flintby Road, and whose dog had wandered out into the road, had passed away from a sudden heart attack. He had been the only witness to the accident, so he was taking the secrets of that night to the grave with him. No-one else had come forward with any information.

He had dithered and debated with himself constantly. Several times he was on his way to the police station – almost at the door – when his fear and paranoia got the better of him and he turned away. With each passing day, the burden of his guilt grew heavier.

Then, about two months after the accident, Mikey rang him to say he and his family were emigrating to Australia. The garage business had been sold, and they would be leaving in two weeks' time.

What ironic twist of fate had presented him with this state of affairs, Dom wondered? The only witness to the accident had died, taking his knowledge to the grave. Soon Mikey would be all but out of the picture, so Dom had his 'get out of jail free' card that made it even more difficult for him to give himself up to the police and face the consequences of his behaviour.

It was then Dom began to seriously loathe himself. When he looked in the mirror, he saw a different face. He looked mean and cruel, to his eyes, his features sharpened by his lack of honesty and integrity. He was sure people were looking at him and seeing it too.

Day by day, his mental torment had increased.

CHAPTER FORTY-FIVE

Walking like an automaton, as his mind whirred over the past, Dom found that he had arrived at the marina. He ambled towards the harbour entrance, drawn by the vast emptiness of the sea that lay beyond it.

Momentarily, Dom's attention was diverted by the sight of a yacht, slowly slipping out of the marina, its navigation lights illuminated - pin pricks of red, green and white - in the growing darkness. Laughter and shouted instructions carried across the still night as the crew moved swiftly and efficiently around the boat, preparing for a night sail.

Observing the boat glide smoothly through the jaws of the harbour, Dom remembered the time he'd done the same – headed out into the black emptiness of the sea at night, its smooth surface broken only by an occasional ripple of shimmering water, illuminated by the moon.

He had been with his family – his dad, brother, uncle and cousins. A proper boys' own adventure, sailing a 32-foot yacht from Lymington to Weymouth, by night. He'd been so excited, he was physically sick over the guard rail, to the amusement of his older brother and cousins.

Forcing himself to stay awake, when his body yearned for sleep, Dom had marvelled at the break of dawn and the light slowly bleaching the sky. He had watched, open-mouthed, as the burning ball of the sun rose swiftly above the horizon, marking the beginning of a new day. His uncle Joe had descended to the galley from where he produced warm bacon rolls for the whole crew. Dom could almost taste the salty bacon and the drip of melted butter on his chin, as he thought about it. He remembered helping to tie up the boat on arriving at the destination, proud to have participated in a successful voyage.

Looking back, Dom could almost believe those were the happiest few hours of his life.

Whilst his mind wandered over the past, his fingers automatically closed around the keys to the Gypsy Queen. He would stay the night on the boat, he decided, since he had no doubt at all that Morgan meant what she said. There was no way she was going to allow him to lie beside her, their bodies unavoidably touching inside the compact canvas space.

Slowly, he made his way to where Gypsy Queen was moored, familiar feelings of self-loathing and disgust slushing around inside him like the filthy bilge water in the bottom of the boat. Since first setting eyes on Morgan, at Harley Grange, he had been able to shut out some of the bad stuff that had haunted him since that November night a year and a half ago. She had brought light into the darkest corners of his life. Now, the horror came rushing back to him like a torrent of unstoppable flood water.

CHAPTER FORTY-SIX

Unlocking the hatch, Dom descended into the galley, his mood sinking with each step. He laid down on one of the bunks, hands behind his head, staring up at the ceiling. The white light of the moon shone through the portholes and the sea lapped gently against the hull. It was a soothing sound, but there was no ease for his troubled soul.

He couldn't just lie here, hour after hour, endlessly revisiting the past, he told himself. The sea was calling him, like a siren beckoning him forward. He jumped up and began feverishly rushing about the boat, untying ropes, adjusting fenders and cranking up the engine. With a splutter and a grumble, Gypsy Queen responded, eventually ticking over into a steady rhythm.

He should alert the coastguard to his nocturnal activity, Dom knew, but he wouldn't be out for long. All he wanted was to head back towards the cove where he and Morgan had spent such an idyllic afternoon, but which now seemed like a lifetime ago.

He cast off and slowly edged out of the berth, gliding towards the harbour entrance. Once through, his eyes having adjusted to night vision, Dom could make out the distant lights of other vessels, large and small, twinkling in the darkness. It was comforting to know that others were around him, yet he had never felt so alone.

There was no wind for sailing, but Dom remembered the course he must take to reach the cove. The heat of the day still hung heavy in the air and soon his T-shirt was drenched with sweat. He set the boat on autopilot whilst he went below deck, searching through the cupboards for a bottle of water, maybe a beer left behind. Finding only a half empty bottle of Jack Daniels, he grabbed that and took it back on deck with him, wrenching off the stopper and pouring the sweet, smoky liquid down his throat.

Desperate to escape from the turmoil of his thoughts, Dom continued drinking until the bottle was empty. He threw it to the deck, in disgust at its inability to dull his pain.

The night was still and quiet except for the rhythmic pumping of the engine as the Gypsy Queen ploughed through the water, yet Dom's head was filled with the sound of carping voices, strident with recrimination and accusation. He put his hands to his ears to blot out the jarring noise, staggering around the deck as he tried to escape his tormentors.

Then, at last, some peace - a susurration, barely a whisper, making suggestions and offering encouragement. An invisible hand was reaching out to him, palm open, beckoning.

The Gypsy Queen ploughed on, hugging the course her skipper had set.

CHAPTER FORTY-SEVEN

Morgan sipped from her glass of chilled white wine and gazed out over the French countryside.

In the far distance were hundreds of evenly spaced vines climbing the gentle, sun-soaked slopes of the Burgundy countryside. Below her lay the classical splendour of the neatly planted parterre garden of the hotel. She tilted her face to the sun and closed her eyes, appreciating the warmth on her skin.

Morgan had insisted on leaving Spain, the day after Gareth and Petra's arrival, because of her anxiety that Dom might somehow catch up with them. She had wanted to put more distance between them.

"I don't think you need to worry too much, love," her father had said. "For one thing, Dom doesn't have a car, so he'll probably have to catch trains home. Our paths aren't likely to cross."

Gareth was right, of course, but she had wanted to move on, for her own peace of mind. They left immediately after breakfast, having thanked Juanita profusely for her and her brother's kindness.

Morgan had insisted they share the driving between them and make regular stops along the way. They took a scenic route, through small towns and villages, with Gareth and Petra taking it in turns to travel with Morgan and to drive her car.

"I think we need to take some time out," Gareth had said, when it was his turn to be Morgan's passenger. "We've all had a helluva shock and so much to take in. On top of that, Petra and I have done a lot of driving over the past couple of days and we're making slow progress today. When we stop for lunch, I think we should research a nice hotel for a couple of days. We can re-book the ferry. I think we could all do with a rest."

Morgan had readily agreed. She still had a few days' holiday left and wasn't yet mentally prepared to face everyone at Harley Grange. There was a lot she still had to get straight in her head, before she attempted to recount to her friends and work colleagues all that had happened to her since she last saw them.

They stopped for lunch in a quiet, historic French village with narrow, cobbled streets, attractive pale stone houses and a spa hotel in a renovated chateau.

"I think this could be the place for us," said Gareth, as they drove up to the impressive glass fronted entrance of the hotel, from which sweeping stone steps descended to a circular gravel drive and delicately trickling fountain.

They booked into the hotel for two nights, intending to make use of all the spa facilities during their stay. After hours of driving, Gareth and Petra admitted to feeling exhausted, whilst Morgan craved some peace and tranquillity in which to process what had happened to her.

"You look comfortable," said Gareth, stooping down to kiss his daughter on the forehead as he and Petra joined her for supper. They had each enjoyed a relaxing massage, he told her, and, he admitted, a few hours of restorative sleep.

"How about you?" he asked. "What have you been doing?"

"I had the pool all to myself, then I had a sauna and jacuzzi. And now, I'm just soaking up the atmosphere of this beautiful place," she responded, gazing out across the elegantly laid gardens and green backdrop of fields and woods.

Petra glided to a seat opposite Morgan. She looks lovely, this evening, Morgan thought to herself, admiring the layered maxi-dress the older woman was wearing. The blend of yellow, gold and red in the diaphanous material suited Petra's colouring. Presumably her dad thought the same, as she noticed he was holding Petra's hand lightly beneath the table.

They had agreed to try and talk about something other than Dom, over dinner, since they had spoken of little else in their time together during the journey from Spain.

"How are you feeling about going to university, love?" Gareth asked after ordering a zero-alcohol beer for himself and a glass of wine for Petra. Morgan took a deep breath before replying. It was one of the subjects she had been turning over in her mind ever since the dramatic turn of events with Dom. She wondered when her dad would bring it up.

"I'm not going," she replied, with conviction.

"What?" Gareth and Petra asked in unison.

"I said I'm not going."

"What's brought this on, love?" Gareth asked, a frown wrinkling his forehead as he looked closely at his daughter.

"You have to ask?" she replied, a hint of sarcasm in her tone.

"Well, I don't see why Dom's transgressions should prevent you from having the future you want and deserve - if you get the grades, that is," said her father.

"But that's just it, dad. I don't want that life anymore. I want to stay in the place that I know, with the people that I know. End of."

Gareth and Petra looked at each other, without speaking. The look of dismay on Gareth's face spoke volumes. Here was history repeating itself, with Morgan punishing herself for what was not her fault, he was thinking. Yet, he knew better than to try and reason with his head-strong daughter when she was in this kind of mood. Better to move on to a different subject and await the outcome of her re-sits. If her grades were good, then perhaps she would change her mind. The shock news about Dom had turned her whole world upside down again and she obviously needed more time to take it all in.

Gareth opened his mouth to speak but didn't get chance to say anything before Morgan's phone sparked into life, buzzing around on the table like a stunned and angry wasp.

"It's Josie," said Morgan, peering at the screen, before tapping to accept the call. She walked away from the table to the edge of the terrace, where she could not be overheard.

"What's up Jo?" she asked.

"Hi Morgan. Are you ok?" Josie sounded a bit weird, Morgan thought. There was anxiety in her voice which instantly made Morgan's skin prickle. What now?

"Is it Eileen?" Morgan asked, without answering, anxiety clutching at her heart. Please God, don't let something have happened to her grandmother on top of all the horror of the past few days.

"She's fine, hon, don't worry. I was ringing to see if Dom is with you?"

Morgan sighed with relief. She didn't want to get into the whole sorry saga over the phone. She would explain it all to Josie over a few drinks in the pub when she got home.

"No, he's not with me. We've broken up, Jose, but don't ask me about it. I'll tell you everything when I get home. It's a long story. Why do you want to speak to him, anyway? Has something happened to Phyllis?" Morgan's mind was racing over all the negative possibilities she could think of.

"No, Phyllis is ok, as well. It's Eliza, she's been on the phone to Bev, to try and get hold of you. Apparently, she can't reach Dom and she doesn't have your number, so she called Harley Grange to try and get it. Obviously, Bev can't give it out without your permission, so I said I'd ring you and ask if you would call Eliza back."

How bloody typical of Dom, Morgan thought to himself. He's probably on the boat, licking his wounds, not bothering to answer his mum's calls. She didn't want to have to speak to Eliza and explain what had gone on, but she couldn't leave the poor woman to worry.

"Ok," she sighed. "Have you got Eliza's number? I'll give her a ring. There's not a lot I can tell her because I haven't been with Dom for a few days, but I think I know what's going on."

"Well, I'm glad you do," said Josie, with irony. "Where are you now?"

"In France, with Gareth and Petra. It's complicated. I promise I'll tell all when I get back. Sorry Jose."

"Ok. I know better than to argue. Call me if you need me, otherwise I'll see you when you get back."

Immediately after coming off the call with Josie, Morgan tried Dom for herself. Although she had blocked him on her phone, she thought he might pick up for her, but he didn't; his phone rang out to voicemail.

She called Eliza who answered after only one ring.

"Hello?" Eliza responded, in barely a whisper.

"Eliza, it's Morgan. Dom's....." she hesitated," Dom's girlfriend." Now was not the time to get into heavy explanations, she decided, particularly as she didn't know how much Dom had told his mother about her.

"Morgan," said Eliza, "thank goodness you called. I've been trying to get hold of Dom, but his phone just goes to voicemail. Is he with you?"

Morgan pursed her lips and screwed her eyes shut, rapidly assessing what to say and how much to reveal of her last dramatic conversation with Dom.

"No, I'm not with him. I'm afraid we had quite a bad argument and I left him behind at the campsite where we were staying. I can give you the address, if you like."

"Oh," said Eliza, sounding puzzled. "Thanks. Yes please." She hesitated. "Do you mind me asking what you were arguing about?"

God, oh god, Morgan thought to herself. What the hell should she say? She knew how she wanted to reply to Eliza; she wanted to tell her that her beloved son was responsible for her own mother's death and had been concealing the fact for several years, after driving away and leaving Melissa for dead. Of course, she wasn't going to do that to the poor woman, however tempting it might be.

"It's quite a long story," she replied, borrowing the phrase she had used to Josie for the same evasive purposes. "I'd rather not go into it, right now. If you just hold on a minute, I'll give you the campsite address."

She scrolled through her emails to one from the campsite, confirming the booking, then read out details of the address to Eliza.

"You might also try Jake's Place. I can text you the address and telephone number. It's a bar we used to go to. The manager, Jake, let us go out on his boat. He might have seen Dom or know where he is."

"Right. Ok." Eliza sounded doubtful. "Thanks Morgan."

"No problem." Morgan hesitated. Should she ask Eliza to keep her informed? She did want to know Dom was safe, but that was as far as it went. She decided not to say anything. News travelled like wildfire around Harley Grange, not least thanks to Phyllis, so she would probably hear all about it when she went back to work.

"Bye Eliza," she said.

"Bye dear."

Gareth and Petra both noted the grave expression on Morgan's face as she walked back across the terrace towards them.

202

"Everything alright?" Gareth asked.

"I'm not sure," Morgan replied, before proceeding to recount the telephone call. "I think I'll try and contact Jake myself. I'm sure Dom's messing about on Gypsy Queen, so Jake will probably have some idea what he's up to."

"Ok love. Let me know if you need any help."

It took Morgan some time to locate a contact number for Jake's Place, but eventually she found it.

After forwarding the details to Eliza, she phoned the number, listening to the persistent ring and praying someone would bother to answer. The bar was probably at its busiest, right now, in the early evening. Would anyone even hear the phone ring, she wondered?

Eventually, a harassed voice came onto the end of the line. It wasn't one she recognised, so presumably it was one of the staff.

"Hi!" she said in a fake, bright tone. "My name's Morgan. Could I speak to Jake, please, if he's there? I'm sure he's very busy but I won't take up much of his time. Can you tell him it's about the Gypsy Queen?"

"Ok." A rustle as the phone was deposited on a surface, then the hubbub of chatter and music drifted down the line. Morgan waited impatiently, anticipating that she might be forgotten or simply left hanging on indefinitely. Relief surged through her when she heard the phone being handled again.

"Morgan?" She recognised Jake's voice instantly. "What's this about Gypsy Queen? Are you guys out on it now?"

"No, no that's not it. I mentioned the Gypsy Queen to bring you to the phone. I actually wanted to ask if you'd seen Dom in the last couple of days?"

"Hang on. I'm confused here. Gypsy Queen's not in her berth. I went down there this morning to check everything was ok. I assumed you two were out on her. I haven't seen you or Dom since you came into the bar the other night."

Morgan felt her anxiety ratchet up a notch. "Sorry Jake. I should have explained. Dom and I broke up. We had a big fight and I left to come home. Dom stayed behind, or I thought he did. I'm wondering if he's out on the boat right now. I know he wanted to fit in as much sailing as he could before he came home."

"I guess that must be it," said Jake, sounding puzzled. "Look. I've got your number here. I'll ask around if anyone's seen or heard from him. I'm sure he'll be back in a day or so, when it's time to go home."

"Thanks Jake. I'm sure you're right but keep me posted if you can."

"Will do. Gotta go now. The bar's crazy." He rang off.

CHAPTER FORTY-EIGHT

Morgan's sense that something was amiss stole her appetite. Over dinner with Gareth and Petra, she could only pick at the delicious food that was laid before her, course by course.

"I'm sure you're right, Morgan," said Petra, as they mulled over the conversation with Jake. "Dom's probably gone off in the boat, on his own, to figure out what to do next. He wouldn't want to call his mother and worry her, so that's why he hasn't spoken to her."

"I would expect him to call her back after she's phoned and left messages, though," said Morgan.

"Perhaps he just doesn't know how to explain himself," Gareth suggested.

"Maybe."

Gareth tried to steer the conversation away from Dom, as he could see Morgan was worrying about it. He, too, was beginning to suspect that all was not well, but preferred to wait until he had more information before discussing it further. Morgan had other ideas, though, announcing before dessert that she was tired and wanted to go up to her room. He had little doubt she would be social media searching and imagining any number of scenarios. There was little he could do to stop her.

"Promise me you'll switch your phone off when you get into bed," he said. She leaned over and kissed him on top of his head.

"I never make promises I can't keep," she replied, with a sad smile.

Gareth was right to anticipate that his daughter would be spending time on her phone. Firstly, she searched on Dom's social media accounts, but there had been no posts since they went out on the boat together. That didn't necessarily mean anything; as Petra had suggested, he probably wanted to be alone whilst he tried to work out what to say and do when he got home.

She searched and puzzled and searched again, until her eyes drooped with tiredness. What could Dom be doing, she wondered? Troubling answers came back to her, but she didn't want to consider them. Stop being such a catastrophist, she told herself.

As she lay on her bed, drifting off to sleep, the quiet of the room was shattered by the ring of her phone. Grabbing it from the bedside table, she glanced at the screen, noting it was Jake who was calling her.

"Hello again Jake. I didn't expect to hear from you so soon." She injected a lightness into her tone which was fake. In fact, her stomach was clenching with renewed anxiety.

"Morgan. I think there's some shit going down here. About half an hour after you called me, I got a call from the harbourmaster to say Gypsy Queen's been reported drifting out at sea, apparently with no-one on board. Another yacht spotted her and sailed close to check everything was ok, but couldn't see anyone. The coastguard's been radio-ing the boat, but no answer, so they're sending out one of their vessels to investigate and bring Gypsy back, if necessary. I'm not sure what to think Morgan."

"Jesus Christ! Something bad's happened, I just know it. I'm here with my dad – he used to be a police officer. I'll see if he can get more information. Thanks, Jake, and sorry to get you mixed up in all this."

"That's ok. I'm just a bit worried about Dom."

"Me too," she said. "I've got a bad feeling about this."

Tearing down the corridor, she hammered on Gareth and Petra's bedroom door, but no answer. They must still be downstairs, she told herself. Hurtling down two flights of stairs, she ran through the dining room and out to the terrace where her dad and Petra were still seated.

"My God, Morgan, what on earth's wrong?" Gareth asked, taking in his daughter's anxious expression.

"Something bad's happened to Dom, I just know it," she replied. "I shouldn't have said all those bad things about him. This is my fault."

"Sit down, love, and get your breath back. You're not making sense."

With her head in a spin of speculation, Morgan gabbled out the gist of her conversation with Jake, her fruitless search on social media and her imaginings on what may have befallen her ex-boyfriend, not including the one that pulsated at the front of her thoughts. She guessed her dad would figure that one out for himself.

"Leave it with me. I'm not sure what more I can find out, but I'll make a few calls. You go back to your room, and I'll pop along in half an hour or so to let you know how I'm getting on," said Gareth, his face set in a grim expression. "And one more thing. None of this is your fault, so don't be having any more thoughts like that."

Morgan nodded, threw her arms around her father to give him a big hug, then slowly retraced her steps to her room.

It was past midnight before Gareth knocked on Morgan's bedroom door to pass on what he had learned. He had spent almost an hour phoning around ex-colleagues, he told her, calling in favours wherever he could, to obtain more information. In the end, it was his former detective sergeant Jenna Waite, who came up trumps. She had been able to make contact with a Spanish counterpart who, in turn, had spoken to the local coastguard.

"Someone from the coastguard and a police officer boarded the boat and confirmed there was no-one on it. The boat was drifting after running out of diesel, but otherwise there was nothing wrong with it. The coastguard hadn't received any contact from Dom or report of him being in difficulty. The weather conditions have been perfect over the past few days so…….."

"He's gone overboard," Morgan completed his sentence.

Gareth sighed. "It looks like it, on present information."

He decided not to tell Morgan that the police had found an empty bottle of whisky rolling around the deck. It might be that Dom had drunk himself into a stupor, then fallen overboard whilst trying to manoeuvre the boat. The other possibility, which he didn't want to dwell on without further evidence, was that Dom had taken his own life.

"The boat's being towed back to the marina where a thorough examination will be carried out in the morning," he told Morgan. "Until then, love, I think we just have to sit tight and wait for more solid information."

"What about Eliza?" Morgan asked. "Should I contact her?"

"Jenna's going to do that. I can't think of anyone better to break difficult news, so I think we should leave it to her, love."

"Ok, and thanks dad. I don't know what I would have done without you on this wretched holiday."

Gareth enfolded his daughter in his arms and squeezed her tight. He wished he could utter some platitude of reassurance, but he feared that Morgan already knew that this bad situation could be about to get a lot worse. All he could do was be there for her this time and not leave her to struggle on alone, as he had in the past.

"Try and get some sleep, love," was all he could offer. Morgan nodded, knowing full well there was little chance of that.

After receiving so much shocking news, Morgan, her father and Petra all agreed at breakfast, the following morning, that they wanted to go home. None of them wanted to continue luxuriating at the hotel, which felt completely inappropriate. They drove continuously, sharing the driving, and arrived back at Cragview in the early evening of the following day.

Desperate to try and keep her mind occupied whilst waiting for news, Morgan headed straight to her room, where she began pulling her clothes from her backpack and preparing to return to Harley Grange the following day. Although she still had two days of holiday left, she couldn't bear to have only bad thoughts occupying her mind. She needed to have work to do. Whilst she was laying out her clean uniform, there was a knock at her bedroom door.

"Can I come in?" Gareth called out.

"Sure," she said, noting the solemn expression on his face as he entered the room.

"I've just had Jenna on the phone," said Gareth, flopping down onto Morgan's bed. Tentatively she came to sit beside him. When he grabbed her hand and held it tightly in his own, she knew bad news was coming.

"Jenna's been speaking to the Spanish police who've been all over the Gypsy Queen since it was towed back to the marina. It seems they found Dom's phone in the drawer of the navigation desk, where, presumably, he put it for safekeeping. It's taken a while, but they managed to hack into the phone where they found an electronic note."

"What did it say?" Morgan asked, barely breathing.

"It said, *"To everyone I ever met, I'm so, so sorry."*

Morgan studied her dad's face as he said those words, as if seeking verification there for what she had just heard. He closed his eyes when he finished speaking, as if to blot out the images being conjured up by Jenna's harrowing description of events.

"What does that mean?" Morgan asked, her mind struggling to process what she had just been told.

Gareth sighed heavily. "I'm so sorry love," he said, "but it looks as if Dom took his own life. At least, that's what the Spanish police are saying. They're treating it as a suicide."

"Noooooo!" she wailed, bending over and hugging herself tightly, as if to try and hold herself together in one piece.

"It's a mistake," she cried, "a terrible mistake. There must be some other explanation."

She looked appealingly at her dad, praying for him to change his mind and admit he must be wrong. She wanted him to say it couldn't be as bad as feared, but searching his facial expression, all she could see was grim acceptance. She sobbed violently, dropping her head onto her dad's broad shoulder for support. Only when her mouth became dry and her skin felt tight from dehydration did she allow her father to lead her downstairs, where she picked at the supper Petra had prepared for her, before going to bed for another night of disturbed and restless sleep.

CHAPTER FORTY-NINE

December 2016

Morgan cleared a face-sized circle on the steamed-up window of the coach. Landmarks of London swept past the window – the green expanse of Hyde Park, the elegance of Park Lane and the arresting grandeur of Marble Arch.

She gazed out on the streets and pavements, busy with Christmas shoppers enjoying the extravagant light displays around the West End. Parcel-laden people staggered into cafés and restaurants to seek sustenance before resuming their assault on shops decorated to entice customers to enter and spend.

When the coach turned into the Edgware Road, leaving behind the Christmas bustle, Morgan allowed her head to fall back on the padded rest behind her and closed her eyes, relishing the few hours of solitude her journey time afforded her.

What a whirlwind couple of months it had been since she opened the envelope containing her exam results to find they far surpassed her predicted grades. She had read the innocuous piece of paper several times, struggling to comprehend what it meant for her future.

"You might regret it for the rest of your life, if you don't go to university," her father had said.

"You owe it to yourself to continue your studies after doing so well," Bev her manager said, putting on a brave face. Morgan knew she didn't want to lose her.

"It's exactly what you need, after all you've been through," Petra advised.

Different people, saying the same thing, but in the end, it was her mother's voice she heeded.

"You've got this, darling. I have every confidence in you. Don't let your fears rule your life. You've overcome so much in the past couple of years. This is what you've planned and worked for, what *we* planned and worked for together. Go to London and have a blast!"

Morgan smiled to herself. Her mother's was the one voice she could not ignore, even though there were complications from leaving it late to accept the offer of a place at her first choice university in London. Finding accommodation had been a nightmare, and having no time to get her bearings before her course started meant she spent her first week at university lost and late. Now, though, at the end of her first term, she could tell her mum she was settled and happy and determined to make her proud.

Despite fighting to stay awake, Morgan found herself nodding into sleep as the coach became warmer and the repetitive swish of the wipers on the front window lulled her into a doze. Before she knew it, the coach driver was announcing their arrival at Granton bus station, and it was time for her to disembark. She yawned and stretched before dragging down her backpack from the shelf above her seat, sliding into the shuffle of passengers making their way off the coach.

Waiting for her behind the barrier were Gareth and Petra, who waved frantically in her direction, as if she were returning from a gap year or months away. She smiled at their enthusiasm, noting how relaxed and comfortable they appeared together.

Her dad looked years younger than the last time she had seen him, Morgan noted. He'd lost the frown that permanently wrinkled his forehead and he just looked, well, lighter. That was the word that came to mind.

"You look good, dad," Morgan said, after he had released her from a bear hug.

"Thanks love. I feel it," he replied, taking her backpack as he led the way to his car.

"I don't want to say too much about it when you've only just arrived, but suffice to say, I've made my peace with everything," he explained, as he walked beside Morgan, matching his stride with hers. "I'll never understand why your mother ran out into the road as she did. I choose to believe she did it, not just for that poor animal, but to stop Ted Dunlop from trying to rescue his dog. She put her life on the line to save his."

Morgan nodded. It was exactly the sort of thing her mum would do. She was always putting others before herself.

211

"I know, now, that Dom was the driver, which was the big, unanswered question that's been hanging over me," Gareth continued. "I know, too, that he probably couldn't have avoided the accident; the evidence is pretty conclusive on that. As for the rest, I can see that, for different reasons, Dom suffered maybe as much as us. I never got to meet him, but I think he must have been a promising young man; and I know that, because my daughter was so very fond of him."

Morgan glanced across at her father and smiled, a sad, contemplative smile.

"I think I'm finally moving on," said Gareth, putting his arm around Morgan's shoulders, "and I hope, with all my heart, that my darling girl can do the same."

On the drive to Cragview, Morgan patiently answered all the questions being fired at her. How was her course? What was her accommodation like? Was she finding her way around London? Had she made new friends?

Yes, she answered, she was enjoying her course immensely and really enjoying being back in full-time study again. She had been worried that she would be the oldest person on the course, but there were quite a few people studying as post-graduates and a large proportion of the other students had taken a year or more out before starting uni. At first, she had found London daunting and unfriendly, but she was starting to get it and to appreciate how much it had to offer.

She had also made some good friends, she confirmed. There was Chloe, who lived on the same corridor as her, and Felicia and Justin who were on the same course. She didn't mention Luka, whom she met at an audition for the Amateur Dramatics Society, who was the most charismatic person she had ever encountered. With his mop of curly brown hair, dark chocolate eyes and ridiculously sensual lips, she wondered how anyone could resist him, yet she was intent on doing so. He always made a beeline for her at rehearsals and had asked her out a couple of times, but she had declined. It was simply too soon for her to even contemplate another relationship after all she had been through.

"So, you're not sorry you decided to go to university after all?" Gareth asked.

"No dad. I'm glad I allowed you to persuade me," she said, a heavy note of irony in her voice.

"Here we are then!" Gareth announced, as he pulled onto the drive at Cragview.

The house looked exactly like an image from a Christmas card, Morgan noted. Everything was perfect, from the wreath on the front door, to the clear crystal lights draped across the window frames. An enormous Christmas tree had been positioned beside the French doors, it's tip almost scraping the ceiling. Decorated with delicate glass baubles, several of Petra's pottery pieces and vintage decorations Petra had collected over many years, it was a work of art in itself. Although Morgan had turned her face against Christmas after her mother died, she could not fail to be entranced by the magical atmosphere Petra had created.

"This all looks amazing, Petra," she said.

"Thank you," Petra replied. "I can't deny, I'm a bit of sucker for Christmas. Now, your room's ready if you want to settle in," Petra continued. "Dinner about 7?"

"Perfect," Morgan replied, noting, as Petra spoke, that she and her father were exchanging conspiratorial glances. Climbing the stairs to the room Petra always kept ready for her, Morgan wondered what the two of them were up to. Whatever it was, no doubt they'd share it with her when they were ready.

Morgan didn't have long to wait, realising as soon as she came back downstairs, there was to be a major announcement. The table was set with candles, their glow reflecting in crystal glasses, silver cutlery and white bone-china plates. A bottle of champagne leaned invitingly in a bucket of ice.

"What's all this?" she asked, looking quizzically at her father and Petra standing side by side and holding hands.

"You say," said Petra, looking at Gareth. He cleared his throat, as if he was about to make an important speech.

"Petra and I got married in October, love. It was a small affair. No guests. Just us."

Morgan blinked, noting the air of nervousness hanging between Petra and her dad, as they looked at her intently, awaiting her response.

How could she not be happy for them, Morgan challenged herself? Petra was lovely and a great support and source of strength to Gareth. Though she wouldn't say so to her dad, she attributed much of his success in staying sober to Petra's unflagging encouragement and patience. Even so, sadness plucked at her heart strings as she recognised that her dad re-marrying was an affirmation that her mother no longer existed. It wasn't that she hadn't accepted that fact, it was just that each and every step away from the family life they had once led together, faded her mother from the mental tableau she carried in her head. Someone else was taking her mother's place, now, and new memories would be made in which her mum played no part. She couldn't help but feel unutterably sad.

"That's great!" she said, swallowing the painful lump in her throat. "Congratulations! I'm really pleased for you. But how did you pull this off? I had no idea."

"We waited until you were settled at uni," said her father, "then took ourselves off to the hotel where we all stayed together in France. In one sense the place had bad vibes for us, but we remembered how beautiful it was, and we wanted somewhere special. The hotel staff handled everything for us, including acting as witnesses. They laid on a fabulous wedding breakfast for us and gave us the best suite. We were treated like millionaires. We haven't told anyone else yet because we wanted to tell you first."

Morgan rushed over to hug them both, the tears she shed a blend of both happiness and inescapable sadness. Soon they were all crying and laughing together as Gareth poured champagne for Petra and Morgan. Scruff barked excitedly round their feet, unable to understand the emotions he sensed to be pulsating around the room.

"Here's to you dad, and to you, Petra," said Morgan. They clinked glasses and Petra leaned forward to kiss Morgan on the cheek.

"I will never replace your mother, darling, I know that," Petra whispered in Morgan's ear. "And believe me when I say, I will never try."

CHAPTER FIFTY

Morgan reversed her car into a parking space and sat quietly gathering her thoughts for a few moments. She could almost hear the press of silence within the cemetery, radiating from the many souls for whom the place provided a final refuge. She climbed out of the vehicle and made her way slowly along the main avenue, the path in front of her sparkling with a light frost.

She hadn't been able to make her annual pilgrimage to her mother's memorial, this November. Her busy schedule of lectures and tutorials had made it impossible. With the year now drawing to its close, as she walked slowly and thoughtfully towards her grandfather Derek's bench, she reflected on yet another twelve months of tumultuous events. Was she destined to live ten years in every one, she wondered? When might her life become calm and ordinary?

Arriving at her family's plot, she laid her usual wildflowers. This year, she held two bunches, one for her mum, and the other for her beloved grandmother. Eileen had slipped peacefully from life, almost a month to the day that Morgan left for university. It was as if she had waited until her troubled granddaughter had finally found her way, before relinquishing her own feeble grip on life.

"She doesn't want any fuss and she doesn't want a funeral," Gareth told her when he telephoned to break the devastating news. "When she was still well enough to know her own mind, she wrote out a clear letter of wishes. She wants us to have a family celebration of her life, when we're all ready, so there's no point in you coming home. We'll all get together at Christmas."

It was all so typical of her nan, the quiet passing and the strong desire to deflect time and attention away from herself. Hers had been a life of unsung, unselfish devotion to her family, Morgan reflected.

Determined to honour Eileen's express instructions, Morgan's Aunt Jess, her Uncle Charlie and her two cousins were coming to stay at Cragview for several days between Christmas and New Year. It would be good to be in the company of her family – as much of it as she had left - and to laugh and cry with them over the memories of their lost loved ones.

She shivered and rubbed her arms to warm herself up. The air was bitterly cold, today, and not conducive to lingering.

"Bye everybody," she said aloud to her mother and grandparents, after laying her flowers. "I'll be back to see you all again as soon as I can."

Stomping her feet, which were turning to blocks of ice, she walked briskly back down the path to the main avenue, but instead of heading straight back to her car, continued in the opposite direction. Consulting a rough sketch provided by her father, she eventually stopped at a paved area, bounded on one side by an ornate, semi-circular wall, in which brick-sized plaques were inserted at regular intervals. It was easy to pick out those which had most recently been added to the structure, as their granite surfaces and gold and silver carved lettering shone the brightest. She stepped towards the one that instantly drew her eye.

Dominic James Cooper
21 June 1996 – 2 July 2016
Darling boy, you left us too soon
We will forever hold you in our hearts
Your ever-loving family

Morgan traced her fingers over the letters, gouged into the stone for eternity, like the grief in the hearts of those who mourned a life cut short. Tears trickled down her cheeks as she reflected on the awful tragedy that lay behind that short inscription.

For weeks after receiving the dreadful news about Dom, Morgan had been unable to stop herself imagining the scene immediately before he died.

She had pictured him downing the contents of the whisky bottle until he was almost unconscious. He wasn't a heavy drinker, so it wouldn't have taken much for him to become thoroughly inebriated.

He must have staggered up to the deck, she speculated, or maybe he drank himself into a stupor whilst looking out into the total blackness that beckoned to embrace him. At some point, after he had consumed the last of the whisky, he may have fallen off the boat, disorientated; or perhaps he threw himself over the guard rail, descending into the chilling depths of the sea and sinking feet below its surface.

The evening coldness of the water would have seeped into his skin, she imagined, penetrating his veins and arteries and freezing the beat of his heart. She hoped, with all her being, that the shock would have killed him instantly, in his drunken state, but she doubted that would have been the case. It was the height of the summer, and the water temperature would have been moderate or, at least, not cold enough to induce shock or hypothermia.

In that case, she imagined, he must have forced himself to hold his head beneath the water until his lungs were fit to explode and his eyes to burst from their sockets. Did the effort of trying to die wipe out all the negative thoughts that drove him into the sea in the first place, she wondered, or was his soul tormented to the very last second of his life? Was he simply unable to live with himself for another moment and could he not even contemplate that he might be forgiven for his youthful misdemeanours?

Turning over her terrible imaginings, she had always come to the same conclusion. Dom's death represented the tragic waste of a promising life. Had he lived, Dom would have done so much good in the world, she was certain of it. That thought would haunt her for the rest of her days.

Morgan sighed heavily. Kissing the first two fingers of her right hand, she placed them on the granite plaque, leaving them there until the cold penetrated her skin.

Allowing herself to fantasise, for a moment, she imagined that Dom had not died that night on the Gyspy Queen. Perhaps he deliberately jumped off the boat closer to land, swimming in the still-warm waters of the sea, until he reached a different shore, hiding out there or maybe travelling on to some far-distant place where he had assumed a new identity so that he could start over and lead a different life. She knew it was a ridiculous notion, but since his body had never been found, it was one she clung to in her darker moments, and she was not yet ready to relinquish it. Maybe she never would.

A pile of crisply curling leaves crackled at her feet, disturbed by a sudden gust of wind. Before turning for home, she watched as the twisted shapes, carried by the breeze, lifted from the ground and disappeared into the distance.

THE END